THE ICE QUEEN

By the same author:

ELAINE

THE ICE QUEEN

Stephen Ferris

Nexus

This book is a work of fiction.
In real life, make sure you practise safe sex.

First published in 1995 by
Nexus
332 Ladbroke Grove
London W10 5AH

Typeset by TW Typesetting, Plymouth, Devon
Printed and bound by
BPC Paperbacks Ltd, Aylesbury

ISBN 0 352 33039 2

All characters in this publication are fictitious and any resemblance to real persons, living or dead, is purely coincidental.

One

An expectant hush fell upon the small crowd in the great, grey hall as the lights dimmed and spotlights picked out the golden throne set upon a low dais at one end, glowing on the grey velvet curtains which formed its backdrop. A few moments passed, during which speculative tension built, then a heavy oak door at the side opened and a stately figure emerged. She was a woman of indeterminate age. The paleness of her complexion may have been enhanced by cosmetics. In any case, it formed a dramatic contrast with the jet black of her hair, drawn back harshly from her face in a severe bun. A purple dress, which looked as if it had been sprayed on, wrapped her from high collar to floor, revealed by the fact that her black cloak, fastened by a diamond clasp, was thrown back in a theatrical manner.

She swept towards the throne and settled herself into it with considerable grace. Such was the impact of her appearance that it was several seconds before anyone, even the men, noticed that she was closely followed by a near-naked girl, whose perfection of face and figure was in no way spoiled by the filmy wisp of material which floated about her loins. Behind this vision of loveliness stumbled a figure which evoked gasps of amazement from all and subdued titters from the women present. The man was naked and hairless. A shaped, padded leather band over his eyes and a ball-gag strapped across his mouth rendered him sightless and speechless. From a broad leather belt about his waist, a steel crucifix went up his back. The top of it was padlocked to the back of the blindfold, while his wrists were secured by leather straps to the extremities of the arms. More straps about his biceps ensured that no part of his upper body, except his hands, was capable of movement. A metal ring, tightly padlocked about the base of his flaccid penis, was attached to a short chain which the girl jerked, from time to time, to encourage forward motion.

Arriving beside the throne, the girl dragged down on the chain, so that the man was forced, clumsily, into a kneeling position facing the audience, then clipped the chain to a staple in the dais, before passing behind the throne to take up a similar kneeling position on the other side.

From her throne, the seated woman addressed her audience in a voice which, while it did not appear to be raised, carried to the furthest corner of the large room and was clearly audible. 'Welcome, all of you, to Castle Despair. The method of your transportation here was calculated to prevent you from ever discovering our location. Blindfolded and travelling by helicopter, you had no way of knowing whether you were crossing land or sea. Likewise, you do not know if the aircraft flew in a straight line, or in circles, so as to prevent you from guessing any distance from your starting point. The castle has no windows and you are not permitted to pass through any of the doors which might enable you to see outside. In this way you know that at any time, I or my agents can seek you out, but you cannot find your way here. Think about that and the full implications of it.

'I know that you have been most comfortably accommodated overnight and that you have all dined well. You will have appreciated these luxuries, for you all have something in common. You all enjoy the good life but, just lately, have lacked the funds to support such a style. That is why I knew you would accept my invitation. You are here because I wish to offer you the opportunity to return to the glittering social scene you so admire. I shall interview each of you in turn, in private. If I then decide that you are suitable material, I shall offer you well paid employment in my service. I suspect that you will not find your duties too arduous as they will consist of attending many parties and other functions. Additionally, my files contain information about your sexual proclivities and, you may be sure, your work will include ample opportunities to satisfy your own particular preferences.

'I am Matrilla, also known as the Ice Queen. While you are my guests and if you enter my service, you will address me as "Madam". Here in this castle my word is law.' She gestured briefly towards the kneeling man, crouched over the centre of his discomfort. 'You can see that I have no truck with disobedience in those from whom I expect it. ICE is an acronym for "Institute of Corrective Education". There are many wrongs for which the victims of those wrongs have no redress. My life's work, and that of my staff, is to see that the wrongdoer is taught the error of his or her ways. They are brought here and detained for a suitable period, during which time they learn better behaviour. The victims of their transgression are invited to witness, and sometimes to share in, the corrective process. Some of them develop a taste for it. I have several of these on my staff and they derive great satisfaction and pleasure from their work. However, I need people like you to act as my agents. You have the opportunities to listen to gossip; overhear confidences; move in the sort of circles where such behaviour is most likely to occur. Your job will be to collate such information and pass it to me, with appropriate recommendations and a profile of the victim which assesses their suitability for inclusion in the routine of re-education.

'Now, before I end this audience and begin the personal interviews, it is fitting that you should receive a demonstration of the sort of thing we do here, so that you should be under no illusions about what your reports will lead to and what will, quite probably, be in store for you personally if you join my staff and I decide that you need such discipline. You should also take the opportunity to contemplate what would happen if, having decided not to become one of us, you subsequently disclosed to the outside world anything you have seen or heard today.'

The Ice Queen gestured to the kneeling girl who got up and passed behind the throne again to untether the man's chain. The Queen rose and took the lead from her, jerking on it to guide the pinioned man to a point on the dais where a chain led around pulleys in the floor and ceiling, forming a continuous loop. Backing him up to it, she secured the top of his metal crucifix to one of the chains with a large clip through which the chain was free to slide. Going behind him, she drew his lead back between his legs and clipped it to a link, so that he was effectively tethered by his penis to the chain. She went to the rear of the dais and parted one of the velvet curtains to reveal a crank. When she turned it, the part of the chain which was attached to the lead began to descend. For a while, the man resisted the strain, but it was a contest which he could not win and, gradually, his knees buckled until he was in a half squatting position, unable to lean forward because of his crucifix attachment, yet not obtaining any support from that attachment which would take the strain off his thigh muscles. At that point, the Queen stopped turning the crank, came back to the chain and shackled front and rear links together, so that there was no possibility of further movement, either upwards or downwards.

She regarded her handiwork with head on one side, then stepped forward to face the audience again. 'He will remain in that position for as long as it pleases me to keep him there. A simple enough punishment, you will agree, but a very effective one. I assure you that, if he was able to speak, he would tell you that he does not like it one bit.'

The audience took in the scene. Under the spotlights, the purple and black of the Ice Queen's clothing toned most perfectly with the grey background, as did the flesh tints of the two other participants in the drama. It was impossible to see the man's facial expression, but the rapid, shallow heaving of his chest and the quivering of his tortured thighs were enough to indicate his discomfort, so that the men in the audience felt a sympathetic twinge in their own bodies.

As if sensing this, the Queen continued. 'I hope that has been a useful lesson for you men. Now I propose to show you that women are no less sternly dealt with.' At an almost imperceptible gesture from her, the great oak door opened again. As it did so, a woman's high pitched wail became audible to the audience.

'No! Please! I beg you! Not in there! Not in front of all those people!'

Two deeply tanned and muscular men appeared, one pushing and one pulling at a tall wooden frame mounted on a wide, wheeled undercarriage. The men wore only white loincloths. Their heads and bodies were hairless and shone with the application of oil. The crowd barely noticed them. Their attention was on the contents of the frame. From each of the corners, short chains and leather cuffs restrained the wrists and ankles of a completely naked girl, holding her in a widespread, open X position, facing the audience. As they watched, a pink flush spread over her white skin, increasing in intensity towards her head, until her face was scarlet with embarrassment. Her eyes were tightly closed and her head was turned away as though by shutting out her own view of their eyes, she might prevent them from seeing her nakedness.

The men stopped the frame beside the dais and impassively took up positions on either side of it, arms folded. For a long moment, the Ice Queen continued to sit on her throne, obviously enjoying the girl's discomfiture. From where she sat, she had a side and rear view of the pink, imprisoned flesh. For their part, the audience had the benefit of her full, pert, brown nippled breasts and the delicious triangle of brown pubic hair which only partially concealed the pink lips of her sex. She was suspended in the centre of the frame, so that her feet had no support and her full weight was taken on her wrists, which had the effect of throwing her superb upper body into prominence, while the muscles and sinews of her arms and thighs stood out in witness of the strain to which they were being subjected. The sight might have been less erotic had she hung motionless, but her constant wiggling and writhing within the severe limits of her restraint, served only to emphasise her helpless subjugation, so that most of the male watchers felt their manhood stirring into wakefulness, while the females experienced twitching tingles in important places.

It was only when the girl adopted a trivial defence and shook her long, dark hair so that it fell forward, concealing her face, that the Ice Queen lost patience and went over to stand beside the frame, closely followed by her hand-maiden. At the Queen's sign, one of the men went out and came back with a wheeled trolley, on which were arranged various implements, straps, canes and cords. The Ice Queen reached up and swept the brown hair away from the girl's face, twisting it into a thick rope behind her head, which the hand-maiden secured with a short cord. Still grasping the hair, she pulled the girl's head around so that she was forced to look squarely into that implacable face. Matrilla's voice was low and menacing, almost a hiss, yet it still contrived to be heard by everyone.

'Gala. You have been remiss and lazy in your duties. You have been warned many times. It may be that you thought that what we have enjoyed together was sufficient to save you from punishment. Today you learn that no one, however favoured, is exempt from reaping the just rewards of their misdeeds. It is fitting that your punishment should be public and humiliating as a useful lesson to those who have not been privileged to be close to me, as you have.'

Tears streamed down the scared face of the hanging girl. 'Please Madam. Please don't do anything to me. I'll be good. I'll work. I have been bad, I know. Please won't you give me another chance to show that I won't laze around again?'

There was no mercy in the hard, grey eyes which bored into her watery brown ones. 'Too late, Gala. You had your chances and you wasted them. I know for certain that you won't laze about – at least not for the next week, during the periods when the Activator is at work.'

Those words seemed to send Gala into further paroxysms of writhing and pleading. 'Oh no, Madam! Anything but that. You couldn't be so cruel! Ask anything of me. Any service. I am yours. Beat me now. Punish me in some way – I deserve it. But not the Activator, please. Have mercy!'

She might as well have saved her breath. The Ice Queen nodded to the guards and they took a wooden bar from a slot alongside the frame and fitted it into sockets so that it passed in front of Gala's body at the level of her hips. She never ceased her wailing and moaning as they withdrew catches in the centre of the sides of the frame and bent the top half of it down, so that the naked girl, effectively, bowed low to the audience, her breasts dangling free, the brown nipples pointing towards the floor. At another nod, the men rotated the frame so that the naked posterior was presented to the crowd, buttocks upthrust by the bar under her hips and the dark hairiness of her clearly visible between the widely parted legs.

'Lower!' ordered Matrilla, and the men bent the frame even further, until the girl was almost doubled in half and her hanging breasts came into view between her legs. The tension in the upturned buttocks and thighs was now intense and the cleft mound of her vulva stuck out obscenely. Both men and women onlookers stirred uneasily and some hands stole towards groins as this view worked its will on them. The Queen, who missed nothing, noted this small movement and smiled to herself. Passing to the cart, she took up a broad, black leather belt, hung it over Gala's back, brought the ends together underneath her bare belly and, drawing it cruelly tight, passed a D ring through the appropriate slot and secured it with a padlock. Next, she selected from the cart a polished metal cylinder with a rounded end and smeared it with a liberal dose of oil. Standing a little to one side, so that everyone could see what was happening, she carefully parted the brown pubic hair and drew aside the soft labial lips to reveal the pink vaginal entrance inside. At the first touch of the cold metal, the girl screamed. Trapped as she was, struggling was impossible, but the jiggling of her breasts showed the efforts she was making to escape. Remorselessly, Matrilla thrust the thing into her until only the hollow end was visible, then left her like that while she addressed the onlookers.

'You will notice that I have not had the girl gagged, as I could easily do. I find that her screams and protests have a salutary effect on observers and that, after all, is part of the object. However, those you have heard are as nothing compared to the ones which are coming next. I can promise you that I know she really doesn't like this part.'

Returning to the bare backside, she placed one thumb on each soft cheek, pressing and drawing them apart, as if it were possible to separate them more widely than they were already. The hand-maiden came forward and poured a little oil into the exposed cleft, so that it ran down over the tight brown sphincter of Gala's anus. Tantalisingly, the Queen allowed her right forefinger to trail up and down the cleft, while the girl groaned and moaned piteously. With her left arm along Gala's back, Matrilla dabbed at the stretched brown nut with her left forefinger, eliciting little gasps at each touch. Then the touches became taps and the noises grew louder. The taps became spanks and the crowd could see the embedded metal cylinder twitching, as the irregular, unpredictable stimulation of her anus had its effect on her vagina. Below the cylinder, her long erect clitoris was forced back and out. Noticing this, the Queen transferred her left hand to that area, reaching from the front between Gala's thighs and grinding the little nub of flesh against the cylinder, while her right forefinger inserted itself, slowly and gradually, up to the knuckle in her bottom.

Now the girl's squeals of outrage were tinged with the ecstasies of approaching orgasm and Matrilla did nothing to prevent this, masturbating her with one hand and plunging rapidly and deeply into her bottom with the finger of the other. With orgasm, the squeals became one long, sighing moan until the girl hung, limp and unmoving in her bonds. When the Queen picked up a second identical cylinder from the cart, the audience realised that her ordeal was not over – it was only just beginning. Smearing it with oil, she placed it against the abused sphincter and pressed. Gala came rapidly to life again, renewed her screaming and attempted to resist the relentless pressure. Such resistance was quite useless. Slowly yet remorselessly the whole length of the cylinder disappeared inside her. Matrilla stood back to allow a good view of the two hollow ends of the cylinders, one above the other, which was all that could be seen of them now. Working quickly, before either could be expelled, she selected another black belt from the cart. Inside the centre of this were two metal projections which fitted into the hollow ends of the cylinders. The two ends of the belt were swiftly padlocked to the front and back of the waist belt, so that there was no possibility that the cylinders could be removed without the proper keys. Attached to the last belt, so that it rested in the small of Gala's back, was a black box about the size of a mobile telephone.

The punishment, apparently, was complete because, at a nod from the Ice Queen, the guards re-erected the frame and released the girl. She stood, uncomfortably crouched over, rubbing her reddened wrists. The women in the audience appreciated how it must have felt for her to have those instruments immovably embedded inside her and some thighs rubbed surreptitiously together.

'Now, Gala, I think we should show the ladies and gentlemen the true nature of your punishment and how our little Activator works, don't you?' The Ice Queen's smile was as cold as her name.

At these words, Gala threw herself on her knees in front of the imperious figure, clasping her arms about the Queen's legs and nuzzling at the purple-clad thighs. 'Please Madam! Mercy! It's not too late to change your mind. I'll be good, I promise.'

Matrilla grabbed her by the cord about her hair and peeled her away. 'Get up at once, girl. Stand to attention, facing the audience. Hands at sides, please!'

Cowed, Gala rose and adopted the required position, although it was obvious that it took all her self-control to do so. The Ice Queen stood beside her to address the gathering.

'You have seen the fitting of the appropriate instruments. What you don't know is that the little box at the back . . . turn around to show them, girl . . . contains a battery operated magneto and a mercury switch. When this device is switched on, a small current passes between one cylinder and the other . . . I see that you are already imagining the effect that will have on the thin layer of tissue in between. It is a device of subtle ingenuity. At a low setting, it produces feelings of intense pleasure. However, the longer it is switched on, the higher the setting goes, until the pleasure becomes quite unendurable. Imagine an orgasm which is never over. As long as Gala keeps moving, the mercury switch renders the magneto ineffective. If she stops for more than five seconds, the current cuts in. That is why we call it the Activator. Anyone wearing it is guaranteed to remain in a constant state of activity.' She crossed to the cart. 'The device is switched on or off by this remote control, which I keep with me at all times.' She held it up to show them. 'This top button is the on/off switch. This second button is an added refinement. With that, I can activate the magneto and the current and override the mercury switch, which means that wherever I am, and wherever Gala happens to be, I can dictate her periods of rest and activity. Also, should I feel in the mood, I can see that she receives vaginal and anal stimulation, whether she is on the move or not. I will switch it on now so that you can see the effect. Once I do that, Gala will have five seconds in which to decide whether or not she wants to get herself in motion.'

Holding the remote control up for them to see, she pressed the top button. The girl began to move immediately. Her self-control completely gone, she began to tear uselessly at the padlocked belt, trying to rid herself of it, at the same time jigging from foot to foot, the discomfort of the hard cylinders forgotten in her frenzy to ensure that the mercury switch was fully operational. The Ice Queen watched this performance for some time with amusement, then raised the remote control again for all to see and pressed the second button. The result was electrifying. Gala gave a gasp and sank to the floor, writhing and grabbing at her vagina and anus but unable, because of the securing belt, even to touch herself near the aroused and tingling places.

Just as it seemed likely that the girl would be reduced to

gibbering idiocy by the maddening irritation, Matrilla relented and switched off the Activator. It was several seconds before Gala was able to collect herself and rise. With infinite cruelty, the Ice Queen proffered the remote control to her. 'Would you like to switch it on again, dear? Or would you prefer me to use the second button again? That's right. Now you have five seconds to start dancing again. Off you go now about your duties . . . and remember to keep on the move!'

Humiliated and enslaved, the near-naked girl made for the door with a curious jiggling gait which set her buttocks and breasts wobbling. Just as she reached it, Matrilla called her back. 'You have forgotten to thank me for being so merciful. Do you want to come back and do that?'

Gala returned and stood before her, still jogging from foot to foot. 'Thank you, Madam, for being so merciful,' she recited.

'Kiss me nicely, then, and tell me that you'll be happy to do anything I ask of you.'

Still moving, the girl kissed Matrilla on the mouth. 'I'll be happy to do anything you ask of me, Madam.'

As the door closed behind her naked back, the Ice Queen resumed her seat. 'That is a sample of my power. Don't join me unless you are prepared to undergo a similar trial. Interviews will begin this afternoon. Each of you has been allocated a personal body-servant and they will tell you how to prepare for me.' The guards opened the door and stood aside as she swept from the room, followed by her hand-maiden, leaving in her wake some people with a lot to think and talk about.

In the room allotted to her, Pandora Vine lay at ease on the bed and thought about the things she had seen and heard that day. It had been a real piece of luck, she considered, which had brought her an invitation to this place just as her life seemed to have reached its lowest ebb. As the sole heiress to the family fortune she had, during her short life, contrived to fritter it all away on wild parties and high living. A series of brief and unsatisfactory encounters (it was putting it too high to call them 'love affairs') had kept her in style for a while longer, but she had just been given her marching orders by the last of these benefactors and without the invitation, she thought wryly, she might have joined the hundreds in Cardboard City at Waterloo. The offer of well-paid and congenial employment was very welcome, although she had some doubts about her ability to tolerate the sort of treatment she had seen meted out that day. As that scene came back to her mind, so did the recollection of how it had excited her. Now, in the privacy of her room, she was able to do what shame had prevented her from doing at the time. Her hand stole down to her pubic area and she began to rub softly through the material of her dress. Now the image of that bare, white, vulnerable bottom was strong upon her and she gathered up the material of her dress, little by little until her suspendered thighs and the tight white gusset of her almost transparent knickers became available to her probing hand. Her rubbing became more insistent and concentrated upon her point of pleasure, while her other hand fumbled with the top buttons of her clothing and slipped inside her bra to massage each of her nipples in turn. So intent was she upon what she was doing to herself that she failed to hear the soft knock and the sound of the door opening. She suddenly became aware of a presence and looked up to find a very young blonde girl standing over her, watching what she was doing with obvious interest.

Pandora hastily adjusted her clothing and snapped, 'What do you want?'

'Forgive me, Mistress. I did knock, but you didn't hear. I am your servant girl, Melissa. I am instructed to help you to prepare for your interview.'

'Oh, yes. That. Well, I'm sure you will be most helpful. What should I wear, do you think?

'Nothing, Mistress.'

'*Nothing*. Don't you mean nothing special?

'No Mistress. I mean nothing.' Seeing that Pandora was still puzzled, Melissa continued. 'For interviews you are completely naked. The Ice Queen is the only one who is allowed clothing. All the staff were interviewed like that – men as well', she added with a sly smile.

For a moment Pandora considered abandoning the whole idea, but then thought again about her financial predicament. This place and this woman were her last hopes. She shrugged mentally. So what if the daft old bat had a bee in her bonnet about nudity. She knew her body was good enough to stand up to the closest scrutiny.

'Very well, then. Just tell me the time and place and then you may go.'

'Oh no, Mistress. I can't do that. My instructions are to prepare you, personally. I am your body-servant. My job is to satisfy your every wish.' With those words, she looked very hard at Pandora from below half-closed lids and put more meaning into the trite phrases than truly belonged there.

Her voice and demeanour put Pandora's mind back to what she had been doing when the girl came in. 'My *every* wish?' she enquired, with the same unspoken deeper meaning.

'Your every wish, Mistress,' Melissa repeated. 'If I did not please you in all ways, I would expect to be punished and I would deserve it.'

'You enjoy being punished?'

'Oh yes, Mistress. Particularly when it is by someone as beautiful as you. I would consider that an honour and a privilege.'

As Pandora surveyed the girl with her head on one side, she felt a small fire ignite between her legs; the sort of burning which, she knew, only orgasm would quench. She continued her scrutiny. Melissa was young and blonde. She was too short; her figure too plump for perfection and the gaudy print dress she wore did little for her, but there was an attractively voluptuous quality about her and her obvious readiness for sex made her most desirable. Pandora found herself wondering how she would strip down and decided to find out.

She lay down on the bed again. 'Take your dress off.'

Melissa obeyed without question or hesitation, drawing

it over her head and laying it at the foot of the bed. She wore no stockings and removal of her outer layer left her in a white brassière and knickers. Pandora thought that she had been right. The girl stripped well. The areas of flesh now revealed were peachy pink and ripe. The full mounds of her breasts bulged provocatively over the lace at the top edge of her bra and the swelling curves of her rounded belly and thighs were delicious. Pandora took a private bet with herself that her nipples, when revealed, would be small and pink, surrounded by a large area of dark pink areolae.

'Take off your bra.'

Again, the instant compliance. The white brassière joined the dress at the foot of the bed. Pandora had won half her bet, she thought. The areolae of her breasts were darkly pink, but her nipples were by no means small. In fact, they were the longest Pandora had ever seen (except on a sow in farrow, she reflected sardonically). They jutted out a full inch and their state of erection demonstrated that Melissa was really in the mood. Pandora could now see that she had seriously underestimated the size of those breasts. Released from the constraining harness of the brassière, they ballooned out and hung down; two magnificent figureheads on the ship of fertile womanhood. Pandora wanted to see them at their best.

'Put your hands behind your head. Bend forward. Now sway from side to side.' As Melissa obeyed her instructions, her breasts jiggled and slapped together like splendid airships in a light breeze. Pandora's hand groped up her dress again and she began to caress herself.

'Stand up and take down your knickers. Now get your legs apart and open yourself so that I can see you.' Pandora gazed upon the plump pinkness of the naked body thus displayed. Melissa's fingers, splayed in the sparse, fair curls of her pubic hair, spread her sex wide, exposing her pink inner area and an obviously erect and prominent clitoris. Unable to restrain herself, Melissa began to finger this fleshy lump and to pull and twist at her nipples.

'Did I say you could do that?' snapped Pandora, in

mock outrage. 'Put your hands behind you at once!' With reluctance for the first time, Melissa obeyed.

'Would you like to see mine?'

'Yes please, Mistress.'

'Then you may come close and have the privilege of removing my knickers.' As Melissa approached, Pandora pulled up her dress and lifted her hips from the bed. Melissa grasped the waistband of her panties and slipped them down and off. Pandora's breathing was harsh as she spread herself in imitation of Melissa's previous display. She was fast becoming turned on by this mutual exposure and she closed her eyes in bliss. They quickly shot open when she felt Melissa's fingers trailing along the inside of her thigh.

'What do you think you are doing? Who said you could touch me?'

'I'm sorry, Mistress. I can't think what came over me. It was very bad of me. Do you think you ought to punish me?'

'I don't just think. I am certain of it. How are you usually punished?'

'For an ordinary offence, my bottom is caned. If I have been very bad, I am beaten between the legs with a strap.'

'Do you think you have been very bad?'

Melissa smirked. 'Oh yes, Mistress. Very bad indeed.'

'Very well. Do we have a strap here?

'Of course, Mistress. Every room is fully equipped. I will fetch it for you.' Melissa crossed to a chest of drawers and took out a stout leather strap, about one inch wide. Before she closed the drawer and came back with the object in her hands, Pandora had the chance to see that it contained other items of pleasure and restraint and she made a mental note of that for her future entertainment.

'Position yourself for your punishment, Melissa.' Pandora got up and stood beside the bed.

The girl lay down on her back, with her head hanging over the side of the bed towards Pandora. She raised straight legs until they were vertical, then slowly parted them until they were very widely separated, her vulva gaping with the strain and the large tendons inside her thighs prominent, in spite of her plumpness. She grasped the backs of her knees and in a voice hoarse with lust, panted, 'I'm ready, Mistress.'

Pandora stepped forward, aware that by doing so she took the hem of her dress over Melissa's face, affording her a view of her knickerless crotch. She parted her legs slightly, to improve the view, then took aim with the strap at the temptingly vulnerable target which lay beyond the naked, pink belly and between the strained thighs. Knowing how much she herself had enjoyed the few occasions on which she had been spanked on the clitoris, she took care to ensure that the end of the strap, as it fell, curled down over the fair, pubic hair and that the extreme tip tapped in exactly the right place on the fleshy mound directly above that point of maximum sensation. That she was being successful in her efforts was made plain by Melissa's pleased wriggling and satisfied moaning. Presently, Pandora felt hands on her thighs and opened them wider to facilitate Melissa's exploration of her moist slot. She allowed this to continue for a while, appearing not to notice, then stepped back out of reach and pretended annoyance again. 'How dare you? You shall be most severely punished for that!'

'Yes please, Mistress. Strap my pussy harder. Make it sore.'

'I intend to, but first you must hold yourself open, so that your clitoris lacks the protection of all that hair and flesh.'

Melissa sat up, her hand placed protectively between her legs. 'Oh Mistress! I don't think I could stand that!'

Pandora landed a light blow on her exposed back with the strap. 'What's this? Disobedience? I thought the Ice Queen's instructions were that you should please me in every way. When I see her I shall be obliged to report this sad neglect of duty. I shall ask if I can watch while she inserts the Activator in you and then I'll get her to loan me the control buttons. I wonder how long it will be then before you are begging me to strap your open pussy?'

Sullenly and with great reluctance, Melissa lay down

again. 'There. That's better. I thought you'd see sense. Now, then. How shall we have you? Lying back, I think, with a pillow under your chest, so that your head hangs down out of the way and leaves the target clear.' Melissa arranged herself as required.

'Before we start, I think you should lift up your breasts. No, not with your hands underneath. Take hold of the nipples and give them a good pinch. That's right. Now lift them up and out! Now shake them! Harder! I want to see them move!' The sight of almost the whole weight of those giant, wobbling orbs being supported on stretched, pinched nipples, was almost enough to make Pandora come, but she controlled herself and got on with the job in hand.

'Very well. Assume the correct position!' Melissa allowed her breasts to fall back onto her chest, where they rolled over and flopped to each side with their own weight. Pandora was pleased to note that her nipples remained very erect and very long, pointing up and out towards the ceiling. The girl raised and opened her legs as before and fumbled to grip the soft folds of skin on either side of her vulva. Shivering slightly in anticipation, she pulled them apart, revealing the wet, pink inner surfaces and the hard knob of her clitoral protrusion, which indicated the huge extent of her sexual arousal by standing out as hard and stiff as her nipples.

With fierce pleasure, Pandora began a methodical strapping, at first taking care to avoid the open love-slit and aiming for the inner thigh area. Melissa responded in a most satisfactory way, writhing and twisting yet, all the time, keeping her legs wide apart, and pulling her sex lips apart. Finally, unable to resist any longer, Pandora concentrated on that splendid clitoris, striking so that the extreme end of the strap tapped directly on the unprotected target, making the rubbery protuberance jump and vibrate with every stroke.

Melissa's writhing became much more intense. She moaned and raised her head so that, straining forward, she could see what was happening to her as well as feel it. The increase that view caused in what she was experiencing was apparent. Her head fell back again and rolled uncontrollably. 'Oh, Mistress! What are you doing to me? You're going to make me come. I can't help it! Is it all right if I come, Mistress? Please let me!'

'Don't you dare come until I tell you that you may! Control yourself, or it will be the worse for you!' Feeling close to coming herself, Pandora got onto the bed and straddled Melissa's back-stretched head. Taking one of the irresistible nipples between the finger and thumb of her free hand, she pulled, rolled and masturbated it as though it were a tiny penis. 'Now lick me out!' she hissed. 'Finish me, before I pull this right off. Do it! Do it! Yes! Oh yes! More! More!' With a great shriek of satisfaction, Pandora felt her body respond fully to Melissa's eager lapping and her love juices smeared the face beneath her. Mighty orgasmic forces were unleashed which turned her muscles to putty and caused her to collapse onto the helpless body of her slave.

Melissa was still holding herself open and, now that the stimulation of the strapping had stopped, was manipulating her clitoris in an attempt to bring about orgasm. Pandora knocked her hands away and re-opened the inflamed labial lips herself. Leaning forward, she took the taut love button into her mouth, sucking and nibbling. Melissa screamed as though in torment, then Pandora felt her own sex being opened and Melissa's lips and teeth on her clitoris. She realised that she would quickly achieve a second orgasm, which was always bigger and better than the first, so she worked hard to induce Melissa's at the same time. As her feelings mounted, Pandora was very aware of Melissa's big breasts, jiggling like a soft caress against the inside surfaces of her thighs. Melissa's legs clamped convulsively around Pandora's head as she jerked involuntarily under the spell of her peak while she spent copiously over Pandora's mouth and face. The taste and smell of this woman-juice, and what Melissa continued to do to her swollen and over-excited clitoris, induced in Pandora a most exquisite and stupendous explosion of sexual ecstasy. She moaned and gasped until she was hoarse, rubbing her sex into Melissa's face at the same time as she ground her own face into the warm, wet, woman-place beneath her. For some minutes after their maximum excitement had subsided, they remained in the same position, dreamily rubbing their naked bodies together; slowly coming back to their senses and normality.

Two

David Corby waited for his interview on the hard wooden bench in the anteroom outside Matrilla's office and was reminded of those occasions at school when he had been obliged to wait outside the headmaster's study to be dealt with for some infringement of the school rules. Admittedly, what had led up to this position had been pleasant enough. Nadia, a very comely and scantily dressed girl had come to him in his room and informed him that she was his maid and would prepare him for interview. That preparation had consisted of bathing him with some care and tenderness. The recollection of this was most pleasant. He would dearly have loved to screw the girl there and then. Her reply to the request had not been discouraging. Nothing would give her greater pleasure at the appropriate time, she had said, but before the interview it was forbidden, so he'd better forget about it. She had led him through the castle to this room, dressed only in towelling robe and slippers. It had come as something of a shock when, on leaving, she had said, 'I have to take the robe and slippers with me.'

'What?'

'I have to take your robe and slippers. For interviews with the Ice Queen, one is always naked.'

It certainly felt very strange to be sitting there without a stitch on. However, David was getting used to it. From time to time, members of staff had entered and left the anteroom, using doors which, David guessed, led to other administrative offices. Not one of them had taken the slightest notice of him, as though it was the most natural thing in the world to see a naked man sitting on a bench. For this place, he thought, it probably was pretty normal.

The illuminated sign above the Ice Queen's door flashed to 'Enter'. David jumped up and just stopped himself in time from straightening his non-existent tie before he knocked and went in. The room was well but sparsely furnished. Matrilla sat behind a huge and expensive desk. To her right and left were other desks. Behind a typewriter at one sat a girl whom David did not recognise. Her upper half was naked, but he guessed that she would have the same sort of filmy covering below the waist which all the Queen's servants wore. On the edge of the other desk, Matrilla's hand-maiden perched on one shapely haunch, her leg dangling. David, who had not been expecting a crowd, least of all a female crowd, became immediately embarrassed and stepped up to a high-backed chair which stood in front of the Ice Queen's desk, using it as cover.

'Come now, David. Don't be shy. Step away from the chair. Hands to sides, please. We want to look at you. Turn around . . . all the way around . . . slowly.' Matrilla's voice was mocking and she made no attempt to hide the fact that she was staring at his body as it slowly rotated before her. He was very conscious of the fact that her two companions were also enjoying the view. This was a moment which Matrilla always enjoyed immensely. She feasted her eyes on his nudity, savouring every detail of him. His skin was white and unblemished; his shoulders square and his thighs and buttocks satisfactorily taut and unflabby. A thatch of dark hair adorned his chest and the tops of his shoulders. She focused her gaze on his manhood, noting that he was uncircumcised and that, although not erect, his penis was of a very satisfactory length and circumference. Anticipation of what she knew she was going to do to him gave her a surge of delight in her stomach and vagina and she pressed her thighs together to control any movement. The sure knowledge of her complete domination was something she craved, as others crave drugs. Demonstrating that power by deliberate cruelty was the only way that craving could be satisfied.

'Very well, David. You may sit.' Matrilla gestured towards the high-backed chair and David settled himself into it, the polished wood cold against his buttocks and back.

Matrilla flicked through a file on the desk in front of her. 'I see that you have not been fortunate with work and money. Although you have had good opportunities, you have wasted all of them. Your drinking, womanising and gambling have finally caught up with you and you are on the verge of destitution. Is that a fair summary?'

'I can explain . . .' David began, but Matrilla cut off his flow of words with an imperious gesture.

'You are new here, so I will give you the benefit of the doubt and explain things more patiently now than at any time in the future. When I ask you a direct question, or give you a direct order, you will answer or obey with equal directness. I asked you a question to which the answer is "Yes" or "No". Now I will ask it once more. Was that a fair summary?'

David opened his mouth, then closed it again. 'Yes,' he murmured.

Matrilla smiled, but it was not the sort of smile from which anyone could have drawn comfort. 'I see that you are not stupid, at any rate. My estimate is that you are in desperate need of the money I can offer you, if only to pay off your gambling debts. Is that true?'

'Yes!'

'Then you ought to be prepared to go to any lengths to please me. Are you so prepared?'

'Yes!'

'Any lengths?' Was she mistaken, or was there the slightest hesitation before the next reply.

'Yes!'

'This is a severe test. Any hesitation whatsoever, just once, will disqualify you from the job you want. Do you understand?

'Yes!'

'You will obey all my orders without question?'

'Yes!'

'Lean forward and look at the front legs of the chair.'

David was taken aback for a moment, then did as he was bidden and saw, for the first time, that there was a short leather strap with a buckle attached to each of the legs, near the floor.

'Fasten those around your ankles!'

The Ice Queen watched as he fumbled with the buckles. Waves of intense pleasure were coursing through her as she sat immobile, her stern face revealing nothing of her inner turmoil. It was always the same thrill for her. Watching a man change from an independent, self-assertive aggressor to a mere plaything to be toyed with and subjected to her will was what made life really worthwhile.

'Reach behind you, to where the sides of the seat meet the back. Feel the straps there? I want you to push yourself as far back into the chair as you can, then pass them across your lower stomach and buckle them tight. Just like an air-line safety belt,' she added.

David was becoming seriously concerned about what he was being ordered to do, but dared not voice his apprehension. Strap after strap, he continued to obey. One passed around his upper body, just under the armpits, holding him fast against the high back of the chair. One after another, he was forced to secure his thighs, just above the knee, to the sides of the chair, spreading his legs. He strapped his left wrist and elbow to the chair-arm on that side, so that the only movement then possible was in his head and right arm.

Observing this, Matrilla nodded to the girl who was still sitting on the corner of her desk, 'Luna!'

Smiling lazily and swinging her hips, Luna slid off the desk and came over to the chair. She continued to smile straight into David's eyes as she secured straps around his right wrist and elbow, so that he could now move only his head. Her breasts so close to his face and her sweet, pungent woman-smell, together with the novelty of his constriction, had an inevitable effect on David and he felt his penis begin to stir under this double stimulation.

The Queen was quick to notice this and made another small sign. Luna at once went back to the desk and collected a short, thin cord. Returning swiftly, she looped it around David's foreskin, knotted it and pulled it tight. The stinging pain was sudden and acute. Taken by surprise, David gasped and grimaced. Strapped upright, as he was, he was quite unable to double up over the source of the irritation or to do anything to remove it.

Matrilla gloated over his expression. 'That should emphasise to you that you are completely under my control. Nothing about you, body or mind, can happen without my permission. That includes erection. In the fullness of time, one will be required of you but for now it isn't, so I have caused a situation in which any attempt by you, even an involuntary reaction, will result in considerable discomfort.'

David spoke between gritted teeth. 'Why are you doing this?'

Her face black with anger, the Queen rose and came around the desk. Placing her hands on David's arms, she leaned forward and spoke close to his face. 'Here, I am the Queen. You do not question me! Even if you dared, you would address me as "Madam". Understand?'

'Yes!'

'Yes, *what?*'

'Yes, Madam!'

'Very well, then.' Matrilla leant a moment longer, reading the fear in the face in front of her and rejoicing in it. Mollified by what she saw, she relaxed and gave David a wintry smile before stepping away and going back to her seat behind the desk. 'Today I am in an indulgent mood. The impertinence you have just displayed will have to be punished, of course, but I am inclined to answer your question. I am doing this to you because it pleases me. I need no other reason, but today I do have another motive. This is our first close acquaintance and it is necessary to establish clearly in your mind that I am a woman who is completely without mercy or conscience. If I am able to cause you pain and distress when you have done nothing, think what your fate would be should you ever display disloyalty. If I can bring you great pleasure without having cause, think how much greater that pleasure will be if you have first pleased *me*.'

She beckoned to Luna, who came to her with unfeigned eagerness. 'It is time we made the young man uncomfortable, Luna.' She took a metal cylinder and a tube of lubricant from a drawer and handed them to Luna, who brought them over to David's chair with her curious, hip-swaying walk.

David recognised the cylinder as being identical to one of those he had seen being inserted into the unfortunate Gala, when she had been forced to wear the Activator. For the first time, he felt relief at the fact that he was so firmly strapped into the chair. At least he could not be subjected to that fate. He realised how wrong he was only when Luna knelt beside him and reached under the seat of the chair. A sudden relaxation of pressure and a draught of cool air told him that she had released a panel in the seat bottom and that his anus was now completely at her mercy. He threw himself from side to side, struggling frantically to break free of the straps, yet knowing, even as he did so, how futile that was.

Matrilla watched these pathetic attempts as she had watched his face for that exquisite, exciting moment when the realisation of what was to happen to him had dawned. For her, this was sheer bliss. Knowing what was yet to come made her wet between the legs and she knew what would be necessary for her full enjoyment of David's humiliation. Luna was holding the cylinder very near to David's eyes and spreading gel from the tube onto it with lascivious, masturbatory motions. He groaned as his penis began to swell and pressure came upon his already stinging foreskin. He closed his eyes and fought to control himself.

The Queen held up her hand in a peremptory gesture to Luna and shook her head. She sank back onto her heels obediently and waited. Matrilla came round to the front of the desk and half-supported her buttocks on it, leaning back. 'Marla!' she called softly. No other command was necessary to cause the girl behind the typewriter to get up and come to kneel in front of her. Knowing full well what was required of her, she raised the hem of her Mistress's long gown, revealing that she wore nothing underneath. Matrilla held the gown up at waist level and spread her legs. Marla placed both hands on the front of the bared thighs before her face and began to nuzzle gently at the exposed vulva so willingly presented to her.

When David opened his eyes, he was confronted with a good view of Marla's naked and voluptuous posterior. Between the parted thighs, a brown bush framed the split pomegranate of her sex. Although her dark hair hid a lot of Matrilla's body, it was immediately obvious what was going on. David felt his penis stirring again and hastily closed his eyes, trying to turn his thoughts away from what he had seen. The lids suddenly jerked open as he felt the cold shock of gel-coated steel intruding between his bottom-cheeks. He tried to clench his buttocks but there was nothing he could do to prevent the cylinder from being stroked back and forth along his cleft, causing him to jump in spontaneous reaction every time it passed across his anus.

Presently the stroking stopped and the rounded end of the cylinder centred itself on his puckered sphincter. Luna pressed harder and he felt himself being opened. His expression of hopeless degradation as he gritted his teeth and groaned whilst staring at the ceiling, was most stimulating to the Queen, who wriggled and pressed the back of Marla's head, provoking her lips and tongue to further effort.

Luna increased the upward thrust and the full length of the hated object slid smoothly into David's anus. Its size and coldness caused him to cry out. Even as his body sought to expel the thing, its proximity to his prostate gland aroused intensely erotic feelings in him. The bare bottom in front of him; the near-naked girl at his side who was doing this to him and, above all, the knowledge that Matrilla was watching him closely and enjoying his humiliation, did nothing to calm him. Inexorably, his penis grew until the constricted foreskin was strained tight and full. Once more, he managed to control himself and the tumescence subsided slightly, easing the painful pressure. Luna closed the panel in the seat of the chair, making it impossible for the cylinder to be pushed out.

Matrilla quivered slightly. It was impossible for David to guess whether or not she had come to orgasm. She pushed Marla's head away and allowed her gown to fall. Hitching herself off the desk, she came over to David and, as before, placed both hands on his arms in order to lean close.

'Comfortable?'

'No! . . . Madam!' he added, after a micro-second's pause.

'Excellent! You're not meant to be. And now there is the little matter of your punishment.'

'But I thought . . . I mean, surely . . . This thing inside me . . . Madam!'

This time the Queen actually laughed. 'Dear me, no, David! That is only a trivial inconvenience which happens to everyone at interview. Punishment by me is something quite different. Something to think about for quite a while. Luna!'

At her sign, the kneeling hand-maiden got up and crossed to the desk, returning with some metal objects which she handed to Matrilla.

The Ice Queen dangled them in front of David's horrified eyes. They were vicious little alligator clamps with a loop of cord attached to each. Most of the ones he had seen which were intended to be used on the body were padded with rubber or leather. These were not. Indeed, he could clearly see that their jaws were serrated.

'I am going to attach these to your nipples, David. That will be painful for you and I have decided to permit you to cry out, if you wish, just once for each clamp. After that, you will make no sound.'

It was quite impossible for David to move in any way to prevent her as she pinched up the skin behind his right nipple and kneaded the small brown knob into maximum erectness. With calculated cruelty, she made sure that the bite of the steel jaws, when it came, was only on the nipple itself and was in no way eased by the inclusion of chest flesh. David had intended not to display emotion, but the sensation was so intense that he could not prevent himself from giving a shout of pain. He was better prepared for the second clamp and confined himself to a loud grunt, then sat quivering with the effort of withstanding the discomfort.

Matrilla eyed him appreciatively. 'Very good, David! I have known those who scream like stuck pigs when I do that to them. Well, we'll soon see for how long you can maintain your stoicism.'

David's eyes widened in horror as Luna passed over two lead weights and he divined Matrilla's intention. She was going to hook them onto the clamps, exerting a downward pull to add to the already unbearable pain. The weights appeared to weigh about a pound each and the torment as they were attached severely tested his reserves of endurance. However, he managed to make no sound, although he could not control his body's reaction of violent trembling.

'This time, I shall let you off lightly. You will remain like that, in total silence, for five minutes.' She went back to the desk and set up a photographic timer where he could see it. Adding mental torture to her physical one, she deliberately dawdled over setting it at five minutes, so that a minute had already passed before she started the mechanism. 'See how considerate I am?' she said. 'Now you can see how the time is passing. You know that I could gag you if I wanted to, but I prefer to show you that I control everything about you, even your voice. That is simply done. If you utter even so much as a groan, I shall reset the timer. Do you understand?'

'Yes, Madam.'

Matrilla smiled wickedly and went back to the desk to reset the timer to five minutes. 'Now you *really* understand!'

David set his mind to the task of enduring the next five minutes. It required his total concentration. After an initial glance down at his body, which showed him that his nipples were stretched down over folds of chest-skin, he saw nothing but the face of the timer. He was aware, as in a mist, that the three women were watching him closely, but he ignored them. There was nothing for him in the world except terrible suffering and the clock face. One tiny consolation was that the distress in his upper body was so great that there was no chance that he would be overcome by any involuntary erection. The sting of his tethered fore-skin and the discomfort of the tube he was forced to sit on paled into insignificance.

After what seemed hours, the timer reached the appointed time and the bell rang out, loud and clear. None of the women moved. As the mist of concentration cleared, David opened his mouth to point out that the time had elapsed, then rapidly closed it again. He had been caught like that before! The seconds ticked on in dreadful suspense until Matrilla relented and came over to him.

'You have done well,' she said in genuine admiration as she unhooked the weights. 'You will find removal of the clamps almost as painful as having them put on and you are permitted to make a noise again.'

David was happy not to have to suppress the sobbing groan which was wrenched from him by the sudden release of the pinching of the steel jaws on his nipples. For several minutes afterwards, the returning circulation was almost as distressing as having the clamps left on, but that gradually subsided to a heated throb, in time with his elevated pulse-rate. His overwhelming emotion was one of relief that his ordeal was over – a fact which was confirmed by Luna, who, at a nod from her Queen, set about removing the constriction from his penis. The touch of her soft fingers, and her nude proximity, caused his organ to stir restlessly.

Matrilla had resumed her seat at the desk. This was another of those moments she relished; when the victim relaxed a little, thereby laying himself open to an even greater shock when he discovered that there was more torture to come. Although she had admired his fortitude during the recent trial, she knew that she could not wait much longer to hear him scream; to see real tears; to degrade and humiliate; to hear him beg for mercy. The intensity of the urge threatened to cause her whole body to shake and she controlled herself with an effort, so that her next words would be calm, even and emotionless.

'Are you ready for the next stage?'

David was dumbfounded. She couldn't be serious! What else could she be planning? He soon found out. He tried to shrink away as Luna came to him again. This time she carried something which he had no difficulty in recognising. It was the little black box arrangement which he had last seen used with a cylinder like the one in his anus to make it into an Activator. This time, his wriggling and pulling was really furious, but there was absolutely nothing he could do. He felt the cool air again as the trap in the chair-seat was opened. He tried to expel the cylinder while he had the opportunity, but Luna had anticipated that and forestalled him with upward finger pressure on the exposed end. He felt the tiny movements as the plug was inserted into the cylinder, then the trap was closed again and he knew that his fate lay entirely under Matrilla's forefinger, which was already poised over one of the buttons of the remote control which lay before her.

'Please, Madam! I've done nothing! Why do you do this to me?'

The Queen was thrilled. This was only the onset of the begging and screaming which was to come and, already, she could feel herself lubricating fiercely. She forced her voice to composure. 'I've already given you reasons,' she said patiently. 'I will repeat them. Firstly, I enjoy it very much. Secondly, I demonstrate my complete control. As a further example of that, I want you to look down at your penis. Go on, inspect it closely! You may have thought that it was under *your* command. It is not. It is now mine, to do with as I wish. Your thoughts and words are mine. Erection and ejaculation are entirely under *my* control. I have already demonstrated that I can cause it to remain limp, soft and useless. Now see that I have the power to erect it whenever I wish to do so.'

She pressed the remote control button. David had never

felt anything to equal the sensation which he now experienced. The micro-current generated in the metal cylinder was infinitesimal, but its effect was devastating. The internal stimulation caused his penis to shoot into massive and immediate erection, the red glans erupting from his still-sore foreskin. It would be wrong to describe what he felt as pain. In smaller amounts, the tickling, tingling irritation would have been pleasurable. In this excessive dose, it made the pleasure completely intolerable. He felt that he could not stand another second of it, yet it went on and on and on. He heard his own voice as if from a far distance, screaming for mercy, his head thrown back and his body twitching convulsively in time with the pulsing current inside him. It stopped at last and his head slumped forward. Had it not been for his confining bondage, he would have fallen to the floor. His mouth hung open, dribbling saliva onto his bare body. He did not care. The only thing which mattered was that the infernal gadget was quiescent.

Matrilla poised her finger over the button again. 'More?'

'No! Please! No! Madam.' His bottom twitched at the very thought of it.

'You would tell me anything I wanted to hear?'

'Yes! Oh yes!'

'You would do anything I wanted you to do?'

'Just tell me. I'll do it!'

The Ice Queen smiled with satisfaction. This was another of those moments she loved. The admission of her total supremacy. 'Then there is just one more thing to be endured. You have to learn that I can demand anything of you. Even your ejaculation is in my power. Luna and Marla will masturbate you now. They will continue to do so until you come, in spite of anything you may say or do to try to stop them. I can see you are wondering why you should try to stop them and I can provide an excellent reason. I shall be watching most closely to see the emission of your seed. As soon as I do, I shall press this button again and hold it down for a long time. It will be interesting to see how long you can hold back that moment.'

David was appalled. Not only was he to be subjected to

the indignity of forcible masturbation, but he knew that the climax of it would be horrifying. Now the two girls were taking up positions on either side of him, Luna on his right and Marla on his left. He watched as though mesmerised as Luna laid her hand on his chest and, with soft, stroking movements, moved it downwards towards his groin. He had time to notice her long, red fingernails, then the hand encircled the engorged flesh of his erect organ and he jerked, convulsively. Luna's hand moved up and down its length, pumping slowly but most effectively. He fought to keep his mind away from what was being done to him and strained his head back to stare at the ceiling, only to have Marla place her hands on his cheeks, holding him in position while she kissed him, open-mouthed. Her lips were soft and full, tasting of woman and cinnamon. Her tongue, like that of a snake, flickered in and out, lighting up the circuits which connected his mouth to his nipples and his penis. It was quite impossible to think of other things and to ignore what was happening. The cylinder in his rectum was no longer uncomfortable. It exerted a pressure which he found welcome and that was a danger sign. His stomach muscles began to contract rhythmically in time with the movement of Luna's hand, letting her know that she was getting to him.

Luna shifted her position slightly and changed her grip so that only finger and thumb touched his penis with light pressure, just below the glans. She masturbated him at a faster rate. At the same time, Marla removed her lips from his mouth and ran them slowly down his neck onto his chest. The touch of her tongue on his sore nipples was almost more than he could bear, but as nothing compared to the sensation when she began to suckle on them and take them between her teeth for little, nibbling bites. Staring down past her dark head, David could see his distended penis being manipulated by Luna. Her grip changed again, fully encircling his flesh and gripping more tightly. From time to time she forced his swollen penis forward and downwards, away from his body, causing the most exquisite sensation. With her free hand, she sought and toyed with his other nipple, pinching, pulling and rolling it between finger and thumb. These girls knew exactly what they were doing!

Luna's hand moved faster and faster, becoming a blur. David felt the first pulsings of an ejaculation and fought to contain it, his head rolling from side to side as he bit his lip and moaned softly. He could think of nothing else, then, except his penis and the sensations in it. He knew that he was lost. In spite of the dreadful punishment which he knew was coming, he found that he needed release more than he feared the Activator. With a great cry, he gave in to that overwhelming want and allowed himself to come in huge spasmodic gushes which shot into the air and spattered down onto his straining belly and chest. Luna's rubbing slowed to a gentle pace and his head fell forward as he panted with the depth of feeling which his ejaculation had aroused. It was several seconds before he realised that the threatened Activator shock had not been administered. Hardly daring to hope, he raised his head and stared at Matrilla, who stared back with elaborate coolness.

'I'm a tease, aren't I, David?' Her hand was nowhere near the remote control and he realised that, from the first, she had not had the slightest intention of carrying out her threat. The mental torture of being obliged to attempt to restrain his natural instincts had been sufficient. He felt a grudging admiration for her subtle cruelty. This was indeed a woman to be reckoned with!

Now Luna was reaching under him and removing the cylinder, which she did very slowly and with great care, enabling him to control his natural reaction to such a movement. That relief was followed by that of having his straps released, so that he could change his position and stretch his cramped limbs.

'Well, David. You have done well. You can consider yourself to be an employee. I shall be able to use a man like you in many ways. There will be no written agreement. What we have just shared is our contract and our bond. I have no fear that you will ever forget it in the same way that a piece of signed paper might slip your mind.'

'No indeed, Madam!' he replied, with considerable feeling, rubbing his overstressed nipples.

'We will discuss details later. I have other candidates to interview. You may leave now. You will find Nadia waiting for you and she will attend to any discomfort you may be feeling. Should you notice any inattention to detail on her part you will, of course, report that to me and I will deal with the problem.'

David found Nadia as promised, waiting in the anteroom with his robe and slippers. He put them on and she opened the outer door for him. She stepped back in order to allow two other women to enter. The first was a buxom, fair-haired wench with large breasts, obviously one of the servant girls. The one behind her was tall, brown-haired and attractive. From her robe and slippers, David guessed that she was the next candidate for interview. He signed for Nadia to wait and remained in the anteroom, knowing that the robe and slippers would have to come off. The couple stopped before the bench and David could tell, from their agitated whispers, that he was the topic of conversation. The blonde, fearful of the consequences of failing to carry out her orders, was demanding the robe and the candidate was pointing at him, obviously unwilling to strip while he was in the room.

David knew who would win the argument and waited on patiently. Presently, the brown-haired girl shrugged and with no pretence at concealment, threw off the robe and handed it over. Completely naked, she faced David and met his eyes brazenly, hands on hips and legs spread slightly to afford a good view of her dark pubes.

'Seen enough?'

David gave her a mock bow. 'Yes. Thank you very much. Very nice!' Chuckling quietly to himself, he followed Nadia out of the room. He hoped he would have the pleasure of knowing the young woman better one day. At the same time he wondered just how brazen and defiant she would be after her interview with Matrilla.

Back in his room, David threw himself down on the bed and closed his eyes. He was tired after the ordeal of his interview and he had much to think about. For a short while he dozed, but was awakened by the touch of soft fingers on his chest. He opened his eyes to see Nadia leaning over him.

'What is it, Nadia?'

'Forgive me for disturbing you, Master, but I know what the Queen does when she interviews a man. I have a soothing salve here which I thought would help.'

David lay back and relaxed. 'Very well. You may continue.'

'Thank you, Master.' She opened his robe and began to massage a cool cream into his sore nipples. He watched her as she worked, intent on what she was doing, noticing the soft curve of her breasts as they thrust against the gossamer silk of the short tunic she wore.

'Why do you wear that?'

She pinched the soft material between finger and thumb. 'Does it not please you, Master?'

'It pleases me very much, but it would please me even more if you removed it.'

'As you wish.' She stood up and, crossing her arms in the timeless manner of all women since clothing was invented, she took the hem of the tunic in both hands and raised it up over her head. For a second or two it caught in her hair and she struggled, wobbling slightly, so that he had an opportunity to admire her flawless body unobserved. Her pose thrust her firm breasts into full prominence, each strong nipple framed in a perfectly circular areola of darkest brown. Her upstretched arms accentuated her flat, smooth belly and elongated her delectable navel. A swathe of dark curls marched across her lower stomach, spreading outwards and upwards from the intriguing crevice between perfect thighs. David had thought himself drained of all desire for sex, but the sight of that flawless body, so provocatively yet innocently displayed was putting ideas into his mind and his groin. He felt his penis stir beneath his robe.

Nadia knelt on the bed beside him and resumed her ministrations. Her movements caused those delightful breasts to jiggle maddeningly and he reached up to caress them. Nadia displayed no revulsion at his touch. Quite the reverse. She smiled knowingly, and her hands moved down his body to pass beneath his robe. She slipped the knot of the cord which held it loosely to him and drew it aside to reveal his manhood, already stirring into life. Dipping her fingers into the jar to collect more salve, she enquired, with mock innocence. 'Does anything else require soothing?'

'I thought you'd never ask,' he replied, then started as the cool slipperiness was applied with loving care to his penis. Under her treatment, it swelled rapidly to full size and she fixed her eyes on it with obvious fascination. He watched her as she watched him. Already, all trace of tiredness had disappeared and he knew exactly what he wanted more than anything else at that precise moment.

'Nadia, my little sweetness, how would you like a very nice, very long, very slow fuck?'

'Oh Master, I thought you'd never ask,' she replied in pert mimicry of his own phrase then, conscious of her temerity, added, 'If it would please you, it would also give me the greatest pleasure.'

He got up and took her by the hand. 'Come here and kneel in the middle of the bed. Rest your elbows on the bed and put your forehead on your arms. Good! Now part your legs.'

Nadia did exactly as bidden and David marvelled at the wonders thus displayed. Her fabulous hindquarters were set like sculpted statuary on the twin pedestals of her thighs. Yet there was nothing coldly statuesque about the faint, pink blush of youth and health which suffused the acres of bare skin thus exposed, nor about the fascinating black curls which sprouted profusely from the cleft which divided her naked buttocks. Her breasts, firm though they were, swung free below her body and jiggled slightly as she breathed. She was willing, vulnerable, available and completely irresistible.

Without further ado, David got onto the bed and knelt behind her. She reached back between her legs, eagerly, to guide his straining penis to her gaping vagina. David paused for a second to savour the moment, then drove his full length into her until his pubic hairs met hers. He grunted with pleasure as he did so and she echoed that with a gasp. She was every bit as delicious as anticipation had told him she would be and he gave her exactly what he had promised. It was very nice, very long and very slow. He lay along her back and passed his hands beneath her, one caressing her breasts and the other searching the thicket for her clitoris. When he found it, she gasped again and he felt the muscles around his organ clamping convulsively.

'That's so good, Master, but not too much. Make me wait! It's so much better if you make me wait!'

This blissful coition seemed to David to go on for hours. They would approach orgasm, then slow down and rest awhile, moving gently and savouring each other's body to the full. Then they would resume, each doing their best to please the other until the moment arrived when climax could no longer be denied. With a howl of delight, Nadia gushed love-juice over David's spouting ejaculation, as if to extinguish the heat of it inside her, then they fell sideways and remained entwined, panting and slaked.

Three

Lady Grace Crendall was bored. Life in the country could often be pleasant particularly life in this great Tudor mansion with servants to attend to every need. Just now, though, it was definitely boring! She stretched out in her huge, turquoise bathtub and examined her reflection in the mirror on the ceiling. Still an enticing body, she decided. Her auburn hair was concealed beneath a towel which served as a turban, but the parts of her which showed above and through the water were most satisfactory to her. Superbly firm breasts, narrow waist, tapering thighs and long legs. Any man would be eager to have access to that body. Any man, that is, except Sir Malcolm Crendall. She frowned impatiently as she reflected on the way he virtually ignored her. Even now, he was off on some of his good works. Some down-and-out or criminal was getting attention while she got none. Surely that justified her many indiscretions? That train of thought excited her and her mind reran some of the more pleasurable moments spent with other men. And women, she reminded herself. She ought not to forget the ladies – particularly as Pandora Vine would be visiting her that afternoon. Pandora had an exciting taste for the bizarre and that, at least, should ensure that the afternoon was not as boring as the morning had been.

As close as they had been (she drew a sharp little breath as she remembered *how* close) there were still things she had not done with Pandora. She would remedy that this day, she thought. Unconsciously, her hands began to move over her glistening, naked body, caressing her own breasts and stomach, then straying down over the coppery-dark bush to lodge between her thighs, manipulating and massaging. She moaned and moved uneasily, her eyes intent on the mirror, watching what she was doing to herself. Her mind filled with erotic dreams and fantasies. She would go down to the stables and take out her black stallion. She imagined herself riding at full gallop, stark naked, the oiled leather of the saddle forcing her legs apart, her thighs and calves gripping the strong, sweating body between them. Now her husband's valet, Simon, was riding with her, his bare chest pressed against her back, his erect manhood rubbing at the cleft of her bottom with the horse's motion. She had never seen him unclothed, but her imagination gave him a perfect physique.

She reached forward and picked up the flexible shower hose, adjusting the head to a stinging jet and the temperature to blood heat. She parted the lips of her sex to expose her straining clitoris and directed the jet onto it. She jumped with pleasure and her spare hand went to her breasts, her strong fingers kneading and pulling first at one nipple, then the other. As the wave of the first orgasm came upon her, her bent knees trembled spasmodically, making little splashing noises on the surface of the bath. She watched the twitching of her stomach muscles and sighed deeply. It was always that way. The first climax was just a forerunner of better things to come. Today she would be stern with herself and ration herself to two. She wanted to reserve some of her strength so as to be able to do justice to her forthcoming session with Pandora.

Pandora came to her in the big, sunny drawing room just after lunch, shown in by Jameson, the butler. Lady Crendall rose to greet her with a smile, noting in one swift glance that Pandora's fortunes must have changed very recently. Her clothes now had nothing of Oxfam about them, but positively reeked of Valentino. They embraced and although it was only a brief contact, breast to breast, it was sufficient to make Her Ladyship tingle with anticipation. She sat down again and patted the sofa in invitation.

'Come and sit here, darling. You look absolutely splendid. Jameson, ask Laura to make us some tea, please.'

The butler departed on his errand, closing the door softly behind him. As soon as he was gone, Lady Crendall slid along the seat and put her arm about Pandora's shoulders.

'Now kiss me properly, darling, before the tea comes. I can't tell you how much I've been looking forward to seeing you. I've been so bored, you wouldn't believe.'

They kissed, open-mouthed, for long seconds until Pandora felt hands stroking her breasts through the linen of her suit. She pulled herself away and sat up. 'Now, Grace! Contain yourself. We've got all afternoon and you'll get me going if you're not careful.'

Grace pouted. 'You're always so sensible! Still, you wait until you hear what I've been planning for us. I think even you will have to admit that it's a bit special.'

Pandora's curiosity was piqued, but she forced herself to remain the sensible one. 'After we've had our tea, dear. Then we won't be interrupted.'

They gossiped happily until the tea arrived. Grace was bursting to know about the new clothes, but was too polite to ask and Pandora had not the slightest intention of revealing the source of her new income. In due course Jameson returned with a laden tea tray and put it on the low table before them. 'Will that be all, Your Ladyship?'

'Yes. No – wait a minute. No, that's not all. Will you ask Laura to get Cook to make us up some sandwiches and a flask. We're going to have a picnic.'

'A picnic, Madam?'

'Yes, Jameson. It's not supposed to rain until this evening, so we'll eat in the garden. It'll be tremendous fun, won't it Pandora?'

Pandora shook her head in wonderment. She ought not to have been surprised at anything this volatile woman decided to do. 'If you say so, Grace.'

'I do. Thank you, Jameson.'

'Just one more thing, Madam. The maid has had to go into town to shop. Laura wonders if you have finished with your bathroom and bedroom for the time being. If you have, she'll clean them.'

'Oh yes! Tell her to go ahead. We shan't be back until much later. Tell her to bring the hamper here. After that, neither you nor she need be bothered again this afternoon.'

Now that, thought Pandora, was definitely suspicious. One thing for which Grace was not renowned was her consideration for servants. As soon as Jameson had left the room, she voiced that suspicion. 'You're up to something, Grace. What is it?'

'It's what I was talking about. Something exciting and different. Look!' She got up and crossed to a bureau by the wall. She came back with a Polaroid camera. 'What about that then?'

'Well, what about it? That's not different. We've done the candid camera bit before.'

'Of course we have, darling. In the bedroom and in the bathroom and even in here. But never in the garden.'

'Outside? In the open air?' Pandora was genuinely taken aback.

Grace was exultant. Very few and far between were the occasions when she could disconcert Pandora and it was a delight to watch the changing expressions on her face as she considered the odd proposal; apprehension turning to curiosity and then a spark of eagerness. Knowing Pandora's appetite for the unusual, she raised the pressure a few pounds.

'This time, I want to photograph you tied up.'

The jolt between Pandora's legs at that suggestion was so apparent that Grace imagined that she felt it herself.

'Someone might see.' Pandora was temporising but without conviction and it was easy to see right through the deception. It was the very notion that there was a remote chance of being observed which was at the heart of the sexiness of the plan and Grace knew that Pandora knew it.

'That's a chance you'll have to take,' she said, greatly emboldened.

Presently, the housekeeper brought the picnic to them. Laura Bannock was a widow, but a young one. Judging by her appearance, she looked no more than 35. She had a good figure and used make-up effectively. Pandora thought that she must have known the sort of things which went on in that house but if she did, she gave no sign of it, being the soul of discretion and fond of her job. Grace took the basket from her and dismissed her, then went back to the bureau and brought out a canvas bag.

'What's in there?' Pandora asked suspiciously.

'Things we'll need,' was the reply. 'Anyway, we have to have something to put the camera in. It would look a bit obvious otherwise, wouldn't it.'

Grace led the way into the garden. It was very large and not all of it was formal. There were many wild and secret places, well screened by trees and it was to one of these that Grace took her. In the centre of a small clearing, well shielded by dense shrubbery, there was a very large rustic chair.

Grace pointed to it. 'That's where I want you.'

Pandora looked around. 'You've given this some thought, haven't you?'

That was an understatement. Grace had thought of nothing else for days. 'Get undressed,' she said shortly. She leant her back against a tree. There was something extremely erotic about the sight of Pandora shedding her clothes, item by item. Grace noticed that there was none of the brazen boldness and abandon with which she usually stripped. She was behaving as does a woman on a crowded beach, stooping over herself and using nervous, hasty movements in her unbuttoning. Grace's heart leapt. Pandora was actually feeling embarrassed. How splendid!

In brassière and knickers, Pandora paused. 'Won't this do?'

'You know it won't. Take them off. Every stitch. I want you completely naked, otherwise it's no fun.'

Even more hesitantly, Pandora obeyed. Completely nude now, she crouched, with one hand and the other arm protecting her pubes and breasts. Grace came across and gathered up her clothes, taking them back with her to her tree.

'Stand up straight! Take your hands away from yourself.

I want to see you naked in the open air and I want some photographs of you like that. Walk about a bit and pose for me.'

The sight of Pandora, bare, her perfect, peachy body contrasting with the rural green background was very stimulating and Grace's hands trembled as she operated the camera. She wondered what it must feel like to have the breeze playing all over her skin and shuddered, her thighs clamping together.

'All right. Now go to the chair.' Pandora crossed to it and sat down. 'No! Not sitting! Get up and come around the back. Now lean over the back and put your hands on the ends of the arms.'

Grace opened the canvas bag and brought out the things she needed. She knotted a length of cord around Pandora's wrists. It was exactly the right thing, bought for that purpose. It was quite thick and very white, yet soft and flexible. She lashed Pandora's wrists to the chair's arms. Next, she pushed her down into a more acutely bent position and tied her elbows to the chair so that her arms and the chair's arms were as one. She passed rope several times around her waist and knotted that to the back of the chair. She spread her legs and fastened one ankle to each back leg. Finally, she forced her knees apart and tied them to the back legs, near seat level.

Satisfied at last, she stepped back and surveyed her work. The sight was every bit as sexy as she had hoped for and she felt her stomach churning with the familiar urges and her vagina moistening, almost to the point of discomfort. She took her photographs but they were now, she knew, incidental to what she had in mind.

'Can you move?'

'Not an inch, darling. It's quite exciting.' Pandora's unsteady voice and heavy breathing revealed the extent to which this new bondage had stirred her.

'Try! I want to watch.'

Head; fingers; perhaps a slight movement of the shoulders and hips. That was all Pandora could do. Grace observed her struggles with deep satisfaction. She delved into the bag. 'Why, just look what we have here. A rubber glove and a jar of cold cream. Whatever could they be for, do you think?'

Pandora's face was a picture. 'What are you going to do to me?'

'Why, I'm going to fuck your bum, darling. I said today would be exciting and different.'

'No! Please! Grace! That wasn't in the deal. I forbid it!'

'Forbid away,' said Grace as she pulled a glove onto her right hand. Pandora tugged uselessly at the cords which bound her to the chair. On the few occasions when she had experienced it, she had enjoyed anal sex, but like this? Tied down like some sacrificial animal? The thought was too humiliating. She screeched as she felt the coldness of the cream being smeared around her stretched anus.

'I shouldn't make too much noise, if I were you. Someone might hear and come to see what's happening.'

Pandora lowered her voice to an imploring hiss. 'No Grace! I really mean it! You're not to . . . Oooh! Oh! Oh God!' The intruding finger worked in and out and Pandora found herself lubricating profusely, despite herself. Gradually, the insistence of that movement and her total helplessness aroused her animal nature to the full. 'Oh yes! Yes! Do it like that. Don't stop!'

Even through the thickness of the glove, Grace could feel the urgency of Pandora's contractions as they pulsed in time with the forward plunges of her finger. The sensation of power and control was marvellous, heady stuff. Slowly, she withdrew, leaving Pandora panting and distraught.

'Do me! Do me now! Don't leave me like this!'

'You'd like that, wouldn't you?'

'Yes! Oh yes! I'll give you anything. You can spank me, if you like. Only do me, I beg you!'

'Not what I had in mind, I'm afraid,' said Grace, outwardly calm though inwardly seething with excitement. She was delighted to notice that Pandora's voice, when she next spoke, was by no means as confident and assured as it usually was. There was a distinct wobble, not purely driven by passion as she said, 'What are you going to do now?'

'You'll find out.' Grace took some cotton wool and a scarf from the bag. Fashioning the wool into two pads, she placed them over Pandora's eyes and bound them in place with the scarf. The powerful leap of sexual stimulation which shot through her when she saw that blinded head, twisting and turning in its vain search for light was frightening in its intensity.

Grace fought for control over her voice. 'Now I'm going to leave you here. I don't know how long I'll be gone. That's for you to guess. I think it's only fair to tell you that it's the gardener's day, so if you're going to call out, I wouldn't be too loud about it.'

She moved back to her tree and stripped silently. Leaving her clothes with Pandora's she moved quietly to a point a little behind her and to one side and sat down on the grass, absolutely silent. From her position, she had a good view of Pandora's perfect, peachy bottom. Her widespread pose meant that the divided oval of her sex, with its fascinating adornment of curls, was prominent between her thighs, on the inner surfaces of which the gleam of wetness showed how close she had been to orgasm. She could also see her dangling breasts, nipples pointing directly downwards, fully erect from sexual excitement and the breeze. They wobbled in the most exciting way as Pandora fought against the ropes which bound her in that shameful pose.

'Grace!' The blindfolded head turned in every direction. 'Grace! It's a joke, isn't it?' Now the voice was definitely uneasy, all confidence gone. 'Are you there? Come back, Grace!' Pandora's efforts to shout without shouting were a symptom of her uncertainty.

Unable to resist the temptation any longer Grace lay back, rejoicing in the feel of the breeze on her bare skin and the cool grass which tickled her bottom. With urgent speed, she inserted two fingers into her vagina and began to masturbate, feeling for her pleasure spot. She never took her eyes off Pandora's body as she struggled to suppress the moans of pleasure which would have revealed the deception. Each tiny twitch and squirm of the helpless nakedness before her stoked the fire of her lust. Presently, she felt the first few spots of rain on her and almost cried out. The shower grew in intensity, until it was beating down in heavy drops. She watched the drops form on Pandora's back. Some ran down the sides of her pendant breasts and dripped from the long nipples. Some collected together into a rivulet and ran down over her exposed and abused sphincter to drip off her pubic hair. The same rain was beating down on her own body, uniting it with Pandora's; covering her breasts with crystal jewels and collecting in a pool in her navel. Her own pubic hair sparkled like an October spider's web. She opened her mouth to the rain, tasting its sweetness. Her hand movements became faster and faster until, with a great shout of satisfaction, she climaxed.

The spell was broken. 'Grace!' I know you're there. Let me up, please.'

As she unbound her, Grace pretended a severity she did not feel. 'Just let that be a lesson to you.'

'I'll certainly remember it,' said Pandora, with considerable feeling. They kissed, briefly, then dried themselves as best they could and dressed. Fortunately their clothes had been under the tree and were almost completely dry and the shower was passing as fast as it came. They went back into the house, hand in hand.

'We'll warm up, here, in the kitchen. I'll go and get us a couple of robes,' said Grace. In a moment she was back, her face alight with mischief and excitement. 'Quick, give me the camera!'

'What?'

'Sssshhh! Not so loud. Follow me!'

Puzzled, Pandora followed her up the stairs. With elaborate caution, Grace tiptoed along the landing to the door of their bedroom. As she followed her, Pandora heard the sound of a radio, softly playing. Grace stopped in the doorway and beckoned her forward. Looking around the door frame, Pandora could not suppress a start of astonishment. Laura was lying on Grace's bed. Her eyes were closed and she seemed in a dreamy state. This, however, was not induced simply by the music. Her flowered skirt was up around her waist and her knickers were down about her lower thighs, exposing her pubic bush, which was dense and large. A vibrator which Pandora recognised as belonging to Grace was in her right hand and probed this thicket. Her blouse was open and the left side of her bra pulled down to expose one of the largest breasts Pandora had ever seen. The fingers of her left hand pinched and rolled the nipple on this breast in time with the movements of the vibrator.

Grace was able to take several paces forward into the room, unobserved. She raised the camera, centred the image and pressed the button. The flash and the whirr of the mechanism made Laura aware of their presence. With a small scream she shot up off the bed, her face scarlet with shame, pulling her clothing into some semblance of order and trying to hide the vibrator behind her back.

'Why, whatever are you doing Laura?'

It was, thought Pandora, perfectly obvious to anyone but an idiot what Laura had been doing but she supposed that was as good a way as any to open the conversation.

'Nothing Your Ladyship! That is . . . I just . . . I thought you were in the garden. I'm very sorry. It won't happen again.'

Don't you believe it, Pandora thought. If I know our Grace it will happen again, and sooner than you think!

'What have you got behind your back?'

In guilty shame, Laura produced the instrument which, incongruously, was still giving off its buzzing sound. With an imperious gesture, Grace demanded it from her and switched it off. 'You like that sort of thing, do you?'

'Oh no! Well, I mean . . . Yes . . . I get feelings . . .'

'I'm sure you do. Well, Laura, what are we going to do about this, eh?'

'I hope you'll overlook it, Madam.'

'I'd like to. I really would. Trouble is, there's this photograph, you see.' She fanned it in the air, drying it. 'It will keep reminding me. It's such a good likeness. Would you like to see it? No? Oh well, never mind. You can look at a copy when I pin them up in the Church Hall and the Post Office and . . .'

'No! Please! Not that! You wouldn't!' Laura was white with anxiety, her hands fluttering as though she would like to try to tear the photograph from Grace's grasp.

'What do you suggest then, Laura? I mean, you've been misusing my property and that surely deserves some sort of punishment, don't you think?'

There was no reply, so Grace went on, 'But perhaps there is a way out. Perhaps you'd like to buy it from me?'

The faint glimmer of hope which had crossed Laura's face was extinguished. 'Yes, but I don't have any money. Well, not much.'

'Oh, I wasn't talking about money. More a sort of payment in kind. You must have guessed what sort of woman I am and what my tastes are. I like to look at women's bodies and I would like to look at yours.'

'What? You mean with no clothes on?'

'It wouldn't be much fun any other way, would it? Certainly that's what I mean. Naked as the day you were born.'

'I couldn't! No! Really!'

'Fine, if that's your decision. Off you go then.'

Laura hesitated. 'What about the photograph?'

'I've told you what I'll do with that. I have to have my fun one way or another.'

'And if I do . . . what you want me to do? You'll give me the photo?'

'That would be a start. I'd have to see how much you please me as the afternoon wears on.'

Laura's inner struggle was apparent and Pandora sympathised. She had too often experienced Grace's persuasive, erosive bargaining techniques not to know that Laura could not possibly win this one.

'You want me to take them off now?' Laura's capitulation was complete, as Pandora had known it would be.

'Yes please. And here, while we watch. Stand in the centre of the room. As you take each thing off, walk over to that chair and fold them neatly on it, then come back to the centre for the next one.' Grace settled herself on the edge of the bed and Pandora, after a moment's hesitation, joined her, her sympathy for Laura in her predicament mingled with excited anticipation.

The undressing proceeded and Pandora could not help being reminded of her own performance that day; the same shy fear of observation. She wondered if that experience had moved her in such a way that she now burned to see another woman suffer the same feeling of shame. Certainly, that walk to the chair after each piece of clothing was removed was a twist of the knife, carefully calculated by Grace to make the subject of their scrutiny very aware of what she was having to do.

As Pandora had anticipated, Laura stopped when she was wearing only knickers and bra to voice a piteous appeal. 'These too?'

Grace was implacable. 'Of course those too! I want to see you quite naked.'

One by one, those garments followed the others onto the chair.

'Good! Come back to the centre of the room. Don't cover yourself like that. Put your hands behind your head.' Laura stood in the centre of the carpet, face ablaze with shame and embarrassment, her body revealed to their interested gaze. She was, perhaps, a little overweight for modern fashion, but her body was quite splendid in its voluptuousness. Any thickening at waist and thighs was amply compensated for by the size and shape of her breasts. To Pandora they seemed enormous, yet there was no sag about them at all. She was, Pandora was forced to admit, a magnificent piece of womanhood, with nothing whatsoever to be ashamed of.

'Is that it? Can I put my hands down now?'

'No, certainly not. Keep them where they are and turn around. Slowly!' A half turn revealed to them a gorgeous expanse of plump, white bottom, hardly marred at all by cellulite. 'Now turn back!' The arms dropped gratefully.

'Put your arms back up. I'm afraid you haven't finished.'

'Why, what do you mean? I thought . . .'

'You have something you have to sell me before you get the photograph.'

'Sell? I don't understand?' Laura was mystified.

'Let me put it simply. I'll swap you the photograph for your hair.'

Laura fingered her light brown hair. 'My hair? You want my hair?'

'Not that hair. *That* hair!' Grace's pointing finger made her meaning clear.

In spite of herself, Laura dropped her hands to clutch her pubic mound protectively. 'No! My God! You can't mean –'

'That's precisely what I mean. I want to snip it off. Clip it. Shave your pussy. Is that clear enough?'

'No! Absolutely not. Never!'

'Just as you wish. You can get dressed and go now. Just think, though. A little pussy shave which no one would see compared with a very public photo. It should be of great interest. Pretty soon every man in the village will have a copy in his wallet, I should think.'

Pandora could see that Laura was wavering.

'And today's the day to do it. You know that I have only one photograph. There are no copies yet. Tomorrow, there could be hundreds so, if you get it then, you won't be sure of anything.' Pandora had to admire Grace's salesmanship.

Laura was deeply suspicious. 'Once you've done that, there'll be nothing else? I can have the photo after that?'

'You have my word on it.'

'All right then, I'll let you do it.'

'Good! You know it makes sense. Now you will go and fetch the dressmaking scissors you'll find in a sewing basket in the library. On the way back, stop off at the bathroom and collect my razor and shaving cream. No, you won't need your clothes. It's better if you go naked, then you won't be tempted to escape.'

Pandora marvelled. Making the woman run about the house in the nude, dodging the other servants, to fetch the instruments of her shame, was exquisite mental torture, quite up to the standard of anything she herself had done to anyone.

While Laura was away, Grace shucked off her clothes and, at her insistence, Pandora did the same, so that when the woman returned she was confronted by the pair of them, both as naked as she. Her confusion was apparent but Pandora could not help noticing that, in the midst of her embarrassment, she was eyeing their bodies. Grace took her burden from her. 'Turn round. Put your hands behind you!' In a trice, she bound her wrists with a soft scarf.

'Wait! What's that for? I said you could . . .' Laura pulled frantically at the restraint, but Pandora knew how useless that would be.

'It's all right. Nothing to worry about,' Grace said soothingly. 'I just need to be sure that you don't change your mind halfway through. Sit down on the edge of the bed. Pandora, you kneel behind her and support her. Now, Laura, open your legs. Oh, come on, don't be coy. You know you've got to.'

Slowly and reluctantly, Laura parted her knees and Grace knelt between them to prevent them from closing again. She took up the scissors, took a pinch of light brown hair between finger and thumb and snipped. Pandora, looking down over Laura's shoulder, saw the hair being cut and experienced an intense vaginal spasm. Added to that was the fact that her hands were around Laura's waist and those balloon-like breasts were only inches away. She slid her hands up and cupped one under each of the melons, lifting and shaking a fraction. They felt every bit as good as they looked. Laura wriggled uncomfortably but said nothing.

Slowly and methodically, the snipping continued. Soon Laura's dense bush was reduced to a rather ridiculous mass of irregular short hairs. To get at the curls on either side of her slit, Grace introduced a finger between her pink lips and grasped one of them, to pull it out of her way and stretch the skin to make the hair available to the scissors. Laura gasped sharply. Grace peered up into her face with a knowing look in her eye, but deliberately misunderstood. 'It's all right. I'll be most careful.'

When the scissors were no longer useful Grace laid them down and picked up the can of shaving foam. Squirting a little onto the tips of her fingers, she laid it gently on Laura's pubic mound and massaged it in slow circles looking up, all the time, into Laura's face. What she saw there apparently pleased her, because she smiled and her hand moved lower until it was over the hood of Laura's clitoris. Her slow circles continued and a low, mooing noise burst from Laura's pursed lips. Her head went back, her hair brushing Pandora's face. Pandora moved her hands up and grasped one pink nipple in each, extending it and rolling it between finger and thumb. The mooing noise grew louder. Laura's thighs and knees began to quiver. When Grace stopped and took up the razor, Laura was breathing hard and looking down at her soapy body as if mesmerised.

Gently and carefully, Grace shaved her mound smooth and bald, then looked up. 'Sorry, Laura, but to get at the difficult bits, I have to put my finger in you.' She did so, and gripped one lip between that finger and her thumb as before. The razor slid on about its work, then it was time for similar treatment on the opposite side. Soon the job was done and all traces of hair removed. Grace then wiped away any residue of lather with a damp washcloth.

'That's it. It's over now. I was just thinking, though. We interrupted you before you had finished your fun and that wasn't very fair, was it? I just wondered if you might like us to finish the job for you, since we're here? Tell you what. I'll give you a sample of what it could be like. You can tell me to stop any time and I will.'

Grace leant forward, closer and closer, her face now deep between the parted thighs. Her breath huffed softly on the freshly shaved surfaces. Her tongue extended and parted the bare lips, probing inside. Laura gasped and the mooing noise started again. Pandora found that she was able to pull and twist the captive nipples quite freely without provoking any objection. Better still, she felt Laura's bound hands moving, searching out her body. She shuffled closer, parting her thighs more widely until one was pressed against each side of Laura's bare bottom. That contact, and the weight of the breasts in her hands, was definitely exciting. Laura's questing fingers sought and found Pandora's wide-open vagina and she felt them hook upwards and plunge inside her. Her excitement increased and she bounced wildly on the fingers to increase the stimulation.

Laura's time was near, Pandora could tell. Grace changed her position slightly and used her finger and thumb to pry open the slit before her and retract the protective hood. She slipped two fingers of the other hand into Laura's vagina and massaged her, then took the exposed clitoris between her lips, sucking and nibbling. Laura went mad, bucking and jerking as if in agony. Her moans rose to a shrill shriek as she came to her peak and collapsed, her weight sagging against Pandora's breasts. Pandora continued to support her as her breathing slowly returned to normal. For quite a long time after orgasm, her stomach muscles continued to ripple in spasms, dying echoes of her internal turmoil. Pandora's attention to her nipples had changed to a gentle, stroking massage of her whole breast area and Laura sighed, leaning her head back against the supporting shoulder.

Pandora whispered in her ear, 'Was that nice for you, Laura?'

Laura nodded, too shy to say the words.

Grace rose from her kneeling position and reached between them to untie the captive hands. 'Well now, Laura. That wasn't so bad, was it?'

Laura shook her head dumbly.

'Good! I'm glad you enjoyed it, because I rather feel you'll be joining me in similar fun any time I feel bored.'

'Oh no, Madam. Please, I'd rather not.'

'But I'd rather you did, Laura. So I think I'd better keep the photo for a while, after all.'

'But . . . You promised, My Lady.'

'Oh dear, Laura. I tell lies! Didn't you know? Get dressed and get out now. I'll ring for you if I need to be amused again.'

As Laura left, Pandora said, 'You know, Grace, you

don't play fair. Someone is going to catch up with you one of these days, then you'll be sorry.'

'Huh! Who would that be? Not my husband, that's for sure. You couldn't tear him away from his pet charities for long enough to take any interest in what I do. Anyway, be honest. Didn't that make you just the least bit horny?'

Pandora was forced to admit to herself that she had been aroused by what she had just seen and heard, but she prevaricated, not wanting Grace to know how deeply she had been moved. 'Maybe a bit; but it's not as though it was a man, is it? That would be really something.'

'Darling! What an extraordinary thing. You've read my mind. There's a little plot I've been working on for some time. You know Simon, Malcolm's valet?'

Pandora did. It was difficult not to notice the tall, handsome servant with his dark eyes and even darker, curly hair. 'Surely you haven't got anywhere with him?'

'Oh! That's not very complimentary, dear! But as it happens, you're right. He won't give me the time of day, although I've practically flung myself at him. The more I think about him, the more I just *have* to have him and I think I've found his weak spot. He's one of Malcolm's deserving cases, you know. Served a stretch in prison for something or another; fraud, I think. No one but Malcolm will employ him until he builds a reputation again. Are you game for a bit of fun?'

Pandora was well acquainted with Lady Crendall's 'bits of fun'. They usually left a trail of hurt and humiliated people in their wake. On at least one occasion she had been one of them. Pandora had already made up her mind that Grace was an ideal candidate for a spell at the Castle of Despair, but she felt she may as well let her lengthen the rope by which she was to be hoisted, so she acquiesced with apparent enthusiasm.

They went downstairs to the drawing room and Grace rang for Jameson. When he came, she asked him to send Simon to her at once. He left to convey her message and she took a green leather case from a drawer and brought it back to the sofa.

'What's that?' asked Pandora, but Grace would not say. She simply laid a finger along the side of her nose and winked mysteriously.

Simon knocked and came in. 'You wanted me, Your Ladyship?'

And how! thought Pandora.

'Yes, Simon. Can you tell me what this is?'

'Yes, Madam, those are Sir Malcolm's dress studs and cuff-links.'

'And you are responsible for them?'

'Yes, Madam. I keep them in Sir Malcolm's safe in his bedroom.'

'To which only you and my husband and I have a key?'

He was puzzled. 'Of course, Madam, but what . . .?'

'What are they made of, Simon?'

'They are gold, with inset diamonds, Madam.'

'Correction, Simon! That is what they ought to be. If you will inspect them closely you will see that more than half of them are nothing more than brass and glass copies. And not very good copies at that,' Grace added.

Simon paled. 'That's impossible, Madam!'

'Are you suggesting that I don't know fake jewellery when I see it?'

'No, Madam! Of course not! But if they have been tampered with, I can assure you that I had nothing to do with it.'

'You mean Sir Malcolm substituted fakes?'

'Oh no! Indeed not, Madam!'

'Then you must mean that you think *I* did it!'

'No! Of course not!'

'There are only the three of us, Simon. Whom do you think the police are going to suspect?'

Simon's already pale face went even whiter. 'No, Madam! Not the police! It would be ruin for me just when I'm getting back on my feet again. There must be something I can do to put things right. I could save the money to replace them.'

Grace pretended to think this over. 'I suppose I could help you to conceal this thing by paying for replacements, but that would mean you would owe me a great deal, wouldn't it?'

'You would find me most grateful, Madam.'

Apparently changing the subject, Grace said, 'Life in the country gets very boring, sometimes. Don't you find it so, Simon?'

He was perplexed, but answered circumspectly, 'If you say so, Madam.'

'I do say so! Tell me, Simon. Can you think of anything a young, handsome, healthy man who was truly grateful could do to relieve the tedium for two bored ladies?'

Simon's face cleared as the penny dropped. His expression was a picture as he turned over this proposition in his mind. In a second he saw the cunning mind behind the trap which had been set and sprung. Lady Crendall would get his body for her amusement for the price of a few pieces of inferior jewellery. If he exposed her ploy, who would believe him? He saw no way out and bowed to the inevitable.

'You know that I am always at your disposal, My Lady.'

'I knew you would understand, Simon. Shall we say in half an hour's time in my bedroom?'

'Very good, Madam. Will there be anything else?'

'Later, Simon. You may go now.'

When he had gone, Pandora said, 'Grace, you're absolutely shameless!'

Lady Crendall made a face. 'Oh, don't be so stuffy. You know you're as keen as I am to see him strip. If you're going to be nasty to me I won't let you watch.'

Half an hour later they were both in Grace's bedroom. Promptly, at the appointed time, Simon came to them there. Grace let him in and he stood uncertainly, looking from one to the other.

'You know what you're here for, don't you Simon?' Grace said.

'I think I do, Madam, but I would appreciate it very much if you would make it clear.'

'Very well. You are here to please us and you can do that best by taking off your clothes, for a start.'

After only a small hesitation, Simon began to strip. The

chest and arms which came into view were in no way disappointing. He was slim without being skinny and his body was firm, tanned and well muscled. Pandora appreciated the fact that his body hair was not profuse. When his only item of clothing left was a pair of undershorts, he stopped and fixed an appealing gaze on Grace. There was no mercy in her answering look.

'You surely don't expect to keep those ridiculous things on, do you?'

Obediently, he dropped them to the carpet and stepped out of them.

'Turn this way. We want to see.' Grace was enjoying his discomfiture. When all his body was on display, Pandora could not restrain a gasp of pleasure and surprise. His penis, half-erect already, was the largest she had ever seen. Stealing a glance at Grace, she could see that she, too, was impressed.

'Come and take my clothes off for me, Simon,' Grace said. She turned her back to give him access to her zipper and he stripped her with quiet efficiency, laying her clothes, one by one, neatly on a chair. Dressed only in her panties, she sat down on the edge of the bed and beckoned to him.

'Come and kneel here to take these off!'

That was not strictly necessary, but it seemed to Pandora that Grace got her jollies by watching Simon in a position of submission. As he reached for her panties, she raised one foot and placed the sole flat against his penis, pressing it into his body and wiggling her toes. She lifted her hips, thrusting her pubes towards him and he slid the panties down and took them off.

'Very good, Simon. Now lie down on the floor.'

'What?'

'You heard me. Lie down on the floor. Here. By my feet.'

He shrugged and sat down, then lay back parallel with the bed, his head to her right.

'Put your hands behind your head!' Grace sat, staring at his nakedness. His mighty organ was now in full erection, due to the erotic stimulus of being under the gaze and control of this woman.

Grace beckoned to Pandora. 'Come closer and have a good look.'

The combined stare of two pairs of eyes caused Simon to blush red and turn his head away. Grace slipped her feet back into her high heeled shoes. She raised one foot and brought it down on his naked skin so that the pointed heel rested in the centre of his tumescent penis. She pressed gently and Simon shifted uneasily.

'Keep still!' she said, and moved her other foot onto his body with her heel over his left nipple. Again she pressed, this time with both feet and, at the same time, rotated her ankles slightly so that the high heels were ground into his flesh.

'Do you like that, Simon?'

He didn't answer.

'I said, do you like that!' She increased the pressure by lifting herself slightly off the bed with her arms and he winced.

'Yes, Madam. If it pleases you, I like it.'

'Good,' she said and removed her shoes. She stood up and straddled his head, facing his feet, her legs straight and wide apart.

'What can you see, Simon?'

'I can see your body, Madam.'

'Yes, but which parts of my body can you see?'

'Your . . . I can see your private parts, Madam.'

Grace simulated annoyance. 'Really, Simon. I shall begin to think that you are being deliberately obtuse. Did no one ever tell you that it is most exciting to hear a man using coarse words. Surely I don't have to tell you what they are!'

'No, Madam.'

'So?'

'I can see your . . . cunt, Madam.'

Grace gasped and her hand moved, involuntarily, to her nipple. 'Would you like to fuck it?'

'Yes, Madam, if that would please you.'

'It would, but not yet.' She leaned forward slightly, reached around and spread her bottom cheeks.

'Now what do you see, Simon?'

'Your arse, Madam.'

'Good!' Grace shot Pandora a glance of glittering triumph. 'Have you ever licked a woman's arse, Simon?'

Simon's face was very red again. 'Yes, Madam.'

'Excellent. Then you shall lick mine.' She sank to her knees, bringing her crutch within reach of his head. 'You can use your hands again, now. Mine will be busy.' She picked up one of her delicate slippers from beside the bed. 'You can begin now. When you please me, I will rub your dick. Not too much, because you will need it for all the fucking you're going to do. When you don't please me, I shall spank your naughty big dick, like this.' She gave the penis in front of her a few light slaps with the leather sole of the slipper. Pandora thought that it had been fully erect before, but now it increased even further in size, jumping and jerking uncontrollably.

Simon parted Grace's bottom cheeks with his thumbs, raised his head and began to apply his tongue to her sphincter. A dreamy expression came upon Grace's face and she caressed his penis softly. 'Ah! Aaaah! Oh, Simon. You have done this before, haven't you!'

For several minutes, she continued to rock to and fro, savouring the sensation, then she shuffled back so that her soaking sex came within reach of his tongue. 'Give me an orgasm, Simon. Get me ready to be fucked!'

Pandora could tell from the agitated movements of her body and her heavy sighs and groans, that Simon was every bit as good at the front as he was at the back. In a remarkably short space of time, Grace shuddered and came to climax, thrusting hard down on the mouth beneath her and grunting with pleasure. She sat there for so long after it was over that Pandora began to fear that Simon would suffocate, but then she got up and beckoned Simon to do the same. His organ was still in full erection and Pandora could not take her eyes off it. It was enormous! Fully nine inches long and of more than adequate girth. Now that he was standing it jutted from his bush of dark hair in a most provocative fashion and Pandora felt an odd twinge between her legs. Grace was similarly hypnotised for a while, then she said, 'Well? Come on, Pandora. You strip off too!' Somewhat self-consciously, Pandora slipped out of her clothes and stood as naked as they.

Grace gestured to the bed and said, 'You lie in the middle, Simon, and Pandora and I will play book-ends on either side of you.'

Pandora started. This was not what she had envisaged. She had thought that her function was to be merely that of a decorative onlooker, but she reasoned that she might as well be comfortable as stand about, so she lay down in the appointed place. Grace leant over Simon and kissed him on the mouth, then she allowed her kisses to drift down his body until they landed on the tip of his straining penis. She gripped the shaft with both hands and took the head in her mouth, looking Pandora straight in the eye as she did so, as if to say, 'Watch how it's done!' She took more and more of it into her mouth until Pandora wondered how she could possibly do so without choking. Her head moved up and down, massaging it. Unseen by Simon, Grace frowned furiously at Pandora and, by eye movements and such head jerks as would fit into her rhythm, indicated that Pandora should play a more active role at the top end. That didn't seem much to ask, so Pandora propped herself on one elbow and stroked Simon's chest absent-mindedly. It was a nice chest and it was, she thought, not an unpleasant thing to be doing. Simon's hand came up and cupped her dangling breast, his fingers toying with her nipple. That was OK, too, Pandora decided. Presently, when he was worked up, he would roll away towards Grace, they would do the business and that would be that. Mission accomplished!

When Simon rolled, he did not roll towards Grace; he rolled towards *her*! Pandora was stunned into immobility so that, before she could prevent it he was between her legs and the tip of his penis was brushing her pubic hair. This was not in the plan! And what was that silly bitch, Grace, up to? So far from preventing this thing, she was actually helping him, reaching under his body to grasp his shaft and position it correctly. Pandora grunted at the sheer size of the thing as it penetrated the entrance to her vagina, but resisted the temptation to verbalise her protest. Then it thrust further, probing and pushing and it was a very exciting sensation. Normally, her preference was for sex with women but she suddenly realised that there was nothing she wanted more than to explore all Simon's possibilities. Now she had all of it inside her and Simon began a gentle, pumping rhythm which drove Pandora into a frenzy of sexual excitement. Sex with a woman usually involved a dildo or a tongue. This was something completely different. She could feel her vagina sucking and pulling at the giant which was consuming her, trying to drag it further in every time it withdrew a little. She had felt Grace's fingers inside her, but this was not the same. What she did with her body had little physical effect on Grace's fingers, but she could tell that she was having a considerable effect on Simon's penis and that was highly satisfactory. He sighed and began to breathe heavily and she felt her nipples prickling with the stimulation of her sense of power.

When Simon suddenly withdrew from her and rolled over onto Grace, Pandora almost cried out in disappointment. She watched their coupling with the deepest envy, fingering her clitoris and knowing just what Grace was experiencing. She stroked Simon's pumping buttocks and watched in fascination. When Grace came to climax with a groan, Pandora almost came herself, but when Simon rolled off her and lay on his back, Pandora's heart leapt and her vagina twinged with excitement. He had not finished! His tool was just as massively erect as ever. Quickly, she got up and straddled him, leaning forward, her breasts brushing his face as she guided his penis into the hole which so desperately needed filling. She moved her body up and down on him, generating the deep thrusts which she ached for, madly excited by the feeling of her own juices mingling with Grace's. Now she knew exactly what she wanted. She wanted to make Simon come. She wanted to feel his red hot sperm squirt into her with the full vigour of young manhood, bathing her insides with heat. She felt the first faint pulses of his impending ejaculation and now her desire changed. She wanted to come with him, but how could she move in order to accomplish that without bringing him off too early? Then Grace was kneeling beside her, her strong teeth nibbling at her nipple and her hand between Pandora's legs, feeling for her clitoris, readily available because of her wide-stretched straddle.

The problem was solved. Pandora knew that she couldn't wait another minute. She bounced, freely and madly, screaming with pleasure. Simon's hot flood spurted out in perfect unison with her own, squirming, writhing climax. She fell forward, her breasts crushed against his chest. She had just had the most enjoyable sex of her life and it felt wonderful.

Four

As Pandora passed through the anteroom on her way to the Ice Queen's office, she could not help remembering her last visit. Then, she had waited, naked and apprehensive, on the hard bench outside. This time she was fully dressed and there was no waiting. She knocked at the door and the sign above it flashed immediately to 'Enter'. Matrilla was sitting at her desk, intent on a sheaf of papers before her, which Pandora recognised as her own report.

The Queen looked up as the door opened. 'Ah! Pandora, my dear!' She rose with a smile to come around her desk and they exchanged formal kisses. 'Sit down. Sit down.'

Pandora glanced at the high-backed chair, recalling how uncomfortable she had been last time she sat there. Matrilla followed her eyes and laughed. 'No. Not there. That is for interviewees and trainees.' She gestured towards a more modern and comfortable seat closer to her desk and Pandora lowered herself into it, feeling very honoured.

Matrilla went back to her own seat and picked up the folder again. 'I'm most impressed,' she said. 'An excellent report. It seems to me that you must have had some training, which I find unusual in a woman from your walk of life.'

'I did a secretarial course, once, when I was out of money and friends,' Pandora replied.

'Ah! I see. Well, you could certainly give a few pointers to some of my other agents. I shall have to give that some thought. Now then, as to the subject of your report; Grace. Lady Crendall. You say she is a friend?'

'Yes, we've known each other for years.'

'And yet you think she would benefit by coming here for retraining? What, specifically, do you have in mind?'

'Well . . .' Pandora collected her thoughts. 'It's not that she's really wicked, if you understand me. It's just that she gives too little thought for the problems of others. Her servants, for instance. If she wants to achieve orgasm in a particular way, she goes for it and to Hell with anyone else. It seemed to me that she should learn to be more considerate.'

'Quite so.' The Queen resumed her study of the papers and Pandora looked about her. She was off guard when the next question came. 'Anything personal in this? A score of your own to settle?'

Pandora flushed and shifted uneasily in her seat. 'Not really.' She tried to meet the Queen's stare, but found her eyes wandering away. Damn the woman! She seemed to be able to read minds. Even though she could not see it, she could still feel that stare, which seemed to her to be gazing at her very soul. 'Oh well, then,' she said. 'She did tie me to a chair in the garden and stick her finger in me.'

'Mmm! A woman of some imagination.' Matrilla made a brief note. 'But surely a finger in your vagina wasn't too unpleasant for you?'

Pandora met her eyes again, flushing even more deeply. 'It wasn't in my vagina.'

'Aha. That's important!' Matrilla scribbled a few more notes. 'So, you are averse to anal stimulation?'

If she had been red before, Pandora was crimson, now. This was dreadful! 'Not really. It's just that it was so sneaky. I wasn't expecting it.'

'As you know, you're entitled to watch the retraining process. Would that ease your ruffled feelings?'

Pandora did not answer at once. 'I've thought about that. I think I would but at the same time, I would like to remain friends with her. I wouldn't like her to know that it was I who had her brought here. Can that be arranged?'

'Easily! So, your actions are only partially on your own behalf. I see your report mentions . . .' she flicked over some pages, '. . . Laura and . . . let me see. Ah yes! Simon. Do you recommend their presence?'

'Laura, certainly. I have spoken to her privately, without revealing too much, and I know she is itching to have some redress. As for Simon, I'm not so sure. I would be happy to speak to him, once you have made your final decision.'

Matrilla opened her desk diary. 'I make it now. I am scheduling Lady Crendall for corrective education in two weeks' time. You will make yourself available as an observer. Of course, you will be a necessary tool in the process of bringing her here.'

'I've been wondering about that,' said Pandora. 'How do you get your trainees here? Even I don't know where we are.'

'That is as it should be. Only a very few of my most trusted employees know the location of this castle, which is why you are brought here blindfolded and by helicopter. There are several strategies by which my victims are brought to me. Usually, they rely upon the greed or sexual appetite of the person concerned. That pleases me.' She smiled wryly. 'Because of that, one might consider what happens to them here as a sort of "own goal", or self-inflicted wound. In the case of Grace, we will use her interest in bizarre sex against her. I won't go into details. Another of my agents is here and I will brief you both together on several of our most common ploys. Have you met David Corby?'

'No I don't think so.'

'Hmm! Your major interest lies in lesbian sex, doesn't it?'

'Mostly, but not always.'

'You might find David quite interesting. A robust young man, but not good at writing reports. I intend that you should be together so that you can help him in that direction. That will give you the opportunity to look him over.'

The Ice Queen rose, 'I am about to administer corrective education to two of my trainees. Perhaps it would be useful for you to see more of what we do here. Would you care to come along?'

Pandora appreciated the fact that what was, in effect, a command, had been couched in terms of a question. 'Yes. Thank you, Madam.'

'I must ask you to wait here for a moment. Part of the corrective process consists of striking fear into the hearts of those who are to receive it. In this case, one of them is to be a man. I have found that what I am about to do substantially increases his apprehension while he waits to see what will happen to him. Marla and Luna are waiting for me in my private chamber and will prepare me.'

She left the office by her private door and Pandora waited as instructed. She could not help being intrigued by what Matrilla had said. Given a natural feminine curiosity plus time to ponder, she ought not to have been taken by surprise, but she was! The private door opened again and Pandora turned to look. She could not restrain a gasp of astonishment. At first, she did not recognise the tall, menacing figure silhouetted in the doorway. From head to toe, Matrilla was dressed in black. From under the wide brim of a Spanish style hat, her laser eyes now blazed through the slits of a leather mask. Her breasts were encased in a shiny PVC brassière, soft enough to show her nipple erection. Long, black, leather evening gloves came above her elbows, accentuating the white translucence of her upper arms. The PVC bikini bottom of her costume was cut very high on her hips, making her legs appear to go on for ever. That illusion was heightened by the length of white thigh before the start of her long, leather, high-heeled boots. Pandora now understood what she had meant about her appearance being a factor in corrective training. This change of costume had given those eyes new voltage and Pandora found herself gulping nervously at the thought of what this woman could do, should she choose to unleash her unlimited power.

'Follow me,' said Matrilla and led the way out of the office. She continued to lead the way along what seemed to be miles of broad corridors. Trotting along behind, Pandora was struck by the thought that the colour scheme of the castle seemed to have been designed to complement the black leather-clad figure striding before her. The grey of the bare stone walls and the flagstones beneath her feet gave a sombre and menacing feel to the place. Curtains of a rich purple hung at intervals and reminded Pandora of how perfectly the purple of Matrilla's usual clothing set off her black hair and pale skin, particularly when set against a grey background. As in the Great Hall and all other rooms which were intended to convey an atmosphere of dramatic threat, flaming torches were set in sconces projecting at an angle from the walls. Pandora knew that the castle had a perfectly adequate electricity supply; lighting in the bedrooms and other places intended for social activities was normal. Here, though, the electric lighting was deliberately indirect and dim, giving the torches their maximum impact. Even though she knew they were gas-fed and artificial, Pandora could not suppress a little shiver as she came under the spell of the decor and wondered what it was she was about to witness.

Matrilla arrived at a set of double doors. Pandora followed her through them and found that they were in an extremely large room, rather like a gymnasium, with a polished, wooden floor. She had little attention to spare for the room, however. No one entering that hall could avoid giving all their attention to the man and woman detained there. Both were naked and similarly restrained. Their arms were folded behind their backs and kept there by a one-piece leather garment, like a close-fitting sack, which reached to their upper arms and was tightly laced, thrusting their upper bodies forward. Their mouths were stopped with broad leather bands, buckled behind the head. Each wore a set of rubber-tipped nipple clips, from which leather leashes were stretched, attached to a beam above them. The tension on the leashes was such that, by standing on the tips of their toes, they could relieve some, but not all, of the pull on their nipples, which were stretched by the partial weight of their bodies. It was obvious that any movement, however slight, would result in extra discomfort and in witness to that, they both stood perfectly still.

Beside them stood one of the guards Pandora had seen when she was first addressed by the Queen. He had no visible hair on body or head. He wore only a loin cloth and his perfectly muscled, tanned body gleamed with an application of oil. As Pandora and Matrilla approached, he gave them a small, court bow, as though by long custom.

'How long now, Jason?' asked Matrilla.

'One hour, Madam. As you ordered. Shall I take them down?'

'No. In a minute.' Turning to Pandora, she said, 'This is Delilah and this is Mark. They are accomplices in the vile practice of blackmail. She entices men into her bed and he photographs them in compromising positions. Unluckily for them one of their victims happens to belong to the same club as David Corby. So we have them here for corrective education. Even now, their victim is watching what is happening to them and, I hope, deriving considerable satisfaction from it. Naturally, they chose only men in prominent positions with much to lose and it is therefore imperative that he remain unseen and anonymous.'

She stepped up close to Mark and stood looking into his face for long seconds. His eyes were almost the only part of that face capable of expression, but Pandora saw in them the terror which Matrilla's bizarre costume occasioned. As she had done, he was contemplating what the full exercise of the Queen's power might mean for him. With careful cruelty, Matrilla extended a forefinger and gently pushed against his chest. He lost his balance slightly, swaying to recover it. His nipples and the chest skin behind them extended visibly. He moaned behind his leather gag and shook his head in mute entreaty. Matrilla pushed again, a little harder, and this time it was several seconds before he could fully recover his balance, during which time his nipple torment must have been considerable. Apparently satisfied, the Ice Queen left him and stood in front of the woman who, having also seen the dominatrix costume and her partner's treatment, began to shake her head and make unintelligible noises. Matrilla raised the flat of her hand and made a feint towards her victim's chest, but stopped without touching her.

In anticipation of the push which failed to come, Delilah leant forwards to be brought up short by the pull of the leashes. For long moments, she remained in that position, her breasts pointing almost directly upwards, before she managed to recover her balance and resume her tip-toe equilibrium.

Matrilla laughed. 'All right, Jason. I'll have Delilah first. Take her gag out and get her down. Blindfold him, first. No reason why he should enjoy this next bit.'

Jason bound a black silk scarf across Mark's eyes, then unbuckled the girl's leather gag. As he removed it, Pandora could see that the inside of it was formed from a large, pear-shaped piece of rubber, which must have stretched any mouth it filled in a most uncomfortable way. As soon as she was released, Delilah threw herself on her knees, nuzzling Matrilla's leather-clad thighs. 'Please, Madam! Please! I beg of you! No more! I can't do it again. I'll die!'

The Ice Queen seized her by the hair and hauled her to her feet. 'Nonsense! You're a fine, strong, healthy girl and capable of a great many more orgasms than you think.'

'Then not that way, Madam. Any other way, please, but not that again!'

Matrilla ignored her pleading. She signed to Jason. 'Get her ready!' Grinning, he came forward with what appeared to be a metal bar, about a foot long, with leather cuffs attached to each end by swivel joints. Kneeling in front of Delilah, he forces her knees apart, none too gently, and strapped one of the cuffs around each of her lower thighs, just above the knee, so that she was quite unable to close her legs.

'Very good, Jason. You may position her now.'

Grinning, the guard picked up Delilah's dangling leashes and, by tugging at them, induced her to follow him into the centre of the room. She could walk only with a curious, slow, waddling gait. Certainly she could not run and she made no attempt to escape as he dropped her leashes and went to the side of the room. For the first time, Pandora noticed what seemed to be a coiled rope, secured to the wall at a height of some three feet. He came across the room, unwinding it as he came and Pandora saw that it was made of thick silk and was knotted every three inches or so. When he got to Delilah, he passed the rope between her legs, then went on to the other side of the room, where he pulled it tight so that it rose up and pressed itself into Delilah's crotch. He attached it to the wall behind her so that both ends were the same height and Pandora noticed that the last few feet of it appeared to be elasticated. She realised that Delilah would be quite unable to get any slack out of the silk. If she pressed her body weight down onto it, it would immediately spring back and exert the same pressure as before.

The Ice Queen called to her. 'Very well, girl. Off you go! Across and back, pressing your breasts against one wall and your bottom against the other, until I tell you to stop.'

Delilah stood irresolute, not obeying. Matrilla sighed heavily and went over to her. 'You're being disobedient, Delilah!'

The young woman turned a tear-stained face towards Matrilla with a final, hopeless plea. 'Please don't make me! I'll do anything else!'

Matrilla feigned friendly patience. She took Delilah's chin in one hand and forced her head around to look into her face. 'Surely you remember what happened last time you refused. You had those nasty, heavy weights attached to your nipples, didn't you?' The girl nodded miserably. 'Now, you don't want that again, do you?' The dark head shook. 'Very well then, get on with it. The sooner you start, the sooner it will be over. Remember I can either pull you by your nipples or take my whip to that bare bottom of yours, then *I* shall be dictating the pace. If you do it on your own, you can go as fast or as slowly as you like. What you can't do, on pain of a serious bottom thrashing, is stop! Start now, or take the consequences!'

Slowly and resignedly, Delilah set off with her odd, waddling walk. The Queen came back to Pandora and they watched the girl's progress together.

'You see what's happening,' Matrilla said. 'The rope is of softest silk, but still exerts friction along the whole length of her sex. Every time she comes to a knot which, as you can see, is very often, it bumps against her clitoris.'

Pandora *could* see, very clearly. She realised that what

was going on was not only working Delilah up into a sexual frenzy, but was vicariously having a similar effect on her own body. Without realising what she was doing, she rubbed at the front of her dress in the groin area, trying to quiet the demon which had awakened in her loins and was making her knickers damp. Matrilla, who missed nothing, noted the movement.

Delilah reached the wall in front of her and started back. The Ice Queen allowed her to go several paces before she called, 'You forgot to press your breasts against the wall! You'll have to go back and do it. *Do* try to remember next time.'

For a moment, Pandora thought Delilah was going to refuse again but, after a pause, she obeyed, shuffling forward to press her clipped breasts against the cold surface.

'Now that she is going backwards,' explained Matrilla, 'the knots are bumping against her bottom first. Remember what stimulation in that area was like for you?'

Pandora did, and now the sensation in her vagina was intense. Her hand moved a little faster. At that moment, Delilah experienced her first orgasm, evidenced by the clearly visible contractions of the muscles of her stomach, thighs and buttocks, and by her gasps and facial expression.

Pandora tried to imagine what it would be like to be watched by three pairs of eyes (four, she corrected herself, counting those of the invisible onlooker) whilst being forced to bring about her own climax. She could tell that the sex juices between her legs were now too copious for her knickers to deal with and felt them trickling down her inner thighs.

Matrilla stared at her. 'You're getting too sexed up for your own good, Pandora. You have to let that pressure go. Would you like Jason to fuck you?'

Pandora flushed. 'No. I don't think so.'

'Lick you out, then? He will, gladly.'

The flush deepened. Pandora shook her head, too embarrassed to speak.

The Queen nodded, matter-of-factly. 'Maybe you're right. Perhaps we should just masturbate.'

'What!' Pandora was breathless with surprise.

'Do you deny that what you want, more than anything right now, is an orgasm?'

Pandora found that she could not lie. 'Well, yes! But Jason . . .'

'You mean that you take no pleasure in having a man's eyes on your body?'

Pandora could not deny that either. 'No . . . I mean, yes. But here?'

'Why not? This is where the source of your excitement is. For sure, I propose to give myself a thrill and I suggest you do the same, unless you want to burst. I could make that a command, if you wish.'

'No,' said Pandora, slowly. 'That won't be necessary.'

'Good! Help me with my costume!' Matrilla turned her back and Pandora saw that the PVC brassière was fastened with press-studs. She unclipped them and the Queen removed the garment. She turned her hip towards Pandora, showing that the bikini bottom had side-fastening studs, too. When Pandora unclipped those, the black PVC pants fell to the floor and Matrilla kicked them away. She kept on the boots, gloves and hat. So far from serving as any sort of covering, they seemed only to make her more naked than she was. Pandora could not help staring at her body. Her skin was very smooth and white. She was extremely slender, with flat hips, bottom and stomach. Her breasts hardly protruded at all, but her nipples were long and brown and already fully erect. From the jet-back colour of her head hair, obviously natural, Pandora had already guessed that her pubic hair would be black also. It was, but there was very little of it; not because it had been shaved or waxed, she noticed, but because it was naturally sparse, hardly amounting to more than a few wisps, so that the vertical slit between her thighs which denoted the beginning of her vulva was clearly delineated.

'Now you!' said Matrilla, and it sounded like an order.

Without nearly so much aplomb as Matrilla, Pandora stripped, very conscious of being watched. She found that embarrassing, but exciting at the same time. Finally, she too was nude and the Ice Queen stretched out her hand.

'Come! I usually lean against this table.' She went to a table which bore an assortment of whips, straps and canes. Sweeping the front edge clear, she perched herself on it and with a gesture, invited Pandora to join her on her right.

There was an awkward pause. Pandora, in the novelty of this situation, was not quite sure what to do. Matrilla reached across with her right hand and laid it on Pandora's pubic mound. 'Shy? Let me start you off.' She moved her hand down until her middle finger was over Pandora's clitoral bump, then began to make soft, circular movements.

Pandora's head jerked back with a shock of pure pleasure then, greatly daring, she extended her left hand and laid it flat on Matrilla's bare, lean belly. The skin beneath her fingers was very cold and very smooth. She could distinctly feel the hard, bunched stomach muscles.

Matrilla took the questing hand with her left and pushed it down over the thin pubic hair until Pandora's fingers rested over the clitoris below. 'Go on, then. I won't break.'

They sat side by side, gently masturbating one another, while the object of their scrutiny continued to shuffle back and forth across the room. Her first climax having paved the way, ensuing ones – although of lesser intensity – were produced with greater ease, so that she was now in an almost constant state of sexual turmoil. Yet she dared not stop even though, by continuing to move, she was effectively masturbating herself into exhaustion. She now crept along with agonising slowness in a futile attempt to reduce the powerful impact that the rope and its knots were having on her grossly over-sensitised genitals, yet it seemed that every few steps brought on yet another shuddering eruption of pleasure, awesome in its cumulative effect. Now there did not seem to be a single muscle in her body which was not leaping and dancing under the faint sheen of perspiration which covered her skin. Even those supporting her breasts contracted spasmodically, producing a constant, twitching movement which Pandora found fascinating to watch. She pressed herself more urgently against Matrilla's hand, while her own moved to seek entrance for her fingers into the vagina just below them.

Matrilla shifted her bottom on the edge of the table, splaying her legs to permit access. Pandora found the way in, crooked two fingers and plunged them deep into the wetness there. Even Matrilla's vagina was cold, she noticed. Truly an Ice Queen.

Matrilla copied her movement, inserting two fingers deep into Pandora's vagina, causing her to gasp and almost cry out, wriggling in the grip of a preliminary orgasm. She found that the touch of the leather-gloved fingers was, somehow, more exciting than if they had been uncovered and she savoured the unfamiliarity of it all. She was disappointed when the exciting fingers were removed and she found her own hand grasped and pulled out of Matrilla.

Then the Ice Queen was standing in front of her, staring intently into her face. 'Put your hands behind you, flat on the table. Lean back! Stay like that. You are not to move, no matter what.'

At such a direct command, Pandora had no alternative but to obey. Obediently, she adopted the desired pose, though her clitoris was screaming at her to be touched. Matrilla stretched out both hands and took each of Pandora's nipples between finger and thumb. Still staring into her face, she began to milk them, stretching, rolling and kneading with firm but gentle movements. Instinctively, Pandora brought one hand towards the front of her body, but Matrilla stopped her with one word.

'No!'

What was happening to her breasts was having a devastating effect on Pandora. Quite apart from what was being done, there was the smell and feel of the leather which was touching her, exciting her madly. Over Matrilla's shoulder she could still see the unfortunate Delilah, now a quivering wreck. That sight, and the insistent, ceaseless teasing of her nipples was causing waves of contractions to convulse her vagina and uterus. She felt that her clitoris must be jutting out like a man's penis, so stiff and long did it feel. It was pulsing with a life of its own so that it seemed to Pandora that just one touch on it would be enough to send her into hysterical ecstasy.

'Touch me, please! Just a little!'

'No! Your next orgasm is going to be by nipple torture only. I so decree it.'

Pandora closed her eyes and rocked her head to and fro with the awful strain of refraining from masturbation.

'Please! No more! Mercy! I won't come this way.'

'You will!'

In an attempt to relieve one of the causes of her unbearable agitation, Pandora stopped looking at Delilah and cast her eyes downwards. She saw her own strong, brown teats being gripped by soft black leather and manipulated. They were longer than she had ever seen them and the whole of the breast area around her areolae was massively engorged. As she watched, a drop of clear fluid formed at the end of each nipple. Matrilla bent her head forward and licked them off, one after the other.

Pandora's stomach contracted massively, as though she had been punched there. Her legs buckled and trembled, so that she would have sunk to the floor had the table not supported her. Her hands beat a drumroll of frustration on the table top as she fought for breath. The stomach contractions continued, now coming every second and with them, hoarse grunts as she doubled over in time with them.

'Oh God! You're going to make me come! Stop! Oh! Stop, for pity's sake! I can't stand any more. I'm coming! *I'm coming!*' Pandora's voice became one long, continuous shriek as the full blast of nipple-induced orgasm hit her. She flopped forward into Matrilla's arms, heedless of protocol, and sagged there, panting for air and waiting for her uterine contractions to slow down.

Matrilla set her back on the table and smiled. 'See! I told you I could make you come.' She left Pandora to recover and went across to Delilah who was now, clearly, exhausted. 'Want to stop now?'

Delilah leant toward the Queen and attempted to shower her breasts with slobbering kisses. 'Please! Oh, please! Let me stop!'

'Very well. Just get hold of yourself. I never knew anyone to make such a fuss over a few little orgasms. Just stand quietly until you've calmed down a bit.' She signed to Jason, who unfastened the rope and recoiled it, replacing it in its original position. 'There we are,' said the Ice Queen, brightly. 'All ready for tomorrow!'

'No! Oh, please God, no! What can I do? I'll do anything!'

'I wonder if you mean that?'

'I do! I swear it! I do!'

'I see. Well, we'll soon see if you're serious about that or if you're just pretending. Jason! Take off the knee-spreader then bring her over to me.'

Matrilla turned on her heel and walked back to the table. Pandora, who was climbing wearily into her clothes, watched her approach and marvelled at her insouciance. Semi-naked as she was, she ought to have looked vulnerable. Far from that, she exuded imperious power with every swinging stride.

Jason led Delilah back to the table by her leashes and put them into Matrilla's hand. She jerked on them, lightly but with sufficient force to cause Delilah to gasp. 'Want me to take these off?'

'Yes! If you please, Madam.'

'Kiss me first.'

'Yes, of course, Madam.' Delilah leaned forward but Matrilla drew back out of reach.

'Not there, stupid! There!' She leaned back against the table, splayed her legs and pulled her sex lips apart to reveal the glistening interior. Without a second's hesitation, Delilah fell on her knees and nuzzled into Matrilla's crotch, licking and kissing.

'Enough! I want to save myself. Get up! Jason! Free her arms!' As he did so, Matrilla removed the clips and leashes from Delilah's breasts. She heaved a sigh of relief, tinged with the anguish of returning circulation in her nipples which she tried to assuage by rubbing them.

'Sit in that chair! You may rest for five minutes to recover your strength. You're going to need it.' Delilah sank gratefully into the proffered chair, bending forward with her arms folded across her upper body, rocking gently.

'Now, Jason, take him down, bring him here and set him up in position one!' Jason unclipped the leashes from Mark's nipples and he staggered back, cramped muscles inadequate to keep him on balance. He was given scant time to recover as Jason grasped him and marched him to the table. Sweeping the contents to one side, he put his hand on the back of Mark's neck and bent him forward, pressing the side of his face against the table top. He reached underneath the table and brought up one end of a thick strap, which he laid across Mark's back, over the encased arms. He brought the other half of the strap from under the other side of the table and buckled them together, pulling with all his strength so that Mark's body was pressed immovably to the surface.

Going behind him, he spread his legs and cuffed each ankle to the corresponding table leg. Matrilla watched closely. Much as she enjoyed torturing women, what was particularly sweet to her was to see a man being placed in a position of humiliation and complete vulnerability. She allowed herself the pleasure of running her eyes over his nakedness, observing the upthrust buttocks, totally bare and available for the exercise of whip, cane or strap. She shivered in delicious anticipation and fingered her sex. Stepping up to the table, she trailed her fingers down his back and dipped into the crease between his bottom cheeks, delighting when she saw that the touch of her cool hand actually made his flesh crawl and produce goose-pimples on the backs of his legs. She went to his head to remove the blindfold and the gag. He turned his head to stare at her in sullen defiance, not speaking. She was pleased about that. She liked to watch for the moment when defiance and machismo turned to abject surrender and snivelling sycophancy. It was no fun unless there was a will to be broken.

The Ice Queen picked up a black rubber paddle. It was about nine inches long and four inches wide; thick, but flexible, with a handle at one end for better grip. She tested it by slapping it against her hand, then went to where Delilah was sitting, now seemingly somewhat recovered and upright.

Matrilla handed her the paddle. 'Very well! You may commence!'

'What?'

'Are you particularly dense, girl? You are to beat him with this!'

'Oh, Madam! I couldn't . . . I've never . . .'

'So you were attempting to deceive me when you said you would do anything rather than go back on the rope tomorrow?'

'No, Madam! Truly I wasn't. But this . . .'

Matrilla was implacable. 'It's your choice, of course,' she said, casually. 'I shall beat him if you don't, so he's going to get a thrashing one way or another. This way, there's just a chance you may avoid another session of orgasms tomorrow.'

This reasoning was very difficult to argue with. Delilah took the proffered instrument and went rather nervously to the table. She slapped, tentatively, at the bare buttocks, then turned, as if to appeal once more to the Queen.

'Perhaps I should make myself clearer, Delilah,' said Matrilla. 'Now that you have made a start, I demand that you finish the job, but properly. Every stroke is to be delivered with the full force of your arm, in the place and manner in which you deem it will cause the maximum pain. I want to hear him scream for mercy. I want to see real tears. I want to see him spill his seed, involuntarily. If all these things happen, you may escape the rope, tomorrow; I can't promise. What I can promise is that if I don't see and hear these things, you will go back on the rope, today, and make twelve passes. Do you understand better now, exactly how things are?'

'Yes, Madam.'

'Then proceed. I shall be watching you closely.'

'How many strokes should I give him?'

'No specific number. You will continue to beat him until I, not you, decide that your arm is too tired to be effective. You will, of course, change arms from time to time, to avoid getting tired too quickly.'

Delilah took up a position beside the table and

moistened her lips. Finally, she swung the paddle with all her strength so that it slapped across Mark's bare behind. A bright red patch appeared on his white buttocks. His entrapped body jerked as much as it was able and his head came up off the table in a gesture of pain, but he made no sound. The paddle rose and fell again, then again and again, until there was no white skin to be seen, only a fiery pinkness. Still he continued to bear his punishment with stoicism.

Matrilla was fiercely exultant. Knowing that his eventual collapse was inevitable made it all the more exciting to watch his progress towards that state and the longer he could delay the moment, the longer would her pleasure last.

She beckoned Pandora to her. 'Isn't that a marvellous sight?' she said. 'Use of such a paddle spreads the weight of the blows and prolongs the process. It's not so bad for him now, but later, when the skin is thoroughly tenderised, it will be much worse. And yet there can be no cutting of the flesh, which means that I can beat him, or have him beaten, tomorrow. Coming on an already bruised bottom, that should be something to see, eh?'

Pandora noticed that Matrilla was breathing faster, her eyes were alight with lust and her voice was just a little unsteady. The spectacle of a man being humiliated and tortured was a real turn-on for her.

'And now, my dear,' said Matrilla, 'I need you to service me with your lips and tongue.' She arranged herself as before, her bottom half on the edge of the table, her legs apart and her fingers pulling her sex open. Her tone implied that it would have been unthinkable for Pandora to have demurred and she did not. She knelt down and embraced Matrilla's thighs. The feel of the leather against her skin thrilled her. When she moved her hands up onto the exposed section of thigh-skin, it felt cold and hard, as the rest of her body had done. She felt herself drawn to the sparsely-haired apex where those thighs met. She extended her tongue and began to lick at the cool, pink orifice before her face.

Matrilla drew in her breath sharply. 'Good! Very good! Not too much on my clitoris for now. I don't want to come until he begins to scream. When you hear that, you will know that I require my orgasm, and you will supply it.'

Obediently, Pandora confined herself to licking along Matrilla's inner labia, occasionally poking her tongue further into her vagina. As it always did, the taste of another woman in her mouth excited her and she slipped one hand up underneath her dress and eased a finger into her panties to manipulate her own clitoris. Behind her, she could hear the regular, repetitive slap of the paddle falling, except that now each stroke was accompanied by a whistling snort of air from Mark's nostrils.

Delilah's right arm was tiring and she took the paddle into her left hand, swinging back-handed, now. Although the blows were lighter because of that, they were now falling on buttocks which had already received many slaps, so the pain was in no way diminished. Now Mark's snorts changed to heavy groans. He kept his mouth shut and his teeth clamped together so that they were only barely audible, but Matrilla heard them nevertheless. They made her vagina and breasts tingle in tense anticipation and she reached up to pull and knead her own nipples, as she had done with Pandora's so recently.

Delilah changed the paddle back to her right hand and slapped with renewed vitality. This change brought about an almost immediate alteration in Mark's condition. His knees, which had trembled before, now flexed as he bucked and heaved like a madman and wriggled his buttocks as far as he was able in a futile attempt to avoid the cause of the searing pain which permeated his whole backside. He beat his forehead on the table in his efforts to remain silent, but could not do so. His mouth opened wide, tears streamed down his face and he began to scream.

'No more! No more! For God's sake, no more! Mercy!'

The screaming stopped, momentarily, as Delilah hesitated and turned to the Ice Queen, only to find no clemency there. 'Go on! Go on! Only harder. Who told you to stop!'

The beating resumed and so did the screams. Now there were no intelligible words, only animal howls. Matrilla shuddered, her eyes fixed on that point beneath the table where she would expect to see the first spurt of semen and Pandora, mindful of her instructions, directed her attention to the nubby erection of the Queen's clitoris and began to suck and nibble at it. She could see those hard stomach muscles wriggling like snakes and knew that what she was doing was having a powerful effect. Out of the corner of her eye, she could also see Matrilla tugging at her nipples, extending them to great length and pinching them hard. From the greatly increased flow of slippery liquid which covered her face, she could tell that Matrilla was on the brink of orgasm. Without stopping her oral stimulation, she inserted three fingers into Matrilla's vagina and pumped rapidly.

The Queen's triumph was complete. She feasted her eyes on the man's abused body and her mind on his broken spirit. Her orgasm was cataclysmic and exultant, and she pressed Pandora's head hard into her body to extract the maximum pleasure from her attentions. As always, she fought hard to control any outward sign of her climax, but could not prevent her knees from trembling and jerking. With uncharacteristic self-indulgence, she permitted herself several gasps which would, she hoped, be mistaken for deep breaths.

She indicated that Pandora should rise and kissed her full on the mouth, licking her face so as to be able to taste her own juices. Only then did she seem to become aware of the fact that the beating and the screams were continuing.

'Very well, Delilah, you may stop now!'

Thankfully, the girl dropped the paddle and stood, rubbing her sore arm as Matrilla approached. Mark lay completely subjugated on the table top. Beneath his face, a pool of tears had collected and he was, even now, hiccuping and sobbing quietly, his chest heaving.

'Now, Delilah. Let us see how well you have done. I heard screams. I saw tears. But no seed has been spilled, I'm afraid. You know what that means, of course?'

The girl paled and fell on her knees, her hands clasped together. 'No, Madam! Please! You couldn't be so cruel!'

'Don't be silly, Delilah. You, of all people, must know that I could.' She pretended to be deep in thought. 'I suppose there is a way,' she said, at last.

'Tell me, Madam! Just tell me!'

'Well, the requirement was that he should spill his seed. Can you bring that about?'

Her relief was evident. 'Of course, Madam!'

'Without using your hands?'

It took only a second for the girl to understand. 'Of course, Madam. If he is taken off the table and laid on the floor . . .'

'Oh no! I'm afraid he can't be removed from the table until our bargain is complete.'

'Oh! Then I don't see . . .' For several seconds more, Delilah frowned in puzzlement, then suddenly she did see 'Oh! I understand what you mean, Madam.'

'And you can do that?'

'Gladly, Madam!'

'Excellent! Except that I have decided that I don't want to actually see his semen now. No trace of it at all. Ever!'

'I'm afraid I don't understand, Madam.'

'Surely you do. All the ingredients are there. You are to induce an ejaculation with him tied to the table and without using your hands. When that happens, I shall be watching closely. If I see a trace of his emission, you will be on the rope tomorrow. Now, are you sure you can't think of a way of achieving what I demand?'

Delilah's answer was slow in coming, her face working and her mouth screwed up in anticipation of what she was being asked to do. 'I can think of a way, Madam.'

'Good. Get on with it, then. And, to give you some assistance and encouragement, I will beat his very sore bottom for you. The sooner you make him come, the sooner his pain will end. It's up to you.'

Delilah went to the table behind Mark, turned her back to him and sat down. Using hands and bottom, she shuffled backwards between his parted legs and stretched her head back, pushing upwards into his groin in search of his now flaccid penis. Without the assistance of her hands, it took a few seconds of nudging and tongue movements before she was able to take it into her mouth. As she sucked on it, fearful of having it slip out again, Mark awoke from his stupor. His head came up off the table, the tendons in his neck standing out like whipcords and he gave a great gasp of pleasure as his organ sprang immediately to the full extent of its erection.

Delilah moved her head back and forth, sucking hard. Little explosions of sound escaped as tiny amounts of air leaked between her lips and the flesh they encompassed. Matrilla picked up the paddle and began to beat his buttocks. It was a double stimulation for him which it was impossible to resist. She had time for only three stinging blows before his knees jerked spasmodically. He raised his head again and shouted; not in pain this time, but in the throes of ejaculation.

His pelvis thrust urgently towards the source of his delight as his semen spurted into Delilah's closed mouth, and went on doing so for some time. Dropping to her knees, Matrilla stared intently at Delilah, who kept her lips clamped tightly around the deflating penis, desperate to prevent the escape of any of the salty fluid which filled her mouth. She swallowed convulsively, her throat muscles bobbing while her eyes turned to meet those of the Queen.

'Not one drop, remember, Delilah! Not even the slightest bead of moisture, even if you have to sit there all night.'

Delilah nodded as she kept her mouth and lips at work, her tongue sweeping everywhere around the fleshy lump she sucked on, searching for the last traces of his spend so that she could conceal it by swallowing it. When finally she dared to let go, she watched in feverish anxiety as Matrilla peered closely at her work.

'Hmmm! Let me see your mouth. Open wide!' After a final gulp, Delilah opened her mouth so that Matrilla could inspect the inside from all possible angles. 'Hmmm!' said the Ice Queen again, noncommitally, and got up. She picked up her brassière and pants and Pandora helped her to put them on again.

Delilah scrambled out from under the table, hopping from foot to foot. 'And tomorrow, Madam? What about tomorrow?'

'What? Oh, tomorrow! We'll see when it comes, shall we? Lock them up for the night, Jason. Pandora! Come!' Every inch the Ice Queen, she swept out followed by Pandora, who was much impressed by what she had just witnessed.

Five

The bar which was provided at the Castle for the benefit of guests could have been mistaken for any rather superior establishment located elsewhere. The music was soft, the lights low and the booths discreet. It was at one of these booths that Pandora kept her appointment with David. Their meeting at their briefing, earlier, had been something of a shock. She had instantly recognised him as the impertinent young man who had hung about in the anteroom to gape at her nudity. She had been annoyed to find that she blushed at the recollection. However, it was not practical to cold-shoulder him when they would need each other's help and support in absorbing what they were told about the capture and transport of potential trainees, so she had swallowed her anger and her pride.

The ostensible reason for this later rendezvous was that Pandora should give David some assistance with his report-writing. Matrilla had been very insistent on that, but had permitted it to take place in an informal atmosphere, suggesting the bar as a suitable place. Consequently, it was partly at Matrilla's command, and partly at David's invitation, that Pandora now made her way across the soft carpet to join him.

He stood up as she approached, smiled and ushered her into the green leather seat opposite him. 'Drink?'

'Thank you. G and T, please. Ice and lemon.'

He raised a finger, caught the waiter's eye and ordered. 'So, what did you make of our briefing?'

'Pretty ingenious, I thought. How about you?'

He frowned. 'Yes. Trouble is, I'm not sure I got absolutely all the details right.'

'Oh? I did.'

'Yes! I saw you squiggling all over the place. Shorthand?'

'Yes.' Her short answers were not due to his behaviour on their very first meeting. She had got over that, she thought. Rather, she had in mind Matrilla's remarks and was sizing him up as a potential sex toy. She had not made up her mind yet, but had so far seen nothing which would prevent her from using him for that purpose. Fortunately, it was only in olden days that a girl had to wait for the man to chase her. If her decision was in the affirmative, she would tell him of it and he could take it or leave it. Not that he was likely to leave it. Her experience had taught her that all men, without exception, went through life to the marching song of 'Where My Willy Leads, There Will I Follow'. Willies, she knew, pointed to her body as did a compass needle to the North Pole.

Abruptly, she broke off this train of thought. He had been speaking, but she hadn't been listening. 'Sorry! What?'

'I was just saying that I would be glad of the chance to crib some of your notes.'

'Oh sure. I'll type them up for you.'

'Thanks. That's good of you. Especially in the circumstances.'

'What circumstances?'

'Well, you know. Looking at you like that in the anteroom.'

Pandora was deliberately casual. 'Oh, that. Did you enjoy it?'

'Absolutely. You have a gorgeous body, you know.'

Oddly enough, Pandora did know. Start the pumps, she thought, it's getting too thin to shovel. She smiled. 'How nice of you. That's very flattering.'

Her drink arrived and she sipped it, appraising him over the rim. He was reasonably good looking, clean and well-dressed. What she could see of his physique under his clothes was satisfactory. He spoke well and was prepared to be ingratiating. Well, she thought. Why not? It might be amusing to dally awhile in the long, dark hours.

She was about to inform him of her decision when he spoke. 'Do you fuck?'

'What!' She stared at him in disbelief.

'Do you fuck?'

She shook her head, despairingly. 'Sheesh! Don't tell me you've been getting it with *that* hoary old line. It's got whiskers on it!'

She was pleased to see that he had the grace to look a little embarrassed. 'Well, one does one's best.'

'Pretty poor best!' she said. She continued to stare at him contemplatively. 'Anyway, the answer to your question is, "Yes!" I do fuck, but only my way.' She watched the compass needle quiver and swing. The bait was in the water. Would he take it? Here he came now, definitely interested.

'Oh, what way is that?'

Now to jiggle the bait a bit, to make it more attractive. 'I don't really think you're up to it.' Was that too much of a jiggle? Would he be scared off?

'Try me!'

There it was! The float was under. Time to strike! 'I like to be on top with my men tied down.' This was always an exciting moment. Had she got him? Was the hook firmly in his uoper lip?

'Sounds good to me!'

Yes! Hook, line, sinker *and* float! Now to just reel him in. 'My room, then? Eleven o'clock?'

'Great! I'll be there.'

Thank God, thought Pandora, for His great wisdom in making men so bloody stupid!

Pandora had spent some time with her preparations, assisted by Melissa, who had gone to a lot of trouble to find all the things that would be needed. She didn't expect David to be late and she was not disappointed. Promptly at eleven o'clock he knocked at the door of her room. Melissa opened it and let him in with a knowing smirk, which he pretended not to notice.

Pandora dismissed her. 'Thank you, Melissa. I shan't need you again tonight.' The blonde girl grinned like a Cheshire cat, bobbed a curtsey and left.

David crossed the room towards her, but she held up a warning hand before he could get too close. 'Uh uh! My way. Remember?'

He shrugged, amused. 'OK. You're the boss.'

'I am,' said Pandora. 'Take your clothes off.'

He blinked. 'Just like that?'

'Just like that. Or leave. Whichever you prefer.'

'Fair enough, I suppose,' he said. 'After all, I've seen you strip.'

She sat on the edge of the bed and watched him undress. He wasn't bad at all, she thought. Quite a catch. The dark hair on his chest and shoulders was not too much for her. When he had finished, she said, 'Turn around and let's have a good look.'

He revolved under her cool stare and she was amused to see that his penis, which was more than adequate in size, was already beginning to erect itself. She was not unfamiliar with the effect she had on men, but it was always nice to see that it still worked.

'Well? What now?' he asked.

Pandora got up and went over to a wheeled hospital-type trolley and patted its black leather padding. 'You get up here and lie down.'

He looked doubtful. 'Not the bed?'

'No. Not the bed. Here. It's quite solid and the brakes are on.'

He shook his head sadly and Pandora could see him humouring the little woman as he came over and climbed on.

'Lie down on your back.'

He lay down and she saw that the novelty of the situation had caused his penis to become even more erect.

'Tell me, why the trolley and not the bed?' he asked.

'Because it has a metal frame, silly,' she replied. 'Give me your wrist.'

'Oh, I see,' he said, although she could tell that he didn't.

She placed a handcuff on his right wrist, pulled it up and clipped it to the top corner of the trolley. She did the same with his left, then went to his feet. Since handcuffs would have been too small for the purpose, Melissa had found metal anklets. Pandora used these, their accompanying lengths of chain and two padlocks to secure his ankles to the bottom corners.

Satisfied, she stepped back and surveyed her catch. 'There! You'll do!' she said.

'Are you going to undress now?'

'Not just yet, darling. I have to get you ripe and randy, first, don't I?' She came close to the trolley and leant over his helpless, naked body. Very gently, she blew on his penis. It stirred and lengthened a little more. She shifted her position so that she was looking up his body into his face, then slowly extended her tongue to signal what she was going to do next. Very deliberately, she applied it to the base of his penis and gave a long, slow lick, all the way to the tip. She put her cool, delicate hand around it and made tiny, masturbatory movements, then blew on it again so that her saliva created a slight chill. His organ was now massively erect, twitching as it jutted from his pubic hair.

David moaned and rolled his head. 'Christ, Pandora. That's terrific. You're good.'

'I am, aren't I?' she said. 'Now you just hang onto that while I get everything ready.'

She went across to the dressing table and he expected to see her strip. Instead, she came back with a length of broad, red ribbon in her hand. He watched in astonishment as she proceeded to tie it around his penis, just below the glans and arrange the ends in a decorative bow. The touch of her fingers and the minor constriction of the ribbon did nothing to slacken his erection.

'What are you doing?'

'I'm tying a pretty ribbon on your dick. Why? Don't you like it?'

'Well, of course I do. But why?'

She bent over his head and kissed him lightly on the lips. 'You do ask such a lot of questions, David. Just be patient and you'll see.'

He watched as she gathered up his clothes and put them on the shelf under the trolley. She went to the door which led into the corridor and opened it, then she came back to the trolley and let the brake off.

It wasn't until she went to the head of the trolley and started to push it out of the room that David had any inkling of the trap she had laid. He pulled frantically at his handcuffs. 'Pandora! Hey, Pandora! What's going on?'

'Can't you see, David?' she replied, calmly. 'We're going for a little ride.'

'Jesus, Pandora! I'm naked, for Chrissake! Don't take me outside!'

'Not only are you naked, dear, darling David, but you have a big red bow tied round your willie!' To his horror, she continued to push him along the corridor and he could tell that there was no chance that this was just a joke, to frighten him a bit, before she took him back into the room.

'Pandora!' he shouted, then remembered that a noise might attract an audience, which was the last thing he wanted. 'Pandora!' he hissed, *sotto voce.* 'This just isn't funny!'

'No it's not, is it, David? It's not a bit funny to be naked and to have anyone who cares to stare at you. How does it feel when it's *your* body that's on show?'

'Oh God!' he groaned. 'That's what this is about. I thought you'd got over that.'

'Isn't that interesting, David?' she said. 'I thought I'd got over it, too. And then, you know, I found I hadn't. Don't you find that interesting?'

She continued to push him along the corridors and his panic mounted. 'Look. I apologise, all right!'

'And do you apologise for treating me like a cheap tart and expecting me to fall on my back with my legs behind my ears just because you ask me if I fuck?'

'Oh God, woman. Yes! Of course I do. I'm very sorry and I'll never say that to another woman as long as I live, OK? Now just take me back and let me get dressed.'

'I don't think you're really sorry for that,' she said, continuing to wheel him. 'I think you're sorry because I've got you on this trolley, naked, wearing a pretty red bow on your dick and I'm taking you where hundreds of people will see you. And here we are now,' she added, pushing open the double doors of the cafeteria and wheeling the trolley inside.

At that time of night the place was deserted but both knew that, by breakfast time, it would be swarming with guests. She stopped the trolley in the exact centre of the room and put on the brake.

He was aghast. 'Pandora! You're not going to leave me here?'

'Oh yes I am. But before I go, just a little something.' She felt in her pocket for a lipstick, wrote two words across his stomach, then drew an arrow, pointing at his penis. 'Just in case you can't read upside down, I'll tell you what it says,' she said brightly. 'It says, "Prize Prick". That means it *and* you, David. Goodnight.' She planted a light kiss on his forehead and walked away.

He squirmed in futile rage, twisting his head round to watch her departure. 'Pandora! I swear to you that one of these days I'm going to fuck your brains out!'

She paused with the open door in her hand. 'And I swear to you, David, that one of these days I'm going to let you. But not tonight! Goodnight, sweetheart!' Then she was gone; only the swinging door to mark her passage.

Grace didn't know how lucky she was, thought Pandora as her car scrunched up the gravel drive to Lady Crendall's attractive country home. Perhaps it was just as well that Grace was blissfully unaware that her luck was about to change. Jameson came down the steps to greet her.

'Do you have a suitcase, Miss Vine?'

'No, thank you, Jameson. I shan't be staying. I'm just here for the day.'

'Her Ladyship is in the garden, Miss.'

'Oh! Right. I'll go round this way.'

He sighed heavily. 'I'm sorry, Miss. Her Ladyship's special instructions were that I should take you to her myself.'

'I see. OK then. Lead on, Jameson.' She followed him along the path which led around to the back of the house, trying to work out why on earth Grace should think that she couldn't find her way around after all the visits she had made.

When they got to the large lawn at the back of the house, Pandora saw that there were two long chairs set in the centre of it. Grace was lounging on one of them, stark naked. Naked, that is, unless one counted the sunglasses which were tilted back into her hair. A skimpy bikini hung on the back of the chair. Jameson led the way to the sprawling figure. As he approached, Grace raised her knees and parted her legs so that anyone approaching as they were would obtain a splendid view of her crotch. Jameson coughed, by way of announcing his presence.

'Miss Vine, Your Ladyship.'

'Thank you, Jameson. Hello, Pandora. Come and sit by me.' She indicated the other chair.

Jameson turned to go, but Grace called him back. 'Oh Jameson. Could you do something for me?'

'Certainly, My Lady.'

'I seem to have dropped my magazine.' She pointed to it where it lay close alongside her chair. 'Could you get it for me, do you think?'

'Of course, My Lady.'

In order to pick it up he had to stoop over Grace with his face only inches from her mid section. As he did so, she put her legs down and opened them really wide so that he could see all of her pubic area. He straightened up, folded the magazine carefully and handed it to her.

'Will that be all, My Lady?'

'Yes thank you, Jameson.'

'Very good, My Lady.'

Pandora watched him walking away across the lawn. 'You know, Grace,' she said, turning to Lady Crendall, 'your name ought to be *Dis*grace, because that's what you are. You'll very likely give the old boy a heart attack, flashing your bits and pieces at him like that.'

Grace made a face and pouted. 'Oh dear, Pandora. Are you going to be in one of your stuffy moods? I thought your visit was going to cheer me up. This place is so completely boring. You must allow me my bit of fun.'

'Your several bits of fun,' Pandora corrected. 'What about Simon and Laura?'

'I've done them, haven't I? It's no fun unless it's new. Come on, Pandora. Think of something exciting and different. That's what you're here for.'

'Well, there is something now you come to mention it . . . But no. I'd better not tell you. It's far too daring, even for you.'

'Ooh, what fun! What is it, Pandora?'

'No, Grace. I shouldn't have even thought about it. It's far too bizarre and way out.'

'Oh really, Pandora,' said Grace, exasperated. 'What are you holding out for? You have this perfectly scrummy idea and you won't share it. I thought we were friends.'

Pandora capitulated. 'All right, Grace. Calm down and stop your wheedling. I knew I shouldn't have mentioned it. It's this.' She passed over a leaflet.

Grace grabbed it from her impatiently. 'The Wicked Lady Fitness and Social Club,' she read. 'Sounds interesting.' She scanned through it briefly, then looked at her friend in disappointment. 'Pandora, it's just another club.'

'Ah! That's just where you're wrong. It appears to be an ordinary club, unless you know certain people, which I do. Then you are allowed into the part of the club which ordinary people don't see.'

'Really! How fascinating! What goes on there?'

'I'm not allowed to tell you that. All members are sworn to secrecy. If it ever got out what they were doing for women, they would be closed down. All I am allowed to tell you is that the most amazingly sexy things happen to the men and women who are lucky enough to be in the know. Things even you have never dreamed of, Grace.'

Grace put a hand between her legs and clamped her thighs together. 'Oooh! Pandora! I'm getting all juicy just listening to you. Darling, you know I just have to go there. Can you get me in?'

Pandora appeared thoughtful. 'I'm not sure. I could try. I would have to sponsor you, of course. I would have to be sure that you wouldn't let me down. I mean, some of the things we do will be a bit surprising and it would be up to you to just do them without a lot of fuss.'

Grace was hurt. 'Well, of course, darling. What do you take me for? We're friends. Friends just don't let each other down.'

Oh Grace, Pandora thought. Did you have to say that right now, just when I'm feeling as guilty as hell? She smiled at her friend. 'I'll ring you when it's all fixed up, shall I?'

'Pandora, you're a saint.'

Hardly that, said Pandora's inner voice. Certainly not Saint Paul or Saint Peter. One of the other disciples, maybe. Judas, perhaps?

They met early one morning in East Grinstead about a week later and travelled together by taxi to the club, a journey of about ten miles. It was not the low, sleazy dive which Grace had been expecting. At least a mile from the nearest town, it was a long, low, modern building which might have been mistaken for a church hall, had it not been for the flickering neon above the door, which announced to passers-by that it was 'The Wicked Lady'. It had the sort of entrance through which respectable, middle-aged women could pass with ease. That many had done so was clear from the number of them who were to be seen pedalling exercise bicycles, working weight machines or just simply galumphing about in leotards to music, under the tuition of a bronzed Amazon who had, obviously, never had need to shed a pound in her life.

They followed the receptionist who was guiding them through all this activity until she stopped at a door marked 'Staff Only'. She pressed a bell at the side and waited. A TV camera overhead squinted at them with its impersonal electronic eye, then there was a buzz and a click. The door opened, the girl left them and they passed inside. At once, the atmosphere was completely different. The red carpets were deep and soft. The walls were hung with red velvet and even the lighting was red. Soft, sensuous music was all about them and there was a heavy musky smell, like incense, in the air.

Grace squeezed Pandora's hand excitedly, like a child in

a new toyshop. 'Oooh! Isn't it deliciously scary,' she whispered.

A young girl appeared, wearing only a diaphanous wisp of material around her hips. 'This way, please, ladies.' She took them into a side room and indicated another door leading off it. 'Through there is a bathroom. You will go in there and perform whatever bodily function you need to. It may be some while before you get another chance, so I advise you to try even if you don't really want to. Then you come back and disrobe here. Put your clothes; *all* your clothes in those lockers. They will be perfectly safe and you won't be needing them for a while. I will come back for you presently.'

Giggling, they went into the bathroom and did what had to be done, then came back into the locker room. Pandora began to undress. After a small hesitation, Grace did the same. 'Pandora,' she whispered. 'Is this what you do when you come?'

'Of course. Everybody does,' said Pandora. 'Anyway, why are you whispering?'

'I don't know,' Grace whispered. 'It just seems like the sort of place where one ought to whisper.'

They put their clothes in the lockers as instructed, and waited, naked. Grace whispered again, 'Pandora!'

'What?'

'I'm getting all wet with anticipation. Have you got a tissue?'

'Like where? In my ear? Anyway, you get wet when someone says, "the postman's coming". So what's new?'

The girl returned just then. 'Follow me, please.' She led the way into another room, similarly decorated and lit with red. There were just two pieces of furniture in the room, and they were side by side in the centre. On two low platforms were two solidly built and square-looking chairs, made from square-section metal. The seats, backs and arms were padded with black leather.

The girl motioned to them. 'Please sit down.' They each took one of the chairs and settled into it. The leather padding was soft and extremely comfortable. The girl went to

Pandora. 'You first, please, Miss Vine. I know that you have done this before.' Pandora placed her arms along the padded arms of the chair and settled her bottom and back against the cushions. Working swiftly, the girl fastened leather cuffs around her wrists, ankles and knees, attaching her to the chair. She passed a leather belt across her stomach and another across her upper body, just above her breasts, and buckled them.

The girl came to Grace's chair. 'Now you, please, Lady Crendall. Put your arms on the chair, as Miss Vine did.'

Grace hesitated and looked at Pandora who said, 'It's all right, Grace. This is all part of the excitement.'

'It is a bit of a turn-on,' said Grace. 'All right, my dear. Carry on.' She placed her arms in the required position and submitted to being strapped to the chair in exactly the same way as Pandora had been.

'Are you perfectly comfortable?' the girl asked. 'None of your straps are too tight and your position is easy for you?'

Grace wiggled experimentally. 'No, that's fine. Thank you for asking.'

The girl nodded, smiled and left the room. They sat side by side for a while in silence, then Grace whispered, 'I can't wait, Pandora. It's just too thrilling! You've got to tell me what happens.'

'I can't, Grace.'

'Well, give me a hint. Is it men or is it women? My God, it's not both, is it? How fantastic!'

At that moment there was a click and a whirr and a panel slid open above Pandora's chair. Something began to move downwards from it. Pandora craned her neck to look up. 'What is it, Grace? What's happening?'

'My God!' said Grace. 'You mean you don't know?' She looked up again. 'It seems to be a big box, like an upside-down tea-chest. Unless it stops, it's going to come right down over you. Look, this isn't a game, is it? Something to frighten me?'

Pandora was tugging and pulling furiously at her straps. 'Oh Grace, this isn't what's meant to happen. There's something terribly wrong! Quick! Run and get help!'

'I can't! I can't!' Grace screamed. Already the box was down past Pandora's head and her cries became muffled. To Grace's horror, the box came right down, lowered by the wires on which it was suspended. The size of it coincided exactly with the dimensions of the dais on which Pandora's chair was set and, as the two united, there was a click as they locked together, then there was total silence as Pandora's cries became inaudible. Grace struggled madly with her straps but it was useless. There was a click and a whirr above her head and she looked up to see that a similar panel had opened above her own chair. She threw herself from side to side as the box came lower. Looking up, she could now see that the sides of it were of sandwich construction, about an inch thick and filled with a foam. Even in her distress, she was thinking clearly enough to understand that this was an insulating material which rendered the box soundproof.

Lower and lower it came and her surroundings grew dim as it shut out the room's light. Then it locked onto the base and there was total silence and total blackness. To her relief, after a second or two, a dim red light came on inside the box, allowing her to see. At the same time, a gentle whirring came from beneath her seat and she felt a draught of cool air on her legs. Craning about her, she noticed a grill set in the top of the box. At least she was not going to suffocate. Grace was nothing if not practical. What had happened was alarming, but it was, at the same time, bizarre and exciting. It was certainly not boring! Whoever had done it was concerned about her welfare, shown by the solicitous enquiries about her comfort, the light and the air supply. Since no one could hear her, there was no point in screaming, so she sat on in silence, waiting to see what would happen next.

Meanwhile, the latches on Pandora's box clicked open and the box rose back up into its ceiling aperture. The same girl came in and unstrapped her. Pandora got up and went immediately to Grace's box, stooping to listen. 'I can hear the air conditioner going. You're quite sure the light is on?'

'Rest assured, Miss Vine. There is no possibility of error. During the relatively short time she will be in there, she will be perfectly comfortable and safer than if she were riding in a limousine.' She reached down and latched up the sides of the dais, to show that the box was mounted on castors. She released the brake and pushed the box towards the door. 'The van is here already. There will be no delay.'

Shortly thereafter, a fork-lift truck emerged from the rear of The Wicked Lady bearing a large box on which was stencilled. 'ComVac Professional Gymnasium Equipment'. The truck lifted up the box so that it could be trundled off into the back of a large panel van, similarly labelled. The doors closed and the van moved away to its destination; a small, private airstrip a few miles to the north.

Six

The past few hours had been very strange ones for Grace. At first, the sensation of movement had been a little worrying, but she had got used to it. She could hear nothing except the small whirr of the fan which was exchanging the air in her little prison. Being strapped into such a comfortable chair was not a great deal worse than being in a tourist class airline seat, apart from not being able to scratch her nose when she wished to. She had experienced the minor stresses of acceleration and deceleration, side forces which seemed to indicate that the box was being tilted, or was on a vehicle turning a corner. Once, she had thought that she was, perhaps in a lift, although the vibration would have seemed to be more like travelling over an unmade road. Each time the movement had stopped, she had braced herself for what was to come next, but the movement had begun again.

The first indication she had that her journey was over was the seemingly deafening click of the latches beneath her, then a light which was blinding after the red glow she was accustomed to. The light increased as the box was lifted off her and she found herself in a very sparsely furnished room with just a wooden bench along one wall. Blinking, she focused on the young woman beside her; a different one, but similarly dressed in a semi-transparent loincloth.

'Are you quite comfortable, Mistress? You have taken no harm on your journey?'

'Yes, I'm all right. But what is all this? What's going on? Where is my friend?'

The girl laid a finger on her lips in a gesture requesting silence. 'All will be explained to you. My name is Zelda. I am your personal attendant. I am not permitted to tell you more.'

At that moment, the door towards which the chair was facing opened. Before Grace's horrified eyes, Pandora, still naked and strapped to her chair was wheeled out by another scantily dressed blonde girl. Close behind them came a tanned, muscular man, dressed only in a loincloth. He was licking his lips and caressing the leather of a long, coiled whip.

'Grace!' Pandora screamed. 'Help me! Help me please! They're going to whip me! Don't let them –' Her voice was cut off as the man leant over her from behind and thrust a ball-gag into her mouth, buckling the strap behind her head. She continued to twist about in her seat, struggling wildly to free herself as she was pushed past Grace and out of the anteroom. As soon as the door closed behind them, the girl stopped Pandora's chair and began to release the straps, while the man unbuckled the gag.

Pandora got up and wiggled her jaw. 'Thank you Jason, you may go now. Was I all right, Melissa?'

'Very convincing, Mistress.' She reached under the chair and handed Pandora a robe.

Slipping into it, Pandora gazed at the closed door of the anteroom. 'I do hope so,' she said. 'I'd hate to lose Grace as a friend.' She stopped in the act of tying her belt. 'Bother! It's only just occurred to me that if I'm supposed to have been whipped, she's going to want to see the marks later on.'

Melissa smirked. 'I would be happy to help in any way I can, Mistress. There is a cane in your bedroom.'

Pandora eyed her thoughtfully. 'Bet you'd enjoy that, wouldn't you, you crafty little cow? Well, if I must, I must, I suppose. It's in a good cause. Not too hard, mind. Just enough to give me some convincing battle scars!'

'Of course, Mistress. Trust me. You'll like it the way I do it.'

'Hmm!' Pandora was unconvinced. 'Come on then; let's get it over with.'

Back in the anteroom, the sign over the inner door flashed to 'Enter'. Zelda went behind Grace's chair and propelled it forward through that door into an office beyond. Behind a big desk, a woman was intent on studying a file. She did not look up as Zelda pushed Grace to a position a few feet in front of the desk, set the brake, curtseyed and left. The woman behind the desk had very black hair, a strangely pale complexion and wore a tight-fitting, purple dress with a high collar. To her right and left were other desks, each occupied by a bare-breasted young woman. One sat at a typewriter; the other sat on the front corner of her desk. She wore the diaphanous waist-garment which seemed to be uniform in that place and she was swinging her leg and looking curiously at Grace. That look made Grace feel like a butterfly on a pin. She shrank back, acutely aware of her nudity.

The black-haired woman completed her reading and looked up. 'Grace? You are here . . .'

'Lady Crendall to you, please! And I demand that you release me and my friend at once!' Grace said.

The woman stared at her. Those eyes were like laser beams, cutting through Grace's defiance and searing her will. After a long pause, the woman sighed wearily, reached into a drawer and brought out a jar. She got up, came round the desk to Grace, took the lid off the jar and dipped the extreme tip of her finger inside. She reached down and smeared the ointment in slow circles onto Grace's left nipple and the surrounding darkly pink circle. Grace tried to wriggle to prevent the application, but there was nothing she could do about it.

'What is it? What are you doing?'

The woman did not reply, but went back to her desk, leaving the jar sitting on its surface. 'I was saying, *Grace*,' she continued, laying heavy stress on the name, 'that this place is the Castle of Despair. I am Matrilla, the Ice Queen. You have been sent here for corrective training.'

Grace said nothing. During the short time since the application of the ointment, she had become aware of an odd sensation in that area. At first she had thought that it was a fly, crawling over her nipple and had attempted to shrug it off but, when she looked down, there was no fly there; only the faint sheen of the ointment. That feeling grew and grew. It was by no means unpleasant, rather like having her nipple sucked and the area around it tickled with gentle fingers. The trouble was that it went on all the time and she had no way of touching herself to relieve the irritation. She shifted uneasily in her seat, as far as she was able; as if, by doing so, she could remove herself from this touch, even though it was now part of her skin. Looking down at herself, she saw that her left nipple was now much larger and harder than the right; a fat, pink bud which felt as though it would burst at any moment. The area around it was also engorged, as with extreme sexual excitement, so that the tip of that breast stood out from the otherwise smooth curvature as a hard bump.

Matrilla was continuing to speak. 'Your period of detention here may be long or short. That depends on you and how quickly you respond to training.'

'You're mad! You're completely mad! If you think . . .' Grace's voice trailed off into silence as Matrilla shook her head sadly, reached for the jar and got up again. 'No! Keep away with that stuff! I don't want . . . Oh God!' She looked down at Matrilla's finger smearing ointment onto her right nipple. 'All right! I'm sorry. You're not mad! Wipe it off, please!'

Matrilla sat down again and continued. 'You are an intelligent woman, though a little impulsive at times. It ought not to take you long to get the message.'

Now Grace's right breast was beginning to give her the same problem as her left. She watched as the tip engorged, the nipple straining from it, springily erect. Now that both had been treated, the slippery juices were beginning to accumulate in her vagina in an embarrassing fashion as her body interpreted the messages from her breasts as precursors of intercourse and orgasm. To divert her mind, she forced herself to listen to what the Queen was saying.

'During your stay here, I have decided that it will be appropriate if your treatment is regarded as education rather than punishment. Therefore, you will be treated leniently, unless you give me serious cause to do otherwise. You will have a comfortable room and Zelda will be your personal attendant. Her orders are to satisfy your every wish, but there is a proviso. If Zelda says that you are to do something, then she will be acting on instructions from me and you will do it. If you fail in that, there are other, less pleasant, ways of enforcing my will. You will, at all times, address me as Madam.'

'I'm damned if I will!' said Grace. 'If you think for one moment . . . What is it? What are you doing? Keep away!'

Matrilla had signalled to the two girls and they now advanced on Grace in a menacing fashion. Dropping to their knees on either side of her, they slid their hands over the tops of her thighs and between her legs which were, perforce, parted by being strapped at the knees to the chair. She felt fingers groping through her pubic hair, then each girl gripped the set of crinkly labial lips they found on their side and pulled them outwards so that Grace's vulva was stretched wide, revealing a large amount of the inner surface. With sticking plaster, they attached the lips to her inner thighs so that, when released, they remained pulled apart, exposing her completely. As Matrilla advanced towards her, Grace was as much alarmed by the fact that this woman would see just how wet and excited she was as by what was about to be done to her.

Matrilla dipped into the jar and Grace squeaked apprehensively. 'Oh no! Not there! You couldn't! You wouldn't! Oh! No, please!' She looked down at her own gaping sex and watched in disbelief as the Ice Queen smeared the unguent liberally over the pink, glistening surfaces. She dipped her finger again and applied all of that portion to the clitoris and the area directly around it. With deliberate slowness, so that Grace would be fully aware beforehand of what she intended to do, she held the jar up in front of her horrified eyes and lovingly and carefully dipped two fingers into it, hooking them on withdrawal so as to extract the maximum load. Stooping down, she inserted those fingers into the wide orifice of her vagina, pushing hard in order to get them as far up as she could, then twisting and turning them to ensure that all inner surfaces were covered, particularly the G spot under her pubic bone.

Matrilla straightened herself and went to a small wash basin in the corner of the room. In the short time it took her to wash her hands, dry them and go back to her seat, Grace was already beginning to feel the effects of this latest application of cream. On her breasts and nipples, the effect had been considerable. Smeared all over the most sensitive tissues in her body, the result was stratospheric. As with the previous applications, what she felt could not be described as pain, burning, stinging, or even itching. There was just this incredible illusion of a million tiny fingers and mouths, sucking, stroking, gently tickling, teasing, exciting, and arousing. Centred on her clitoris, which she could see standing out like the Eiffel Tower, the sensation spread throughout the whole of her genital area and even reached upwards to connect with her nipples, uniting with them in the task of driving her mad with a pleasurable craving which only orgasm could satisfy. And the worst part of it was that there was absolutely nothing she could do to bring about that relief. She could not touch herself, or even rub her thighs together. She could only sit and squirm, her eyes tight shut and her face screwed up in the effort of concentration required to withstand such emotions.

It was difficult, now, to pay attention to the Queen when next she spoke. 'I see from your file that you enjoy displaying yourself. That is the aspect we shall deal with first. I shall say no more now, as I see that you are distracted by something. We will speak again when you are calmer and more prepared to listen.' She pressed a button on her desk and Zelda returned. Matrilla looked at her watch. 'One hour, I think, Zelda.'

'Yes Madam,' Zelda replied. Unlocking the brake, she went to the back of the chair and Grace found herself being wheeled out of the room. They did not stop in the anteroom, but went on into the corridor outside. The draught of their passage cooled Grace's inflamed wetness a little. She became more aware of what was happening and conscious of the fact that she was very naked indeed.

'Cover me, please, Zelda.'

'I'm sorry, Mistress. The Queen's instructions were very specific. You are to remain as you are.'

To Grace's horror, she saw a group of people walking towards them; two women and a man. She pulled frantically at her straps and attempted to bend forward, but was held firmly in her upright position, wide-legged pose. As they drew closer, one of the women pointed and said something to the other woman. She laughed and whispered in the man's ear. By the time Grace passed, they were openly staring and laughing. Grace's face was a flame of mortification. Her skin crawled every time she thought of those eyes and those laughs. Zelda pushed her onwards and through a set of double doors into a great, grey hall. She stopped the chair in the centre and put on the brake.

'Why have we stopped, Zelda?'

'It's by the Queen's order, Mistress. You are to remain on exhibition, here, for one hour. I will come back then and take you on to your next treatment.'

'But suppose somebody comes in?'

'I'm afraid that is not a matter of supposition, Mistress. The Queen will see to it that very many people do come in and see you like this. That is the object of the lesson. To save you the embarrassment of a refusal, I must tell you that it will be useless to ask them to help you or to touch you in any way. That is not permitted.'

Zelda walked away. Grace opened her mouth to call her back, then closed it again, realising that this would have no effect. She set herself, grimly, to endure what was to come in the next hour. Now that she had no distraction, the sensation in her vagina and nipples returned with new force. With that feeling came the renewed longing for the relief of orgasm and she became aware that a small puddle of liquid had collected on the leather seat between her thighs. She pushed it from her mind, but it refused to go away. Just when she thought she had it under control, some fresh twinge would intrude to remind her of that overwhelming urge. Added to that was her recollection of what Zelda had said. There was to be another 'treatment' after this, and she had no idea what that could be.

It did not help when the door opened and the first group of people sauntered in; the first of many. Some just came, stared for a while, then left. Some stayed for longer and one woman even knelt down in front of her, the better to view her obscenely exposed private parts. At first, Grace blushed every time she was inspected, but then became hardened to it and sat on, stoically enough, helped by the fact that the effects of the ointment were at last beginning to wear off and she found that she could control her emotions better.

Nevertheless, it was a relief when Zelda returned to collect her. As the girl pushed her through the maze of corridors, Grace said, 'Where are we going?'

'To the Training Room, Mistress.'

Grace was as wise as if she had not asked. 'What happens there?'

'I am not permitted to tell you that, Mistress. But we are nearly there, now, and you will find out.'

They passed through more double doors and Grace found herself in a large room with a polished wooden floor, rather like a gymnasium. Zelda stopped the chair, braked it and left without a word, giving Grace time to take in her surroundings. She looked around apprehensively and what she saw was not reassuring. She had scratched only the surface of bizarre methods of restraint with her previous sexual experiences, but she knew enough to recognise some things when she saw them. Her eyes took in a padded bench with leather straps for securing various parts of the body; a stout wooden table and vaulting horse with similar fitting. On hooks and brackets attached to the walls there hung a profusion of whips, canes, straps and paddles; handcuffs, chains, cords and heavy padlocks. She shivered in spite of herself.

She was left alone with her thoughts for several minutes, then the doors opened and the Ice Queen came in, dressed in her floor-length grey gown. She was attended at a respectful distance by the two girls Grace had seen in the office. She came and stood in front of Grace, who wriggled uncomfortably as those laser eyes stared brazenly at what was to be seen between her parted thighs.

'Well, Grace? Have you learned anything about exhibitionism?'

Sullenly Grace answered. 'Yes!'

The Queen pursed her lips and frowned. 'The answer should have been, "Yes Madam!" Perhaps I have been too patient with you.' She stood for a while, apparently deep in thought, then shook her head. 'No. I will persist, but my forbearance is not unlimited. Maybe this is the time for a more detailed explanation. You have had an opportunity to see the things about you. Have you any idea what they are for?'

Grace nodded.

'Let me give you a closer look.' Matrilla signed to Luna and she brought over a trolley laden with an assortment of implements. The Queen picked up a cane and flexed it in her hands. 'You know what this is for?'

A little paler, Grace nodded again.

'And this?' Matrilla exhibited a black rubber paddle, obtaining another nod.

'These?' She dangled two tiny metal objects from short chains.

Genuinely ignorant, Grace shook her head.

'Ah! These are nipple clamps, not clips. Like tiny vices. The frame is placed over the nipple, then this screw is tightened –' she held one close in front of Grace's appalled eyes as she demonstrated – 'until unbearable pressure is exerted. Look! The two parts close together completely, with no space in between. Do you understand their use now?'

The fact that Grace's colour had changed from white to pale green was answer enough, without requiring another nod.

The Queen held up other objects. 'These weights are intended to hang from those clamps. They are quite heavy, but can be added to. Now, I want you to imagine this. See yourself naked, bent double and strapped over that horse with clamps and weights on your nipples, while I and others take turns to thrash your bare bottom with this riding whip.' She picked up a thin, black, whippy implement and flexed it for Grace to see. 'It lies completely within my power to do that to you. Think about that and also think very carefully about the manner in which you are going to answer my next question, which you will do by speaking, not by nodding. Now, here comes the question. In view of what I have told you, and what I have invited you to imagine, do you not think that I have been extremely lenient with you so far?'

Grace's skin had been crawling for some time. She had a good imagination and it was not hard for her to see herself as Matrilla had bidden her to do. She had long ago decided how she would address this woman in future.

'Yes, Madam,' she said, the words tumbling over themselves in their haste to escape her lips.

Matrilla exulted internally. Another broken spirit! She felt the first stirrings of sexual excitement. She had to press home and prolong the moment of triumph. 'And are you not extremely grateful for that leniency?

'Oh yes, Madam. Extremely grateful.'

Matrilla smiled, indulgently. 'Then I see no reason why it should not continue for a while longer, now that we understand one another better. I feel that we can now proceed with the next stage of your re-education. I learn from your file that you take pleasure in humiliating those over whom you exert power. You may have thought that you had some expertise in this matter. You will learn today that, compared to me, you are a rank amateur.' She signalled to Maria and Luna and they went to a large wooden frame which stood against the wall. It was mounted on wheels and was about fourteen feet square with a large wooden box attached outside one lower corner. It was very heavy, so that they had to exert considerable strength to drag it out and place it squarely in front of Grace's chair. When they were satisfied with the position, they slid bolts from it into brass sockets in the floor and latched them in place, so that the frame was immovably fixed. From holes inside the top corners of the frame dangled two thick white cords with leather cuffs attached. They pulled on these, extending them, then unstrapped Grace's wrists and fastened one cuff round each. Two similar holes in the bottom corners of the frame contained similar cords and cuffs and they extended them, unstrapped Grace's ankles and put on the new cuffs. She noticed, with relief, that although the cuffs were of leather, they were lined with padded silk. Next, they unbuckled all the other straps holding Grace into the chair, so that she was at last able to move and exercise muscles which had remained unused for so long.

Her respite was short-lived. Matrilla went to the wooden box and opened a flap, to reveal a set of controls. She operated one of them and, with a whine, an electric motor started and the top cords began to retract slowly into the frame. As they tightened, Grace was obliged to lean forward and then to stand. The cords continued to be reeled in until she was standing almost directly underneath the top bar with her arms stretched above her and widely parted, pointing to the top corners. To ease the tension in her arms, she stepped up onto the bottom bar of the frame and the motor whined again as Matrilla immediately took up the tiny amount of slack thus obtained.

There was a short pause during which the Ice Queen admired her handiwork, then the motor sprang to life again. Grace gave a little scream and scrabbled for support with her toes as she was lifted clear of the bottom bar and hung suspended by her wrists, her feet at least a foot away from any resting place. There was another momentary pause before the motor operated again and her ankle cords retracted. She tried to cross her legs and resist the pull, but her efforts were as nothing when set against the power and gearing of the motor. Her feet were irresistibly drawn apart until she was stretched in an X position, completely suspended within the frame. For a while she was able, by flexing her elbows and knees, to draw herself up and let herself down a little, and she did so. Matrilla, observing these minor movements, made minute adjustments to the controls until she was so tightly stretched that even that small relief was denied to her. The Ice Queen came and stood in front of her. This was another one of those enjoyable moments. The victim, unsuspecting of what was to come, was naked and vulnerable to anything that might be inflicted on her person. As if to test this, Matrilla reached up and flicked each nipple in turn with her fingernail. Grace jerked a little in reaction, but could make no other movement.

Matrilla moved away to the table but soon came back, holding a little jar. Knowing now what torment that jar held, Grace began to whimper and plead. 'Please, Madam. Please don't do that to me. Not that stuff again, I beg you. I've learned. Really I have.'

Matrilla paused. 'Oh, really? What have you learned?'

'I don't know, Madam. Whatever you say, Madam. Only please don't put it on me.'

'You see, you don't even know what you are supposed to have learned,' said the Queen calmly. She dipped her finger into the pot and smeared Grace's right nipple and breast, as before. She dipped again and repeated the dose on the left side. With terrible dread, Grace guessed what she would do next and was soon proved right. The Queen removed two fingers full of cream from the pot and inserted them into Grace's vagina. Because of her widely stretched legs, Matrilla was able to push her fingers much further into her this time, and completed the task with the same care and thoroughness as before.

The effect was as it had been the first time, perhaps even a little worse, since the first dose had hardly had time to wear off. Grace felt the same erection and engorgement of nipples and clitoris. The same pleasurable, unbearably sweet sensations in breasts and vagina. The same thwarted craving for orgasm. Tears of frustration rolled down her cheeks as she hung defenceless, naked and exposed.

'Now I have to cause you a little pain, I'm afraid,' said Matrilla. 'Your sticking plaster has to be removed and several vaginal hairs will come with it. Would you like me to rip it suddenly, all at once, or would you prefer it to be done slowly, one by one?'

This was an unanswerable question. Grace would prefer neither, so she said nothing.

'But perhaps there is someone who can help you,' said

Matrilla. She clapped her hands and the doors opened to admit a woman who came across to them. Grace was in such a dither of emotions that the woman was standing right in front of her before she recognised her as Laura, her housekeeper.

'Oh God, no!' Grace was humbled beyond her worst nightmares that her servant should see her thus, a powerless captive hanging before her with dripping vagina taped open for inspection.

'I understand that watching a woman having her pussy shaved gives you a thrill, Grace,' said Matrilla. 'Well, this will be a little treat for you. You can watch Laura shave yours. And, by the way, you *will* watch, unless you want me to take the whip to you. Don't forget, she'll be helping you by saving you from having that plaster ripped off.' She retired to the table a little way off and sat down on the edge of it to watch.

Grace watched with thudding heart as Laura went to the trolley and sorted among the things on it. She came back with a tiny pair of nail scissors. Mingled with the shame and the uncertainty of what it would feel like to have her pubic hair removed was the knowledge that the area around her clitoris was going to be touched. In the seething turbulence of her lust for climactic satisfaction, this was a side effect which she very much desired.

Laura began gently and carefully, lifting the corners of the plaster and snipping at the hairs beneath it before they could be plucked from the tender flesh. Heedful of the Queen's command, Grace craned her neck forward, but still could not see that far underneath herself to be able to watch the process. Laura was not completely successful and Grace was obliged to yip with pain a couple of times but at last the plasters were discarded and her labia were released. Laura exchanged the small scissors for large ones and now Grace could clearly see the auburn curls of which she was so proud coming off in clumps and falling to the floor.

Matrilla watched Grace's face intently and saw resignation being replaced by lust. Grace was being fired up by what was happening. When Laura reached the point at which she had to insert her fingers to pull and stretch the pink labia, Grace's breathing became noticeably heavier and her head began to revolve in slow circles. Her eyes closed and she began to whisper, almost to herself, 'Yes! Oh yes! Yes!'

When Laura's fingers, perhaps not entirely by accident, contacted her yearning clitoris, Grace shuddered into orgasm at that single touch. The scissors clipped and snipped. Gradually, the mass of hair around the division of Grace's sex diminished into a wispy stubble. She knew that there was nothing to be gained by protest or struggle. She remained motionless, only craning her head forward to watch as her only bodily covering was removed from her against her will. When Laura smeared on the first dabs of shaving cream, Grace climaxed again on the spot, but tried to control her body's quivering. She did not want to do anything to interfere with the exquisite, scraping touches around her groin as the razor did its work. Laura had two fingers inside her most of the time and that was delectable.

Laura completed her work and stepped away, allowing Matrilla to get a good view of the result for the first time. The part of Grace that was now completely revealed, instead of being hidden by hair, was just as perfect as the rest of her. The bald mound over her pubic bone, her *mons veneris*, was flawless in its symmetry and lovely to look at. From the base of it, the hood over her clitoris projected enticingly, directing the eye downwards to the soft pink lips of her sex, now without any protective hair to conceal them.

Matrilla could not resist the temptation to approach and plant a kiss on that beautiful mound. The skin beneath her lips felt soft and cool. Grace shuddered with pleasure.

'And now,' said Matrilla, 'on to the next phase. My records tell me that you forced Laura to undress by blackmailing her. You, of course, are already as completely naked as any woman can be. Still, it isn't the act which is important, it is the principle which lies behind it. Undressing is something one usually does in private, unobserved.

To be forced to do it in public was shaming. I intend to shame you in the same way by forcing you into a public performance of something very private. I want you to pee for us, while we watch. That's something personal and private enough, I feel, to do the trick.'

Grace was aghast. 'I couldn't do that. Not with you watching. It would just be impossible.'

'Oh well, then. Never mind. I'll give you another dose of ointment, then we'll go off and leave you to think about it. We'll come back in an hour or so and see if you've changed your mind.'

'No, wait! Don't go!' Grace gave in. 'I'll try,' she whispered, hanging her head in embarrassment.

Laura fetched a plastic bucket and held it in position between the strained legs. She and Matrilla then stood really close to Grace, their arms over her thighs and around her back, holding her, their faces only inches away from her shaven crotch.

'I can't do it if you're so close!'

Matrilla gave her bottom a sharp slap. 'Yes you can! Try harder!' She gazed up into Grace's face. That face was grimacing, now; eyes closed in concentration. Grace's stomach muscles clenched and unclenched. Matrilla stared with intense concentration at the pink lips in front of her face. As she watched, they puckered and parted a little. They pouted again, momentarily, and a small squirt of golden liquid trickled out. Matrilla slapped again, harder this time. 'Come on! We're waiting!' There it was again. That fascinating pout of the pink lips followed, this time, by a continuous, steady stream into the bucket. Matrilla couldn't take her eyes off the source of the flow and watched intently until it stopped. Only then could she take the time to study Grace's face again. Her eyes were closed and she hung her head in deepest shame.

Still Matrilla had not finished with her. 'It's time for your spanking now. I have decided that, as Laura is one of the injured parties in your case, she shall be the one to administer it. I have left it entirely to her as to how she sets about it. She has my permission to use any of the instruments in this room to achieve the results she wants. We shall not supervise her in any way, but simply return when it is over to pick up the remains.' She and her handmaidens swept out, leaving Grace alone with Laura.

Grace had trouble in meeting Laura's eyes. 'Look,' she said. 'What I did was all in fun, you know. It was a game. Perhaps it wasn't very funny, now I think about it. Can't you let me off?'

Laura said, 'You do agree that you deserve a good spanking, don't you?'

Grace's voice was barely audible, 'Yes.'

'Louder, please!'

'*Yes!* Just get it over with, will you!'

As Laura came towards her, pulling on a black leather glove, Grace said fearfully, 'What's that for?'

'Well, I don't want to hurt my hand, do I?'

Grace's face was pale. 'Oh God!' She braced herself, tightening the muscles of her bottom, closed her eyes and gritted her teeth. 'All right! I'm ready!'

Laura stood behind her and to her left, to give her right hand full access to the bare bottom, so helplessly available. Grace shivered as she stroked the target area quite tenderly. 'Well? Get on with it! Do what you have to do and get it over with!'

As the first smack fell on her bare buttocks, Grace's eyes popped open in surprise. That was not a hard, stinging slap. It was a most pleasing contact; hard enough to be felt, but by no means unpleasant. Just how she liked them! She gasped with pleasure and relief, wriggling her bottom and concentrating her attention on that area so as to extract the maximum enjoyment as the delightful spanking went on, making her bottom warm and pink and her need for orgasm greater – if that were possible. Then she was forced to gasp even louder as Laura thrust three fingers into her vagina and began to pump them in and out.

'Ah! You teasing bitch! Oh yes! Oh yes! Do it to me! Spank my bum! Fuck me with your fingers! Just like that!'

Laura stopped her spanking but continued to move her fingers. Grace's straining nipples were at face level and

Laura took one into her mouth, sucking and nibbling, without for one second breaking the rhythm of her pumping action lower down. Grace's head shot back, her neck muscles standing out. Her tongue came out and licked feverishly at her lips; the only touch she could give herself.

'Don't stop! Please don't stop spanking me! Keep doing it!'

Laura removed her mouth from the nipple. 'I think I know where else you'd like to be spanked.'

Grace craned her head forward to see, mewing in ecstasy as Laura put her left elbow against her navel and slapped at her bald mound; a machine-gun volley of light smacks, making the hooded clitoris jump and dance. Her hairless mons reddened and glowed. Now Grace's whole body was quivering and shaking as though attached to some giant galvanic apparatus. A great hollow appeared in her already flattened stomach, to be sucked up and down with the violence of her pre-orgasmic contractions.

She screamed; her voice harsh and almost unrecognisable: 'Yes! Harder! Faster! Oh God, I can't wait! I can't stand it! I'm going to come! Do me! Don't stop!'

Her orgasm went on and on and, even when it was over, her vagina still sucked greedily at Laura's fingers and her naked belly continued to jerk and pulse with the aftershocks. When, at last, all was stilled, she hung quite motionless in her frame, her head drooping in exhaustion.

Grace stirred, but tried hard not to wake up. Her dream was much too pleasant. She snuggled into the soft pillow and tried to recapture it, but it was fading fast and that insistent though gentle shaking would not permit her to concentrate on it. She opened her eyes. 'What is it, Zelda?'

'I'm sorry to wake you, Mistress, but it is time to get up. I cannot permit you to sleep longer.'

With a sigh, Grace heaved herself into a sitting position. Zelda handed her a cup of steaming coffee and she buried her nose in it gratefully. She remembered how good Zelda had been to her when she had been brought back to her room in a state of near collapse. The soothing creams; the all-over body massage; the light meal and then bed! Glorious, wonderful bed! She felt rested and refreshed. In the artificial light which was all there was in the windowless castle, there was no way of telling whether it was night or day.

'Zelda! How long have I been asleep?'

'Three hours, Mistress.'

Only three hours! It was incredible. She could have sworn she had slept round the clock. The creams and the massage must have been very special.

'What time is it?'

'Almost nine o'clock, Mistress.'

'In the morning?'

'No, Mistress. It is still the evening of the day you arrived.'

'Really Zelda! Why did you wake me? I thought I had finished my education for the day.'

'I was ordered to wake you so that you could eat, Mistress. You need to keep up your strength.'

'For tomorrow, I suppose.'

'No, Mistress. For tonight. You are to receive a visitor.' Zelda put the finishing touches to a little table with a white cloth on which she had been arranging the contents of a tray of food. Grace went over to it and sat down. She was suddenly ravenous and realised that she had eaten very little that day.

With her mouth full, she said, 'What sort of visitor? No, don't tell me. You're not permitted to say.'

'But I am, Mistress. It is to be a gentleman.'

'Really?' That was interesting! 'What does he want.'

'He wants you, Mistress.'

'What does he want me for?'

'I told you, Mistress. He wants you. He wishes to make use of your body in the way of men.'

'What!' Grace coughed and almost choked on her food. 'I thought I was being retrained. How is that educational?'

'It isn't, Mistress. It happens that way, sometimes. This man has seen you; perhaps when you were on exhibition in the hall. He has approached Her Majesty; maybe he has paid her. No one knows but she. Whatever the reason, she has given you to him for his entertainment this evening.'

Grace thought for a moment, then shrugged. 'Well, it might be fun at least. What time is he coming?'

'At ten o'clock, Mistress. You must hurry; have a bath and prepare yourself.'

'I'm not going to hurry. If he wants me that badly, he can wait a bit.'

'Please, Mistress. I must have you ready on time. If you will hurry now, I will help you with your bath by washing you all over.'

Grace was quick to catch that subtle nuance. '*All* over?'

'Yes, Mistress, but only if you will hurry.'

Grace lay at full length in the bath and watched Zelda's hands moving over her body, which was a most pleasant sensation. The half naked girl seemed quite fascinated by her hairless mound and had washed it several times already, awakening sexual thoughts in Grace's mind.

'Zelda.'

'Yes, Mistress.'

'I like to have a small orgasm as a preliminary to sex. Would you like to give me one? Perhaps your soapy fingers would be nice.'

'If you wish, Mistress, but I would consider it a privilege if you allowed me to do it with my tongue and lips. Let me dry you, then we can go to the bed.'

Grace agreed willingly and got out of the bath. Zelda patted her dry and they went into the bedroom.

'Mistress, if you will sit on the edge of the bed and then lie back, I will kneel on the floor.'

Grace remembered Matrilla's instructions that she should obey Zelda and smiled to herself. She was willing to bet that 'Madam' hadn't reckoned on her being given such a sweet order. Zelda knelt between her spread legs and gazed at her. 'You are so beautiful down there, Mistress. I can see everything so clearly. I have never been close to a woman who has been shaved.'

Grace was pleased. Being shaved off had been pleasant enough. Being told that she was more beautiful because of it was even nicer. Zelda had a very long tongue, which reached right inside Grace's vagina. She was also very skilled in the ways of dealing with the clitoris. Perhaps it was those things, or perhaps it was the lingering traces of the ointment. Whatever the cause, Grace came to her peak quickly and with only small groanings and shudderings, as was her wont with the first one of the evening. Now she felt fully prepared to take on her gentleman caller.

As Zelda got up and moved away, Grace called after her, 'What should I wear, Zelda?'

The girl was already digging into a drawer. She held up a pair of wide-legged French knickers with lace around the bottom. 'These, Mistress.'

'Yes, but what else? What outer clothes?'

'None, Mistress. Just these. By the Queen's order.'

'Oh! Well, I'd better wait for him in bed, then.'

'No, Mistress. I am not permitted to allow you to be in bed. The gentleman has requested that you be in a special position.'

'What position?' said Grace, with deepest suspicion.

'I am to have you stand at the bottom of the bed, facing it, then bend over and spread your arms along the rail there. I am to bind you in that position.'

'Why like that?'

'I understand that the gentleman wishes to take you from the rear, Mistress. Some men like that.'

Grace's vagina was already tingling with wetness at the prospect, but it did seem like a bit of a cheek. 'Well, tough! I'm not going to let you do it.'

'Please, Mistress. For my sake. If it is seen that you have not obeyed me, I shall be beaten. All that will happen is that strong men will come and force you and that would be worse than having me do it, wouldn't it?'

Grace considered this. She had grown fond of Zelda and she didn't want to see her punished. Anyway, what the hell! She was game for a sex romp and it wouldn't be the first time she'd volunteered to be tied down for it although, admittedly, that was with people she knew. 'Oh, all right,' she said.

She put on the knickers, went to the foot of the bed, bent over and spread her arms along the rail. Zelda bound her wrists to the rail with silk scarves, then passed more around her upper arms and tied her down so that she could not move her upper body up, down or sideways. She took an elasticated blindfold, such as sleepers and airline passengers wear, and passed it over Grace's head so that she could see nothing.

'Hey! What's the idea?' said Grace, struggling a little.

'It is by the Queen's order, Mistress. Your visitor must remain unknown to you.'

Grace heard the door open and close. Had Zelda gone out?

She called out, 'Zelda!' There was no reply. She was alone. Or was she? Was that just the tiniest rustle of something?

'Zelda, is that you?' Again the smallest rustle. Grace's flesh crept and she felt her sex urge jump up a gear. There was a man in the room with her! Her imagination made him huge and hairy and menacing. She could not see them, but she knew that the nipples on the ends of her dangling breasts had lengthened into erectness. She felt a little trickle of love juice beginning to escape from her. Now her imagination added another man; then two more; then ten. They were all going to have her, one after another, to the point of exhaustion.

She listened intently. Nothing! She had imagined it. She was alone after all. She screamed in surprise as hard fingers dug into the waistband of her knickers and ripped them down to the floor, before she had a chance to cross her legs or spread her knees to prevent it happening. She sucked in her breath and waited for the thrust of a penis into her wet vagina. Oh God! Maybe not into her vagina at all. What had Zelda meant when she had said that she was to be taken 'from the rear'. That could mean . . . She braced herself.

Silence! Nothing! What was happening? What was he doing? She became suddenly much more mindful of her nudity. He must be looking at her. Now! At this very moment! At her bare bottom. At her shaven pussy. Why had she been tied down? Did he like to spank his women, unable to enjoy his thrusting unless it was against fiery, hot skin? Was he fetching a whip? There were some in the room. She had seen them. She was lubricating furiously now and her trickle had become a flood, running down her leg.

The first touch, when it came, was like an electric shock. Someone had placed both thumbs on her bottom cheeks and was forcing them apart. God! She *was* going to be bum-fucked! She prayed that he knew enough to use a lubricant. That was his penis now, pressing against her sphincter! She gasped.

Wait a minute! That wasn't a penis! It was a tongue! It flickered to and fro across her bottom hole in the most delightful manner. Her gasp of anxiety turned into several gasps of ecstasy. She could not restrain herself from little, cooing noises of delight. Disappointingly, the tongue stopped. Had he moved away? No! She felt something between her legs, pushing against them to widen them. Then it became clear that he was sitting on the floor with his back to the bed. His hands went around the backs of her thighs and she felt beard shadow scrape against their inner surfaces as his face reached up towards her bald sex. She stood on tip-toe and spread her knees as far as they would go to give him access. Now that gorgeous tongue was licking up and down her slit and intruding into it, flickering on her clitoris. She thought she would burst with desire. The hands behind her thighs moved higher and grasped her bottom cheeks, pulling them apart again. She felt a finger on her sphincter, rubbing in small but insistent circles, demanding entry. She longed with a passion for him to shove it into her, lubricated or not, but it just went on circling and rubbing, driving her crazy.

She sobbed, moaning, 'I don't care who you are. You've just got to fuck me. Now! Please!'

She felt him remove himself from between her legs, then he was behind her and she felt the weight of him press gently on her back. From the feel of his hairs on her body, she could tell he was naked. The extreme tip of his penis entered her vagina and she jerked her bottom up and down in an effort to get more of it. He advanced it a little way with gently pumping strokes, titillating the sensitive area just inside. She felt hands slide forward along her sides and then jumped with pleasure and surprise as her hanging breasts received a light slap on either side. The slapping went on. It was very gentle, but it made her breasts wobble and flop together, tingling in an excruciatingly wicked way.

'Yes! Do it to me! Spank my tits! Fuck me hard! Do it to me! Oh, do it, please!' With a great sigh, she came to a peak of pleasure. She had been right to take that first climax from Zelda. She knew her own body. For her, multiple orgasms built from a low point, each succeeding one being just that bit better. She felt this one much more deeply, tearing and pulling at her vagina and uterus with the old, familiar surges.

His movements did not stop. His penis thrust a little deeper and he stopped slapping her breasts. She felt his right hand slide back over her stomach and dive into her groin. His fingers spread themselves flat on the hairless flesh right above her clitoris and began to massage it.

Her head thrashed from side to side and her knees jerked in time with his thrusts. 'Wonderful! Yes! Like that! A bit lower! *Yes!* Oh Jesus, *yes!*' Her climax ripped through the whole of her pelvic region like a tornado, devastating every pleasure nerve in its path. It left her drained and satisfied. It was the best sex she had known.

Still he did not stop! Now the full length of his penis was plunging into her very rapidly, driving her wild. She could feel his testicles slapping against the backs of her thighs every time he pounded into her. She felt the fingers of his left hand spread her sex lips even wider, exposing her clitoris to direct stimulation and knew that if he so much as touched her there she was going to be forced into another orgasm. He trapped it between his finger and the sliding, pumping organ above and rubbed it in small circles. She could feel her bottom leaping with frenzied activity, driven by the twitching of gluteal muscles which were entirely out of her control. At the same time, his weight came off her. She felt the fingers of his right hand on her lower back, then his thumb slid over and down into her crack to rub against and press at her anus.

She was lost. 'Oh my God! You'll drive me mad! What are you doing to me? Yes! Go on! Push! Put it right up my bum! Do it! I want you to! Make me feel it! Oh! Yes! Fantastic! Don't stop! Now! *Now!*' Head back, she howled like an animal. She felt the geyser of his sperm shoot into her, bathing her insides with heat and came for a third time, her violent contractions sucking and pulling at the instrument of her pleasure. For a moment, her senses became confused and she thought she was going to faint as her orgasm consumed her in great gushes of sensual delight which threatened to last for ever. Slowly, very slowly, she came down off her peak and relaxed, her knees still quivering like jelly. She glowed with the thought that she had just received a great gift; an absolutely perfect fuck which someone ought to put in a text-book!

Their movements slowed and stopped, both breathing heavily. After a moment or two, she felt his organ withdrawn from her and felt empty and alone without it. She listened, but heard nothing.

'Who are you! I've got to know. I've just got to! Who are you?' There was no reply.

Seven

A thin, cold drizzle made the pavements of Victoria Street gleam in the lamplight. It was not the sort of weather to encourage loitering and the young man under the large black umbrella had his coat collar turned up as he walked briskly towards the station. He was preoccupied with recent events and thought the streets deserted. Consequently, he was startled when a voice broke into his reverie.

'*Monsieur!* Excuse me, please!'

He spun on his heel and, for the first time noticed the figure of a girl standing in a shop doorway. His immediate reaction was that he should continue on his way, but there was something about this frail waif which distinguished her from the usual woman of the streets. Dark-haired and very young, probably hardly twenty, he guessed, she was very unsuitably dressed, having on only a light jacket over her thin, blue dress. He could see that both these garments were soaked through already and she was shivering with cold. From the form of address she had used he deduced that she was French and spoke back to her in that language. 'Can I help you, *Mademoiselle*?'

'Oh! *Monsieur* speaks French. What good fortune! I have great need of assistance. I am lost in this great city and all my money and my valise were stolen on the train. I have been afraid to speak with anyone, but now I am cold and tired and you have a good face. Will you help me, please?'

The young man thought rapidly. There was always the possibility that this was yet another begging act but, somehow, he did not think so. He could not believe that those large, dark eyes, set so solemnly in the luminous face, could be capable of deception. He made up his mind quickly.

'The first thing we must do, *Mademoiselle*, is to get you into a warm place. Just around the corner, there is a coffee shop which stays open late. Perhaps you would come there with me?' He shared his umbrella with her and steered her towards the warmth and light of the tiny establishment. There were very few customers on such a night. He sat her in a booth and, having enquired her choice, brought her a large mug of steaming coffee. She wrapped her hands around it for warmth and sipped gratefully.

He watched her large, round eyes peering at him over the rim of the mug and warmed further towards her. She was like a baby fawn, lost in the forest. 'I regret, *Mademoiselle*, that it is *café Anglais*.'

'Nicole,' she replied, lowering the mug. 'Nicole Foret. And it is very good coffee. You are most kind Mr . . .?'

'Corby. David Corby.' They shook hands gravely.

'So, tell me all about it, Nicole.'

'I am from Foret-sur-Marne – a small village. I am to be *au pair* with English ladies, to make better my English, you understand. I have taken the train this morning to Calais and crossed *la Manche* to Dover. All marches well until I arrive at Victoria Station, then, when I seek my valise on the rack, it is not there. Someone has stolen it. I have in it all my money, my clothes. Everything except the passport in my pocket. Even the address of the ladies I was to be with. What can I do? I know no one. I do not know London. I do not have money to make telephone to *mon père*. I had great fear until you came.'

David lapsed momentarily into English. 'You poor thing. You have had a rotten day, but I think I can sort you out. Can you remember the names of the ladies?'

'But yes. One called herself Miss Carteret.'

'Good! At least it's not "Smith". Would you remember the address if you saw it written down?'

'Yes, I think so.'

'Then that's your problem half solved already. Let me

get you something to eat.' He grinned. 'I'm afraid it won't be *haute cuisine*. Just a hamburger.'

She giggled. 'But I love much the hamburger. In France now, the McDonald's is *très chic*.'

He went to the counter and spoke to the proprietor. When he came back with her hamburger, he also had a telephone directory. As he leafed through it, he watched out of the corner of his eye as she sloshed tomato ketchup on her burger. So much for the French *gourmet* tradition!

'How about this?' He turned the directory so that she could see it. 'Miss K. Carteret. St John's Wood.'

'But yes, that is the one! You are very clever, David.' Then her face fell again. 'How to get there? I was to go by *Metro*, but I have no money for the ticket now.'

He took out his wallet and pushed a ten pound note across the table. 'Now you have a little spending money.'

'No! Really, *Monsieur*! I cannot borrow money from you. It would not be proper!'

'It's not a loan, it's a gift. Consider it my payment for the privilege of having dinner with a most amiable and charming companion. I know men who would gladly pay many times more than that. If we should chance to meet again, perhaps I'll let you buy me a beer. Otherwise, let it be simply for the sake of *l'entente cordiale*.'

He telephoned for a taxi and when it arrived, he put her in, paid the driver and made sure that he knew where to go. Through the open back window, he handed Nicole his card. 'If ever you have need of me, Nicole.'

She smiled radiantly. 'I have heard much of the English gentleman. Now I know it is true. *Au revoir*, David.'

He stood on the wet pavement and watched the cab's rear light disappear out of sight. Now that was a nice girl!

The taxi deposited Nicole at the entrance of a thirties' style apartment block. Directed by the hall porter, she made her way to the third floor and rang the bell. For the correspondence she had had, Nicole was expecting her host to be elderly, or at least middle-aged. The woman who opened the door was neither of those things. She was, Nicole judged, in her late twenties, red-haired and beautiful. She peered out at the pale and bedraggled figure on her doorstep. 'Yes?'

'*Mademoiselle* Carteret? I am Nicole.'

'Who? Oh, the *au pair*. I was expecting you hours ago. Gracious, child, whatever has happened to you? You look dreadful. Come in, come in!'

Karen's flat was larger than Nicole had expected. She had been conditioned by film and television to believe that all apartments near the centre of such a large city had to be tiny and not very pleasant. It was clean and neat, comfortably furnished without being garishly modern. Karen ushered her into a very pleasant sitting room and poured her a generous gin and tonic. She settled Nicole into the large sofa; switched on the electric fire and pressed the drink into her hand. Nicole settled back and relaxed. It really was rather pleasant to be in that place and with someone who was obviously concerned about her welfare after all the traumas of the day. The glow of the fire left dancing patterns on its back-plate and the drink warmed her. She began to feel more normal.

'Now tell me how you got into such a state and where you've been,' said Karen. 'I was getting worried about you.'

Nicole recited all her woes again, while Karen listened with attention. 'You say you've had only a hamburger since breakfast! That's dreadful! I'll make us a nice omelette.' said Karen. 'When you've had that, I suggest a good, hot bath. That always cheers me up. While you're soaking, I'll sort out something for you to wear. You're not going to be very comfortable in those wet things.'

She bustled off into the galley kitchen, from which arose the clink of pans and dishes; the sizzle of frying and, presently, a most enticing, herby smell which had to be the omelettes. Nicole suddenly decided that she was hungry again. Now it would take very little on top of her gin and tonic to start her tummy rumbling. That would not be very lady-like.

Karen brought the meal to her, where she sat. Nicole noticed that it was garnished with fresh parsley and tastefully arranged, accompanied by a side-dish of crusty bread, on a tray with a snowy white napkin. It was remarkably pleasant to be on the receiving end of such care and concern. She lingered over the omelette, which tasted as delicious as it smelt, reluctant to let the moment pass.

When, finally, she was done, Karen took the tray from her and guided her to the bathroom where the tub was already full and steaming, the air redolent with some very pleasant-smelling bath oil. Alone, Nicole slipped out of her clothes and slid gratefully into the bath. She lay there totally relaxed, not bothering to soap, admiring the decor. It certainly was a most beautiful and luxurious bathroom. She wondered idly, what Karen did to bring in enough money to pay for such a flat. Her thoughts came to an abrupt halt as the door opened without warning and Karen breezed in, pink towelling robe in hand. Nicole's hands flew in panic to cover her body. She had never been naked in the presence of another woman. Karen appeared not to notice. Indeed, her eyes never once strayed towards Nicole as she bustled about, hanging up the robe and collecting cast-off clothes. Such matter-of-fact behaviour reassured Nicole. After all, some women thought nothing of undressing in front of others. Probably, she was being terribly old-fashioned. She did not want Karen to think that of her so, after a while, she began to move her hands in gentle soaping movements so that they ceased to hide her breasts and her dark pubic hair would have been clearly visible had anyone been interested enough to peer down through the water. No one was. Was that just a trifle disappointing? She was not sure. Karen continued her chores, then left without a backward glance.

In case of a return, Nicole worked up a little lather with her hands and so arranged it that it partially concealed her breasts and pubic zone. Thus prepared, she felt no need to leap nervously when Karen came back with a couple of glasses. She had changed into a white, silk housecoat. Settling one hip on the edge of the bath, she proferred one of the glasses.

'Hair of the dog?'

To Nicole, this was completely incomprehensible. 'Pardon, *Madame*. Dog hair?'

'That's colloquial English, dear. That's what you've come to learn. It means another drink, like the one you had before. The hair of the dog that bit you, see? And it's Karen, by the way.'

Nicole took the glass, her nervousness returning at such proximity but grimly determined to see the thing through. That was what sophisticated ladies did every day, apparently, and she wasn't going to commit any *gaucherie* before Karen who was so obviously the epitome of sophistication. She sipped her drink and made herself relax. Unfortunately, she made rather too good a job of that and her head, falling back struck the top end of the tub with a resounding *clonk*. She was embarrassed again, but Karen showed no sign of noticing. Instead, she reached for a small bath pillow, raised Nicole's head and slipped the pillow beneath her neck. She did not remove her hand immediately, but softly massaged the neck beneath her fingers. Nicole could not contain a great sigh. That massage was the most comforting feeling. She was sorry when it stopped, but it was immediately replaced by a most gentle hand, which stroked her forehead. No word was spoken; no glance exchanged. There were just the two of them. In close contact, yet far apart. How nice that stroking was, thought Nicole. So soft. So gentle. So reassuring. So . . .

She jerked awake with a great start, water splashing everywhere. How long had she been asleep? It couldn't have been too long because the bath water was not really cold; just a bit tepid. She scrambled out, got into the robe provided and dried the bits it did not cover on a fluffy towel. When she poked her head, cautiously, into the living room, she could hear that Karen was in the galley kitchen. She joined her there and found her washing up.

'Hello, sleepy! Back with us, then?'

Nicole was embarrassed. 'I must excuse myself. It was most impolite to sleep so. Perhaps it has been a very difficult day, or perhaps it has been the drink.'

Karen took both her hands. 'It wasn't. If I'd gone

through what you have, I would have wanted to sleep for a fortnight, not just for half an hour. When you nodded off, I just left you. You need to sleep. Knits up the ravelled sleeve of care, and all that.'

'Ah! This I understand. Shakespeare, no?'

'Shakespeare, yes! Very good! Coffee's perking. Want some?'

As they sipped their coffee, Karen said, 'Actually, my dear, there is a weeny bit of a problem. The bed in the spare room was not good and when I knew you were coming, I threw it out and ordered another. The silly men have failed to deliver it, so I have a room for you, but no bed. Still, never mind! We'll just have to manage until it comes. Tomorrow morning we must enquire to see if your bag has turned up at lost property. It could be that whoever took it wasn't interested in the contents when he opened it, and he just threw it away. In the meantime, you're close to my size and I can loan you whatever you need until we can buy replacements. I've got a brand new toothbrush you can have, and I'll loan you a nightie. Tomorrow afternoon, we'll go shopping. Nothing like a bit of shopping to raise the spirits.'

Nicole found that her eyes were prickling with tears at this continued kindness. She knew that her spirits were rising already. It seemed as though it was going to be quite impossible to be unhappy for long in the company of this nice woman. She had never had a real, female friend, and was therefore unaware of the myriad delights such a relationship had to offer. Just a few of those delights became apparent as the evening went on. They gossiped and chattered without pause about hair, clothes, men, politics, employment and taxes. Karen was not turning out to be the sort of person Nicole had thought she would be when she volunteered for *au pair*. By bed-time, Karen knew all about Nicole and Nicole knew, amongst other things, that Karen was an actress and had a flat-mate who was also an actress but was away on tour with a play.

The promised toothbrush having materialised, Nicole prepared herself for the night. When she emerged from the bathroom, she could not immediately see Karen. Investigating an open door, she found herself in a large bedroom with a huge bed. Karen turned as she came in. 'I've sorted you out a nightie.' She held a peach silk creation against Nicole's shoulders and surveyed the effect. 'That'll be OK, I think. Try it.'

Nicole was a little disconcerted at the prospect of removing her robe in front of Karen. Having completed her bathroom ritual, she could hardly use that as an excuse to hide while changing. Anyway, what did it matter? Karen had already seen her naked in the bath. It was sheer prudishness to worry about such things. She turned her back, slipped out of the robe and wiggled the nightdress over her head. She had seldom worn silk and the caress of the soft material against her skin was quite delightful. On to the next problem.

'I'll sleep on the sofa, shall I?'

Karen stopped dead in the middle of climbing into bed. 'Why would you want to do that, when there's a perfectly good bed. Come on in. I don't bite or snore.' She flipped back the other half of the sheet, invitingly. Nicole shrugged and got in. The sheets were starched linen and felt amazingly good. Karen sat up to reach the light-cord and the bedroom became dark. On the way down from the light-cord, she leaned over and kissed Nicole briefly on the cheek. She did this as though it was the most natural think in the world and for Nicole, it was. She snuggled down. She hadn't felt so cared for in years. The kiss reminded her of the happy days of her youth, when her mother would kiss her goodnight. She wondered if she ought to return it, or to say something about how grateful she was to Karen for all her care and concern. She was still wondering about that when she fell asleep.

It was good to wake up to the smell of coffee and fresh rolls.

Finding slacks and a sweater at the foot of the bed, Nicole slipped into them and found Karen in the little kitchen. She looked up as Nicole came in, surveying her critically.

'That's better. You needed the sleep. We'll get some breakfast into you, then we'll be off.'

'It should be I who makes breakfast for you. I feel so guilty, having you feed me this way.'

'No need to feel guilty. Guess who's doing the washing up!'

Nicole grinned and took the proffered plate and coffee from her. Over the breakfast table they fell into the same relaxed, easy conversation as they planned their day. Telephone enquires revealed no trace of the missing luggage and Karen proposed that they should shop in Oxford Street for replacements.

Nicole protested. 'But I have no money.'

'Did you have travel insurance?'

'Oh yes! I had forgotten! But it will be a while before I get paid.'

'Not to worry,' said Karen. 'We'll put everything on my account and you can pay me back when your claim comes through.'

This made the shopping trip entirely possible and it proved to be as hugely enjoyable as everything else Nicole did in this woman's company. It wasn't that they spent large amounts of money. The did spend large amounts of time in browsing and trying things on. By now, Nicole had no inhibitions at all about sharing a changing room with Karen and stripping down to undies – or less – in front of her. Karen, for her part, clearly felt no misgivings about doing the same thing.

That night, they sat together on the sofa in front of the fire with their drinks, chattering and giggling together. The conversation moved around to relationships with men.

'Do you have a regular boyfriend?' Karen asked.

Nicole blushed. 'No. I have been out with boys once or twice, but it is not easy for me. I do not seem to be like other girls. For them it is easy. I do not seem to find boys I like. The ones who took me out were not good. I found their attentions . . . unpleasant. Do you understand that?'

'Oh, only too well,' said Karen ruefully. 'I've had a few like that. Makes orgasm just about impossible.

There was a long silence. Nicole was having enormous difficulty with the question which was uppermost in her mind. Finally, the confidence she had built up in her relationship with Karen won out over her natural shyness.

'Tell me about orgasms, Karen. I've read about them in the magazines but, as far as I know, it has never happened to me.'

'You have had sex, of course?'

'No! Never!'

'You poor thing. Do you mean to tell me that you're twenty and still a virgin? That you have never . . . Well! I'm lost for words. What about when you do yourself?'

'I don't know what you mean. Do myself?'

'You know. When you masturbate.'

Nicole was fiery red with embarrassment. 'I don't . . . I've never . . . It wasn't nice. *Maman* told me . . .' Her voice trailed off miserably.

'Never fooled around with the other girls at school?'

Nicole was shocked. 'No. Of course not.'

'There's no "of course not" about it. Most girls have some small experience of sex with another girl, in the same way that most boys have a passing interest in other boys. It's a natural part of growing up and sorting out preferences. It may get no further than a schoolgirl "crush", but sex is lurking in the bushes. Pity you didn't dabble, really. At least you would have learned to give yourself an orgasm. Believe me, you have really missed out there.'

'What's an orgasm like?' Nicole's curiosity was rapidly overcoming her shyness.

Karen laughed. 'That's a bit like trying to describe "red" to a blind person. It's something you can only find out by having one. Have you ever thought about having sex with a woman?'

'No.' That was a lie. Nicole *had* thought about it, in a vague sort of way. Not that she had ever considered putting her fantasies into effect. Even the half-thought was sinful enough. A sudden impulse made her ask, 'Have you, then?'

'Of course.' That answer was truly amazing. 'My philosophy is, if it's fun, do it and to hell with what the world thinks.'

Nicole sat in silence, trying to accustom her mind to this revelation. The more she thought about it, the greater her curiosity became. Her old fantasies came flooding back as she realised that Karen was, in effect, offering sex. Presently, that offer was repeated in a more concrete way.

'Tell you what. I'll make a start on the education you should have had as a girl. I'll kiss you, now, and you can tell me if you like it or not. Put your drink down.'

That was cleverly done, Nicole realised. Now, she did not have to agree, or say the dreaded word, 'Yes.' All she had to do was put down her drink and anyone might do that, mightn't they? That was a perfectly normal and straightforward thing to do. She set her drink on the little table. Karen put her arm around Nicole's shoulders and, drawing her close, kissed her firmly, full on the lips. It was the sweetest, most tender kiss Nicole had ever received and it seemed to go on for ever. It stopped at last and Karen sat back, her eyes scanning Nicole's face intently.

'Well? How was that?'

Nicole was a little breathless. 'Strange. It made me a little afraid.'

'Nasty?'

'Oh no!' Nicole was sure about that, at any rate.

'Exciting?'

Nicole was certain that Karen already knew the answer to that. Everyone in London must have been able to hear her heart thudding.

'Again?'

Nicole nodded, feeling slightly faint. This time, the kiss lasted even longer and she felt the tip of Karen's tongue emerge gently to add to the sensation. She was not ready yet, she felt, to respond to this stimulation, but she noted, with heightened awareness, the compound interest added to the sensation of sexual desire which the first embrace had aroused.

When that kiss ended, the sensation of dizziness persisted, so that it was some while before Nicole noticed that Karen had left her and gone into the kitchen. She was able to sit for a while, trying to recover some of her poise and analyse the feelings she had experienced. She knew that she had been deeply moved and excited. Was that latent lesbianism? She felt a little ashamed but, strangely enough, that shame was all a part of the excitement. When Karen came back with two steaming mugs of cocoa, she waited for her to interrogate her further, or to foster the sexual tension. She did neither and that was, perhaps, a little disappointing. Karen resumed their conversation as if nothing had happened and continued it until it was time for Nicole's bath.

She soaked for a long time, waiting for Karen to come in. She didn't and Nicole knew then that she was definitely disappointed. Was that all that was going to happen? Was this the 'education' Karen had spoken of? When she went into the bedroom, Karen was already in bed, reading a magazine. Nicole was too shy to say anything to her, but simply went about brushing her hair and other night-time rituals. It was not until she was ready to put on her nightdress that Karen spoke. 'I've put out two nighties, tonight,' she said casually. 'There's the one you wore last night and then there's that other one that buttons all down the front. You choose which you want to wear.'

There it was again. The clever and subtle invitation. She was not being asked to voice any desire for further intimate contact. She was simply being invited to choose which nightie to wear. A simple, humdrum question and a perfectly ordinary decision which anyone could make without embarrassment. She turned her back, took off her robe, put on the nightdress with the buttons and climbed into bed alongside Karen.

Karen reached up as before to put out the light but instead of the goodnight peck, she sought out Nicole's lips this time, her tongue moving more urgently. Nicole allowed her own tongue to extend and match Karen's movements. When she did so, Karen's mouth opened and sucked Nicole's tongue inside, which was a wildly exciting sensation. The cessation of that kiss left Nicole breathless and palpitating, a state which Karen did nothing to assuage by caressing her face and allowing little butterfly kisses to pepper her forehead and eyes, murmuring endearments as she did so. Presently, Karen's hands left her face and wandered down her neck, stroking and feeling. The first touch on her breast was so light that at first she thought she must have been mistaken. No! There it was again; firmer now and unmistakable; Karen's forefinger circling and delineating her hardening nipple through the flimsy material of her nightgown. Nicole gasped and squirmed, thrusting her upper body up towards the tickling sensation. She knew that there was nothing she wanted more than for Karen to unbutton the nightie so that there should be greater contact, flesh with flesh, and she waited impatiently for that to happen.

The questing, circling finger continued its work, first on one nipple, then on the other, while Karen's mouth sought hers again in the darkness. Nicole responded eagerly to that kiss, her mouth opening readily to receive Karen's tongue, sucking on it fiercely, then inserting her own into Karen's mouth to be similarly received. Now Nicole did not want Karen to unbutton her. She wanted her to kneel over her and rip the nightdress away, buttons spraying everywhere. She wanted to feel cool air on her skin and to be completely naked, vulnerable and available. Never before had she reached such a fever pitch of sexual arousal.

The unbuttoning, when it came, was soft, gentle and almost imperceptible. Slowly, gradually, Karen's fingers dealt with the obstacles one by one, then laid the material back. Nicole bit her lip to avoid screaming out, 'Touch me! Touch me!'

The first touch on her naked breasts was not of fingers, but of lips. Little fluttering kisses, first on one breast, then on the other. Nicole could feel that they were getting closer and closer to the nipple and could hardly contain herself. When Karen's mouth fixed itself on her right nipple and sucked it in, Nicole could no longer hold out and gave a great, gasping shout of excitement. The sucking continued, more urgent now, while Karen's tongue circled the long nipple with sweeping caresses. She stopped and withdrew her mouth. Nicole felt the coldness of cooling saliva on her nipple and, sensing that Karen's head was moving across to the other side, thrust up her left breast eagerly to receive similar treatment.

The clamping of that nipple between sucking lips and nibbling teeth provoked the same gasp as before. Now Nicole was thinking the unthinkable. She knew that she wanted Karen's hand between her legs, where she could feel an unaccustomed wetness. She put her own fingers to the lower buttons in an attempt to undo them, but found her wrists grasped and replaced, firmly, at her sides. Karen was going to make her wait. Nicole wriggled and moaned as her nipples underwent further torture. Surely Karen could not be so cruel as to stop now? Again, she reached for her lower body but, again, her wrists were seized in a steely grip and replaced at her sides. She found that the only movement she was allowed was to stroke Karen's hair where it lay spread over those tenderised breasts. Nicole moaned and sighed, finding her thighs chafing together against her will.

At last, Karen began the long-awaited unbuttoning, her lips following her fingers down over each freshly uncovered area of nakedness. Nicole heard her own voice, hoarse and slurred, murmuring, 'Yes! Oh yes! Please! Oh yes!' When the nightdress was completely undone and thrown back, useless as a covering, Nicole threw her thighs wide apart in invitation, every nerve in her body concentrated on that one, longed-for place where the first touch might come. It came as a gentle, tickling sensation, as Karen's fingers gently brushed the extremities of the hairs at her pubic bush. Moaning uncontrollably, Nicole thrust her pelvis up towards the stimulation, but Karen was not to be rushed and withdrew her hand so as to avoid contact.

Now all pretence of shyness or inhibition was gone. Nicole was squirming in the grip of an erotic stimulation which was not to be denied. When Karen's forefinger found her pink slit and slid along it, she screamed in ecstasy, arching her back to increase the stimulation. When the searching fingers found and gripped the hard nubbin of flesh which was her clitoris, moulding and rubbing, Nicole gave a great shout and thrashed in the throes of orgasm, her head falling back, mouth open and slobbering, eyes glazed and unseeing, uncaring of anything except the sensations of joy and release which oozed out of every pore. She knew, now, what the magazines had been talking about and she was overwhelmed with gratitude and love towards Karen, who had so proficiently brought the matter to her attention. She clung to her, sobbing with happiness and relief from tension.

Karen was still asleep when Nicole awoke the next morning. She slipped out of bed without disturbing her and made breakfast preparations. The coffee was nearly perked before Karen put in an appearance, tousled and sleepy. She surveyed the kitchen activity with an appraising eye and said, 'Well! Just look at you! You look like the cat who got the cream. Something's cheered you up. I wonder what it could be?'

Nicole flushed and remained silent, suddenly embarrassed at the recollection of her uninhibited behaviour of the previous evening. She remained uncommunicative during their meal, very badly wanting to discuss her emotions but not knowing how to broach the subject. Karen seemed completely oblivious to her difficulty, chattering away and inspecting the Jobs section of *The Stage* and *Variety* between hearty bites of toast and marmalade. They shared the washing and drying of the dishes, then Karen said, 'Well, I don't know about you, but I feel sticky all over. I'm for a shower. How about you?'

Nicole wasn't quite sure how to take this and temporised. 'Perhaps I should have a bath when you've finished.'

'Nonsense. Waste of hot water we can't afford. Share my shower.' Karen's direct gaze challenged her.

Did she dare? Nicole made up her mind. After all, her body was now no secret. Karen's hands had already sought out its most intimate places and it seemed that she thought her education still incomplete. Still without speaking, Nicole stretched out her hand to take Karen's and allowed herself to be drawn into the bathroom. Karen slipped out of her dressing gown with total unconcern and stood naked. Nicole could not resist the temptation to peek with shy, lowered eyes. Karen's body was magnificent; flawless; her skin peach-coloured with the flush of youth and health. The areolae on the proud and perfect orbs of her breasts were darkly pink and very large. Below her clearly delineated rib cage and flat stomach, a generous triangle of red hair sprouted profusely between gorgeous, inviting thighs, tapering to long, shapely legs.

Still shy, Nicole turned away to take off her own robe, acutely conscious of the fact that her body could not match Karen's. She stooped to pick up a shower cap, tensing her gluteal muscles as though that would, somehow, make her miraculously less naked. She jumped at the tiny sting as Karen flicked at her bare bottom with the corner of a towel.

'Hey! Not fair! I saw you peeking at me. Stand up and turn around so I can see you too.' Nicole turned, her arms covering her vital parts protectively, and saw that Karen was grinning as she pushed a rebellious lock of hair into her shower cap.

'Take your hands away. I want to look.'

Slowly and nervously, Nicole obeyed, flushing the deepest red.

'Better still, put your hands behind your head.'

Amazed at her own temerity, the flush deepening, Nicole locked her fingers behind her neck and endured the close scrutiny which followed. She saw Karen's eyes drinking in her vulnerability and felt shame at what she was doing. Yet she found that shame was very much a part of the deepening excitement which was causing her nipples to erect themselves. She was a little comforted to observe that Karen's nipples were also becoming stiff and long, losing the flaccid crinkles which were the result of being compressed beneath her dressing gown.

Karen drew the bath's shower curtain across and turned on the water, adjusting the temperature. When that was to her satisfaction, she held out her hand to Nicole and they stepped into the bath to stand face to face, almost touching, under the stinging spray. They were of similar height so that when Karen leant forward slightly, her nipples threatened to brush against Nicole's. Nicole stood as though in a dream and made no attempt to withdraw her body from this attention. Their nipples came together lightly then, suddenly, they were locked in a fierce embrace, open mouth to open mouth, the water hissing and trickling down their bare bodies.

Presently, Karen broke off to turn off the water and pick up soap and a washcloth.

'Turn around. I'll do your back for you.' Dreamily, Nicole revolved and delighted in the sensation of having her back thoroughly soaped and scrubbed.

'Arms up!'

Nicole submitted to this ordering and Karen, reaching from behind, transferred her attention to her armpits and breasts.

'Put your foot up on the side of the bath!'

This order, when obeyed, gave easy access to the crease between the cheeks of her bottom and her stretched vagina. The soapy washcloth on her anus was particularly stimulating, culminating as it did in passes to and fro between her legs. Nicole shuddered as Karen soaped and scrubbed, perhaps more vigorously than was strictly necessary. She felt the overwhelming urge to increase her body's pleasure, sliding her hands down over her breasts towards her stomach and beyond. As on the previous night, she was thwarted by Karen, who grasped her wrists and forced her arms back up to where they had been.

'No! I said "Arms up". No touching unless ordered. Understand?'

Nicole nodded, submissive and wildly excited by this evidence of control.

'Turn around! Shut your eyes!'

Now Nicole's face and ears were subjected to thorough washing. She wanted to giggle. She had not been scrubbed like this since her mother bathed her as a little girl. It was somehow comforting and reassuring.

Karen turned on the water again and Nicole revolved under it, washing away all traces of soap.

'Now you!' Nicole could hardly believe that she was saying this. She turned off the water and stood, washcloth and soap at the ready, to see if Karen would obey. With a barely perceptible smile, Karen turned her shapely back towards her and waited. Nicole's hands trembled as she applied the soapy washcloth to that beautiful back. She thought that she had never seen anything so perfect. Unable to resist the temptation, she abandoned the washcloth and, soaping her hands, permitted herself the first flesh to flesh contact. She bit her lip to suppress a hiss of excitement as she felt the full effect of that slippery, peachy skin on her palms. Working slowly downwards from shoulders to waist, she paused to let her thumbs explore the delightful dimples which adorned each side of Karen's lower back, just above her creamy buttocks. Extending her fingers and using each dimple as a fulcrum, she rotated her hands so that they encased that perfect bottom, one cheek in each hand, lifting, moulding and shaping those fascinating orbs.

Remembering the thrill which recent treatment had occasioned in her own body, she felt the need to see if she could move Karen in the same way.

'Now you put your foot on the side of the bath!'

She was delighted when the order was instantly obeyed, Karen widely parting those buttocks and thighs for her further investigation. She trailed her fingers lightly down the crease which was now so available, then rubbed more insistently up and down, knowing from the way she jerked that Karen was feeling each pass over her anus just as Nicole had done. She pushed her hand forward between the parted thighs and allowed the flat of her palm to massage the red curls which concealed Karen's sex. Karen moaned softly, arching her neck back and rolling her head from side to side. Her hands came up to her nipples, rubbing and pulling, only to find her wrists grasped and pushed down to her sides.

'No! That is for me to do. I will say when.'

It was clear that these actions and words excited Karen, just as they had excited Nicole. Her soapy bottom began to jerk convulsively in rhythm with the movements of Nicole's hand, while her moaning and head-rolling grew in intensity. Nicole watched Karen's fingers opening and closing jerkily as she fought to prevent them from straying to the places she wanted touched, and took pity on her. Maintaining her left-hand massage, she reached around with her right and began to play with the stiff nipples, noting with pleasure the definite increase in symptoms of excitement. When she felt it had gone on long enough, she tested her authority further.

'Turn round! Eyes shut!'

She exulted in the fact that her command was obeyed, albeit a little more slowly than before. A submissive Karen stood before her, soapy and naked, trembling with passion and breathing heavily, but with eyes closed and hands at sides, as ordered. That felt really good. She washed Karen's face and ears, as her own had been washed, then turned on the shower. They embraced again as the water washed away all traces of lather, then they got out and helped to dry each other, laughing and touching from time to time. Karen put on her robe. Nicole made to put on hers, but Karen reached out a restraining hand.

'You don't need that just yet. I think we have some unfinished business to attend to in the bedroom.' Nicole could feel her juices still boiling and couldn't have agreed more. She followed Karen willingly into the bedroom, where Karen made her lie down on the bed.

Giggling, Nicole complied. Karen slipped out of her robe and tossed it onto the bed.

'Raise your knees! Part them! No, not like that. Really wide!'

Nicole looked down between her breasts at her exposed condition and marvelled. Could this really be her doing this? And loving every minute of it?

Karen knelt, equally naked, between the parted thighs, holding a largish hand-mirror.

'Now then! You take hold of this and adjust the angle so that you can see everything clearly.'

There it was again, thought Nicole; that same feeling of

mingled shame and excitement. She peered into the mirror at the vulgar display of her own genitalia, observing a glistening of moisture at the slightly-parted pink lips. Karen's touch, when it came, was like an electric shock, causing her to jump, convulsively. With a thumb on each side of her vulva, Karen spread her open to reveal the inner labia, pinkly shining.

'See how the inner surfaces are reddened and engorged. You *are* in a sexy mood, aren't you, Nicole?'

Nicole nodded, stifling giggles.

Karen held her labia open with one hand and passed the forefinger of the other lightly along the inner surface. Nicole jumped and gasped, clamping her thighs together.

Karen said, 'Knees wide apart again, please! That's better! Now we test for virginity by gently inserting a forefinger – like this.' Then, as Nicole moved apprehensively: 'Keep still, girl! I'll be careful! Mmmm! So you are still a virgin! We will deal very carefully with that problem and stretch you a little at a time, until you can enjoy every delight.'

'Still that does not prevent us from concentrating on the most important place of all. See this little hood of flesh here, right at the top. I'm amazed that you didn't find it on your own before now. When I pull the hood back and spread the lips – like this – you can see a small white button, like a pointed mushroom. That is your clitoris – the centre of all female delight. In its exposed and erect state, as it is now, it is extremely sensitive, which I can demonstrate with the lightest of touches. Ah! I see that excites you! For masturbating though, the hood is not retracted but left in place. Manipulation of the clitoris takes place through the thickness of the flesh so that the pleasure can be prolonged and all chance of pain or soreness avoided. From now on, everything is a matter of personal preference, so I shall masturbate you in different ways, and you can tell me how it feels.'

'I'll start with one finger pressing lightly, directly over it, making small circular movements. How's that, Nicole?'

'Oooh! It feels good!'

'Now I'll change to two fingers, one on either side, gently squeezing and rubbing. How does that feel?'

'It's lovely, but not quite so comfortable.'

'OK. How about several fingers, or the palm of my hand, spread over a wide area and rubbing harder?'

'That's nice too, but I think I prefer the first way.'

'Then that's what you shall have, *ma petite*, but it would please me very much if you would tell me what you feel as I bring you towards your climax.

Nicole blushed. 'I couldn't do that, Karen. I would be ashamed.'

'Feelings of shame and guilt are perfectly natural in the inexperienced. We'll get into the swing of it gradually, to help you along. I notice that you haven't tried to stop me. Could it be that you like what I'm doing to you?'

Nicole nodded, scarlet by now.

'Was that a "yes"?'

'Yes!' The answer was torn from Nicole's throat as if by hot irons.

'Does it make you feel sexy?'

'Yes!' The answer came more easily this time.

'Describe that feeling for me. I want to understand.'

Nicole searched for words. 'It is warm, like morning bread. It makes my insides like the molasses. They melt and run, I think.'

Karen continued her manipulations, then suddenly bent to take one of Nicole's nipples in her mouth.

'Ah! Oh God! Oh! It's going to happen again!'

'What's going to happen, Nicole?'

'The same as last night . . . That thing . . . You know! Oooh!'

'And that was nice?'

'You know it was.' Nicole jumped and gasped in time with Karen's movements.

'Then why are you feeling guilty and ashamed? The places I am touching were given to you as sources of pleasure. How can it be wrong to enjoy what you are designed to enjoy? Take and take again and think of nothing else but your own pleasure.'

Nicole was almost incoherent now. 'Yes! Oh yes! I love it! I love what you're doing.'

'What am I doing to you, Nicole? Say the word! I need to hear you say that I am masturbating you!'

'You're . . . You . . . You're masturbating me! And I love it! I don't care! I love it!' There! It was out!

'You see? That wasn't so difficult, was it? Now I'm going to slow down and hold you on the edge.'

'No! Oh no! Don't stop! Please don't stop!' Nicole's hands moved frantically to stimulate herself, but Karen slapped them away.

'No you don't! You get it when I'm ready, not before. Keep your hands away or I'll tie them so you can't interfere.'

At that, all Nicole's recollection of the excitement of the previous evening came flooding back. The exhilaration and shame of being controlled; of having her wrists held. She writhed and moaned, clawing at her nipples, her head rolling as if in agony; her voice an animal howl.

'Ah! It's coming! It's coming! Now! Help me! Oh God! Please!' As Karen increased her stimulation, Nicole came to climax with great, gasping shudders, spending vast amounts of fluid over Karen's fingers. Karen fell forward beside her and they lay, holding each other. Presently, they slept.

Eight

The rattle of a key in the front door of the apartment woke Karen and Nicole from their siesta. A cheery voice called, 'Karen! Are you in?'

Nicole looked at Karen in bewilderment. Karen sat up in bed, the sheets clutched apprehensively around her nakedness. 'God! Oh God! It's Jane!'

'Who is Jane?' asked Nicole, infected by her companion's alarm and similarly clutching the bedclothes around her.

'Jane Hunter. My friend. My flatmate. Oh God!' Karen sat, paralysed, like a startled rabbit.

The cheery voice came nearer down the hall, 'Come *on*, darling! I'm dying for a cup of tea. Damned play closed on me. Bloody provincial critics . . .' The voice trailed off into silence as the bedroom door opened to frame a buxom, black-haired woman. About the same age as Karen, she was a little taller and much more solidly built. For several seconds the trio remained in their positions, frozen into immobility.

Karen was the first one to break the silence. 'Jane! Oh Jane darling . . . Let me explain . . .'

'Explain! I should bloody well think you will explain. I can't go off for a couple of weeks and leave you alone without you having to have some trollop in my bed!' Jane's towering rage was apparent. Her face was suffused with dark blood and her whole body shook with anger.

'Dearest . . . It's not what you think . . . It's . . .' Karen got no further.

'You'll find out what I think, you harlot! Come out of

there! Come out of there, now! No, not you, Missie. You stay where you are. I'll get to you in a minute!' As Nicole shrank back beneath the covers, Karen set them aside and slunk out of bed. White and shaking, she stood naked before her partner who, in spite of the small difference in height, appeared to tower over her.

'Well? You know what you have to do, don't you?'

Dumbly, Karen nodded then, to Nicole's astonishment, she sank to her knees, took the hem of Jane's dress in her hand and raised it to her lips.

'More!'

Piteously, Karen gestured towards Nicole and said, 'Please, Jane! Please no . . .!'

'More, Karen!' Beneath that steely gaze, Karen wilted. Slowly and reluctantly, her head bowed lower and lower until her red hair was brushing the carpet.

'I don't see you doing it, Karen. They're really dusty after my long journey.'

Nicole was aghast to see Karen's tongue emerge and begin to lick the shoes in front of her face. She had heard and read of such things, but never believed that they happened. For a long moment Jane allowed Karen to continue her degrading performance, while she transfixed Nicole with a look of contempt and triumph.

'Up, slut!' Karen climbed to her feet and again stood before her tormentor with bowed head.

'Fetch the bag!'

Karen opened her mouth to protest, then obviously thought better of it. She shuffled despairingly to the wardrobe and, standing on tip-toe, took a canvas hold-all down from an upper shelf and took it to Jane.

Jane took it from her. 'Down! Right down. Flat on your face! Hands at your sides!' Jane waited to see her adopt this submissive pose on the carpet at the foot of the bed, then said, 'Now stay!' She reached into the bag and brought something out. As she came towards the bed, Nicole realised with a thrill of horror, that she was holding a pair of handcuffs.

'Now it's your turn, Missie!'

Taken by surprise, Nicole attempted to scramble out of the far side of the bed but, being encumbered by the sheets and inhibited by shame at her nudity, she didn't move fast enough to avoid Jane's snake-like strike. She felt a hand of unbelievable strength grasp her ankle and she was unceremoniously hauled back onto the bed. Nicole fought as best she could, but her twenty-year-old frame was no match for the older, heavier woman who sat astride her squirming, heaving body and easily hauled her arms up, one by one, and pushed them through one of the uprights of the brass bedhead then cuffed her wrists together. Jane fumbled for the discarded robe and removed the belt. Reaching into a bedside drawer, she took out a bundle of handkerchiefs and tried to stuff them into Nicole's mouth. Nicole set her teeth together and pursed her lips. Calmly, Jane pinched her nose then, when she was forced to open her mouth to gasp for air, she rammed the bundle of handkerchiefs in and secured them there with the belt, pulling it tight and knotting it. As Jane got off her, Nicole turned onto her side and curled into a ball, her legs pressed together in an attempt to cover herself. Jane was hardly out of breath as she climbed off the bed and stood, looking from one to the other while straightening her dress.

'Up, Karen!'

Karen rose shakily from her undignified position and once more stood to attention. Jane reached into the bag again and brought out a bottle and a tablespoon.

'No, Jane! Please not that! I won't do it again. You know how I hate –'

'Shut up! Head back! Right back. Open wide!' Karen stood with mouth agape as Jane uncapped the bottle and tipped a liberal amount of the contents into the tablespoon. Stepping up to Karen, she poured the whole spoonful into her open mouth. 'You know all bitches need cod liver oil to keep their coat in good condition. Close your mouth! You know the rules. You don't swallow until I give you permission. Now swill it round to get the full taste!' Jane stood, enjoying Karen's expression of disgust as she worked her cheeks and jaw, allowing the hated substance to penetrate every crevice of her mouth. It was a full minute before she said, 'Now swallow!'

With a convulsive effort, Karen gulped, clearly having some difficulty in controlling the desire to retch. She wiped her lips with the back of her hand.

'Now for our mutual friend, Mr Whippy.' Jane reached into the bag again and withdrew a slender cane. 'You remember him, Karen? He's the one who reminds you how things ought to be from time to time, when you forget. I do believe he's itching to meet your bottom again. Come and give him a nice kiss.' She held the cane horizontally between both fists and Karen, face scarlet with shame, slunk forward and dutifully kissed it.

'I think we'll have you at the foot of the bed with your back to your little friend, so that she can see exactly what's going on.'

Karen moved at once to the foot of the bed and for the first time Nicole began to obtain a dim grasp of the relationship between these two women. One was the master and the other the slave! The amazing thing to Nicole was that Karen's subservience seemed to be voluntary, almost as though she actually enjoyed being ordered about.

'That's right,' snapped Jane. 'Now bend over! Legs apart and grasp your ankles.' Karen adopted this shameful pose without demur, willingly presenting her body for punishment and confirming to Nicole what she had begun to suspect. Nicole was treated to a full view of her perfect bottom, her red, pubic curls and the pink slot of her sex obscenely revealed. Jane saw Nicole looking, wide-eyed with horror. 'Ah, good! You're watching! You'll be getting the same soon. Six, to start with, I think. You'll find that Karen knows what to do. She counts the strokes for me. If she miscounts, or lets go of her ankles, or cries out, we start again.'

Jane raised the cane and brought it down with the full strength of her arm. The willow made a hissing whine in the air, then a sharp slap as it struck across both buttock cheeks near the top, causing them to wobble and jump. A bright red weal sprang up to mark where the blow had fallen. Karen's knees bobbed and straightened convulsively, but she maintained her grip on her ankles and hissed, through clenched teeth, 'One!' Again the cane was raised and the stroke repeated. This time, the mark sprang up a trifle below the first. The knee-bobbing, an involuntary reaction to the pain, was more pronounced this time but as before, Karen recovered herself to stand still after the stroke and present her bottom as a stationary target for the next. 'Two!'

The beating went on, each stroke falling a little below the one before it. Nicole could see the upper part of the front of Karen's body between her legs, her breasts dangling and jiggling with her movements in response to the pain. Her face was bright red with the shame of being watched and the effort of containing her yells of agony, but she counted on, bravely: 'Three! Four! Five! Six!' The caning stopped, but Karen, as if by long custom, maintained her position, her bottom and the backs of her thighs marked with six distinct horizontal stripes.

'Get up! No, don't rub your backside. It has more work to do. Another six, I think, but this time, you shall face your friend and look her in the face, so that you can see the cause of your predicament and she can see just how painful my canings are and prepare herself for hers.'

Karen's face was streaked with tears. 'Please Jane! No more! I beg you!'

'Arguing will get you another six if you're not careful. Turn around! Down you go again, but this time, we'll have a change. You can bend over the bed rail and put your hands on the bed. That's right. Don't forget to look at her. I shall be watching to see that you do.' Again without demur, Karen draped herself over the brass rail at the foot of the bed with her bottom in the air and Nicole realised that, in this position, the rail under her hips would mean that even the trivial relief of knee-bobbing would be denied to her.

Jane laid the cane lightly across the stretched bottom and stroked it, absent-mindedly, to and fro while she addressed herself to Nicole. 'You won't be able to see it, but I shall place these exactly between the first six. I'm good at that, aren't I, Karen?'

Karen nodded without speaking and braced herself, her arms stiff and straight and her head craned back in order to meet Nicole's eyes, as instructed. For Nicole, it was almost worse to watch the beating from this angle than it had been to see the strokes landing. Karen's constant grimace of anguish and her hissing intake of breath between clenched teeth at every blow were expressive enough of her torment, even without the demented dance her body performed each time the cane fell. 'Seven! Eight! Nine! Ten! Eleven! *Twelve!*' This last was wrenched from her mouth as a gasping shout. As before, she held her position, her tears splashing onto the foot of the bed.

'Get up!' Karen rose very slowly and carefully. 'Turn around and show her!' She revolved and Nicole saw what the last six strokes had done to what had been an exquisite, peach-coloured bottom. Now, it was one continuous sea of fiery red from hip to thigh, the weals blending into one another with no discernible gap. Nicole even imagined she could feel the throbbing heat coming off it.

'Now you can rub it!' Karen's hands appeared and caressed her sore posterior. 'Not too much! You'll make it worse. Go into the kitchen and fill an ice tray.' As Karen went out, Jane turned her attention to Nicole. 'Put your legs straight and let's have a look at you!'

Nicole shook her head vigorously and curled herself into an even tighter ball. Jane laughed shortly and went to her bag again. She took out some lengths of cord and came back to the bed. Nicole fought madly, lashing out with her feet, but Jane seized her right ankle, tied a cord around it, pulled the leg straight and secured it to the brass rail at the bottom left corner of the bed, obliging Nicole to roll over onto her face. She went around the other side. Nicole continued to lash out wildly, careless of the fact that her flailing was revealing her to this woman at every kick. Her other ankle was just as easily attached to the bottom right corner so that she was fixed to the bed, face down, by her cuffed hands above her head and the cords about her ankles which widely parted and stretched her legs.

She was all too well aware of the reason why she had

been turned on her face and she felt the skin of her bottom crawling in anticipation. Yet even with the dread of a caning upon her, she was unable to prevent her mind from returning to the thrill she had felt when Karen had gripped her wrists, controlled her and told her that she might be tied down. She did not understand the reason for it, but she felt herself getting some strange sort of arousal from her bondage.

'That's better,' said Jane. 'Now let's see what we've got.' Karen returned at that point, carrying a wide, shallow tray covered with crushed ice. Jane pointed to the bedroom armchair. 'Put it there and sit!' Karen put the tray on the chair and gingerly lowered herself onto it, shuddering and sighing with relief as the cold ice soothed the burning sting of her abused buttocks.

Jane inspected her prize, noting with satisfaction, the translucent whiteness of her firm young body, the plump ripeness of her neat bottom and the attractive display between her parted legs. Turning to Karen, she said, 'Well now! You picked a rich little plum this time. I ought to thank you for bringing her to me. I'm going to enjoy spanking this nice little bottom.'

'Please don't do that, Jane,' begged Karen. 'She didn't do anything. It wasn't her fault, it was mine. Spank me.'

'No,' said Jane, 'I won't. And I'll tell you why. I really believe it will hurt you more if I do it to her than it would if you got it yourself. Now you can sit and watch it happening, knowing that it's all your fault.'

She knelt on the bed beside Nicole and put her left hand on the small of her back, pressing down to hold her steady, then began to slap her bare bottom with her right. They were hard, stinging smacks and Nicole jumped and wriggled with each of them. First on the right cheek, then on the left, each leaving a clear imprint of palm and fingers in glowing red.

For Nicole, the pain of her spanking was as nothing compared to the humiliation of having it done with an audience. She shouted her protests, but they were muffled by the gag and she could do nothing but try to endure it.

She thought nothing could be worse, but soon found that it could. The smacking stopped for a moment and Nicole felt Jane's left hand trying to insinuate itself under her hip. She pressed her body against the bed to try to prevent ingress, but the hand continued to intrude. It passed down under her pubes and she felt a finger curl up to grope through her pubic hair and align itself with the slit of her sex, nestling between the labia. Mercifully it did not move once it was there and she froze into immobility to avoid any stimulation from it.

The spanking recommenced and Nicole immediately realised the full cruelty of the positioning of that finger. If she moved at all, even so much as quivered, in response to what was being done to her bottom, she rubbed herself against it and that produced the most lascivious feelings in her. The only thing which could be worse than having her bottom smacked was to be aroused by it! She fought to control herself, but her clitoris seemed to have a mind of its own and was determined to chafe itself against the intruding finger, no matter what her will bade it do. The burning sting in her bottom seemed to become a pleasurable glow and she realised with horror that she was now getting a sex thrill from that, too.

She didn't know whether to be pleased or sorry when the spanking stopped. Jane withdrew her finger and said to Karen, 'You're two of a kind. See how she enjoyed that?'

'No, Jane. I'm sure she didn't,' Karen murmured. Nicole, who knew the truth of the matter, blushed red.

'Oh?' said Jane. 'I suppose you think you're the only one she loves? I tell you, I know the type. Anyone will do. Didn't you see her nearly come all over my finger, just now. No? Well just watch this.'

She went to the foot of the bed and Nicole felt her right ankle being untied. Jane pulled it over to the right corner and re-secured it, then untied her left ankle, pulled it across to the other side and attached it there so that Nicole was turned onto her back and fixed there, legs spread wide apart.

Jane resumed her inspection of Nicole's bound body, her

eyes running the full length of it, noticing the youth and tautness of her breasts, the flatness of her stomach, and the elegance which tender years and fitness imparted to her legs and thighs.

Nicole tried to shrink away as Jane reached out and began to pass her hand, quite gently, over her stretched stomach. The hand moved downwards and rubbed, more roughly, in a circular motion between her legs. She squirmed with disgust and impotent rage, which brought a smile to Jane's lips. She removed her hand and began to caress the bare breasts. Nicole tried to twitch her upper body so as to evade the questing hand, but this only made her soft flesh dance in an even more exciting way. Her wide eyes above the gagged mouth craned down as she saw Jane pick up a nipple in each hand between finger and thumb. Pinching gently and lifting, she made the soft white mounds wobble and dance. Nicole made noises of protest and shook her head violently, annoyed to find that her body was accepting what her mind was rejecting. Jane's fingers exerted more pressure, pinching harder. The feel of that seemed to reach right down into Nicole's womb and she felt her vagina moistening. She shook her head even more violently.

'Don't shake your head at me! Nod!' Nicole screwed up her face in pain and continued to shake her head.

'You heard me. You like what I'm doing, so you nod. Understand?' Slowly and reluctantly, Nicole nodded. Jane released the tortured nipples and returned to a stroking action. 'That's better. I can see we're going to get along fine.' She slid her hand down between the parted thighs again and carefully separated the hairs which defended the entrance to Nicole's sex. Nicole squirmed uneasily and stared at the ceiling in an effort to keep down the thoughts which were flitting through her mind.

Karen interjected, 'Please be careful with her, Jane. She –'

Jane interrupted her. 'I think you've cooled off enough now. You can get your nipples done the way I like them, then do hers, while I get undressed.'

Nicole did not understand this in the least, but the order became clear to her as she saw Karen go to the dressing table and take a large crayon of red body-paint from a drawer. Standing in front of the mirror, she painted large circles of red around each nipple, then filled the centre, including the nipples, with a heavy layer of colour. She turned away from the mirror and displayed herself. 'See, Jane. I've done them for you.'

'Of course you have.' In brassière and panties, Jane paused on one leg in the act of removing her skirt to glance briefly at the bared breasts so obscenely tipped with violent red. 'Now do hers!'

As Karen came to the bedside with the crayon, Nicole's eyes were wide in mute entreaty. She watched, powerless to prevent it, as the tips of her own breasts were similarly encircled, then those circles were filled in. She was annoyed with her own body when she saw that her nipples were erecting themselves under the rubbing touch of the crayon and, in spite of her repugnance at what was being done to her, she felt her vagina lubricating even more. Naked now, Jane stood beside the bed, hands on hips and legs astride, looking at Nicole. Without shifting her gaze, she addressed herself to Karen. 'Come over here and sex me up!' Karen came over and knelt in front of her. She shuffled forward on her knees between the parted legs, bending backwards like a limbo dancer as she did so, until she was strained in a backward arch, painted breasts taut and thrusting, hands grasping ankles behind her, her face upturned just below the black thicket which hid Jane's vagina. Delicately, with her tongue, she parted the hairs which concealed the pink entrance, then thrust that tongue inside and began to lap.

Jane moved her hips in dreamy circles, a beatific expression on her face. Her hands came up to pinch and roll her nipples. 'Mmmm! Oh yes! Do it! Higher! Go for the clit! Mmmm!' She began to breathe deeply, her stomach muscles twitching with each vaginal contraction, then, 'Stop! Enough! I don't want to come until I've seen to your friend. Go and sit on your ice until I need you again.'

Karen resumed her seat and Jane sat down on the bed beside Nicole. 'Now, Missie. I'm going to make you come and you're going to love it, like the randy little bitch you are.' She placed the fingertip of her left hand on Nicole's clitoris and began to move it in slow, irritating circles. Nicole stared at the ceiling again, but there was no way her body could ignore that finger. She looked down at herself; at the painted nipples, the lewdly splayed legs and above all, at the hand which was doing such incredible things to her. She knew that no matter how hard she tried to prevent it happening, she was going to be forcibly masturbated to the point of orgasm. She could see Karen watching and the knowledge that she could see her did nothing to quiet her rapidly increasing arousal. She rolled her head from side to side, moaning into her gag and trying to tell her clitoris to be numb. It was no good. What was being done to her was driving her mad with lust. She was going to be forced to climax against her will.

Jane sensed Nicole's acceptance of the inevitable and turned to Karen. 'You! Come!' As Jane lifted her left knee onto the bed, separating her legs, Karen knelt between her thighs and, parting the black curly hairs of her pubic bush to reveal the slit of her vulva, she leaned forward to insert her tongue and lick at the soft, pink, inner surfaces. Jane moaned softly and her left hand ceased its masturbation. She used it instead to smack the fleshy mound over Nicole's clitoris. Not hard slaps, but light, fast ones, calculated to drive the recipient wild. For Nicole, each smack was like an explosion of ecstasy. She had never felt anything like it. She felt the forces rising in her and realised that, with the extraordinary feel of the spanking her clitoris was getting, her orgasm was going to be huge and impossible to hide.

Jane's climax was fast approaching, too. Her stomach was pulsing and quivering with the forces generated by the licking of Karen's tongue at her own clitoris. As her emotions climbed towards a peak, a muscle in her cheek twitched convulsively and she panted for breath, moaning and sighing. The pace and severity of her hand's tattoo on Nicole's pubes increased and she screamed, 'That's right!

Wriggle and come! I said come, you little bitch! I want to see you come!'

It was just too much for Nicole to withstand. As the orgasm washed over her, she screamed into her gag, her whole body a juddering, quivering mass. Even as she heaved and jerked in the throes of pure pleasure, tears of anger and humiliation at her own weakness welled in her eyes and overflowed onto the pillow. At the same time, Jane, wildly excited by the sight of her victim's complete surrender to lust, screamed loud and long, clamping her thighs about Karen's head to ensure that the sweet stimulus should not stop until the final throes of climax were over.

Completion of the sex act had vastly different effects on the two women. For Nicole, bound in an obscene position as she still was, it brought feelings of degradation, anticlimax and embarrassment. She was ashamed of the way she had revealed her emotions to Jane. The paint on her nipples was now not even remotely exciting – it was hateful and she longed to take a bath.

For Jane, the release of tension had changed her mood entirely. She was no longer tense and angry, but tender and remorseful towards Karen. She put her arm around her shoulders and they went out of the bedroom together in a most amicable mood. Nicole waited, listening to the low buzz of their conversation. She caught the tail end of that conversation as they came back. They had obviously reverted to their roles as partners rather than master and slave, and had been discussing the content of the refrigerator and the larder.

'Well, we've got to eat,' said Jane. 'I'll go to the store and get something in. When I come back, I'll show you how sorry I am. Tell you what. I'll let you give her a caning. You'd like that, wouldn't you?'

Nicole listened in horror, her reddened bottom already feeling the sting of the cane. This was dreadful. The two were going to gang up on her.

'Now, what to do with you both while I'm out. Obviously, she'll have to stay tied up . . .'

'That's all right, Jane. I'll just tidy up and wait for you.' Karen said.

Jane scoffed. 'Oh, I'll bet you'd just love that, wouldn't you? You think I'm going to leave you alone with her tied up ready for you to fool around with again, you randy harlot? Some hope. No, darling. I'm afraid I'm going to have to make sure that neither of you gets into mischief.'

Jane untied Nicole's ankles. She closed her legs gratefully and pressed her thighs together to try to sooth her sore places. Jane, still naked, climbed onto the bed and straddled her. Shuffling up the bed, she put her knees on Nicole's upper arms and leaned forward to uncuff her. Nicole tried not to be moved by the close proximity of those pubic hairs and bulging breasts, but it was not easy. She felt her hands being freed from the bed-head but was unable to struggle as Jane pulled her arms down in front of her and cuffed her wrists again. Jane got off her and hauled her by her hair into a standing position.

'Come here, Karen. Your bottom's nice and cool now, so you can use it to good purpose. Stand back to back with Missie here. Now link arms.' At her instruction, Karen put her arms back and through Nicole's, then forward again in front of her, where Karen tied them together.

She surveyed her handiwork. 'No, that won't do. You could wriggle out of that.' She fetched more cord and passed a length right around both of them, at waist level, knotting it very tight so that there was no separation at all possible between their bottoms. She knotted another cord onto this over Nicole's navel, then took it down and passed it back between her legs and Karen's, looping the other end over the waist cord at Karen's navel. She adjusted the cord between their legs to ensure that it coincided exactly with both their sex slits, then pulled it tight and secured it with a knot. Next, she wound cord around their upper bodies, above and below breast level and pulled that tight, too, so that they were joined irrevocably from shoulder to hip, neither able to move without causing the other considerable discomfort. For her part, Nicole found herself quite unable to raise her arms high enough to reach her gag.

Jane stepped back. 'That's better. Now I can be certain that there'll be no hanky-panky while I'm out.' She left them standing while she prepared herself in leisurely fashion for her shopping trip. Because Nicole and Karen were in considerable discomfort from the chafing of the rope between their legs, this seemed to take for ever, but she was finished at last and with a bright wave, left them to their own devices. Nicole heard the front door close behind her and stood on in abject misery.

Karen spoke over her shoulder. 'Nicole! I had to wait to make sure she wasn't going to sneak back to peek. I'm so sorry, my dear. I've just got to get you out of this before she comes back. Do you think you can move . . . Oh! You're still gagged, of course. If you understand what I'm saying, pull on my arms a bit.'

Nicole did so and Karen went on. 'There's a spare handcuff key in the dressing table drawer. Move with me and we can get over there.'

The journey to the dressing table was most uncomfortable for Nicole. Forced to shuffle sideways, crab-fashion, every slight misstep on the part of either of them jerked the cord which bit into the division of her vulva so that she would have cried out if she had been able to. When they finally arrived at their destination, Karen said, 'I'll have to get the key. I know where I put it. Then I'll put it on the dressing table and we'll turn round so that you can pick it up and use it to unlock your handcuffs.'

In order to reach the drawer, Karen had to bend quite a long way forward. This not only bent Nicole backwards, but lifted her off the ground by the crotch. She waved her legs frantically, flapped her hands and screamed into her gag until Karen straightened up.

'It's all right. It's over now. The key's on the dressing table. Shuffle around and for God's sake don't drop it when you've got it.' They shuffled around and reversed positions. This time, it was Karen's turn to have her feet lifted off the ground and to feel the savage bite of the cord between her legs. She gasped in pain until Nicole could set her down again. There was an agonising pause, then she felt Nicole tearing the gag from her face and heard her sigh of relief. A few more minutes and the ropes around them were unknotted, then Nicole was untying her hands.

For a few seconds, Karen was engaged in rubbing her sore wrists, then she noticed that Nicole was dabbing at her breasts with tissues. 'What do you think you are doing? There's no time for that. She'll be back any second. The supermarket isn't far. You've got to get out of here. Now!'

While she was scrambling into her clothes, Nicole stopped, suddenly. 'Karen! You are not dressing. Are you not coming with me?'

'No, I have to stay here.'

'But why?'

'Because I love her. She is my whole life,' said Karen simply.

'Will she not be enraged by this?'

'You bet she will,' Karen replied with feeling.

'And she will beat you again?'

'Yes, I expect so.'

'And yet you still love her?' Nicole was genuinely puzzled.

'It's hard to explain and there's no time. Kiss me, my dear little Nicole, then go. Go!'

Without a backward glance, Nicole fled down the stairs and out of the building.

David Corby paid off the taxi and hurried through the driving rain to his front door. In the darkness of the Edwardian portico, he fumbled for a moment with the key in the latch. A voice behind him called, 'David? That is you?'

He turned. 'Nicole! What are you doing here?' Then, appraising her state: 'And wet through and cold again!' He opened the door and switched on the hall light, standing aside to allow her to pass. 'Come in. Come into the warm at once.' She entered and he closed the door behind them. 'Are you in trouble again?'

'Oh, David. I am in such big trouble. The women I was with . . . It was not good, that. Again I have no money and no clothes and I know no one. When you gave me your card I have looked at your home on the map and remembered where it was. So, when there is no one else who will help me, I remember how you are kind and I wait for you to come home.'

'How long have you been standing out there?'

'I do not know. I do not have even my watch. It seems like very long.'

'Well, come in and get warm.' He led the way into his sitting room and knelt to light the gas fire. Rising, he looked at her. 'Cognac, I think.' He poured her a large one and kicked a footstool over so that she could sit close to the fire and get the best of its growing warmth. She sipped gratefully, choking a little over the fiery spirit. A reaction to the day's events set in and she shivered violently. He went to the bathroom and turned on the tap to fill the tub.

When he came back, he said, 'Look, you've got to get out of those wet things and get warm, otherwise you'll be a pneumonia case. The bath is running. Take your drink in with you if you like. There's soap and towels and you'll find a bathrobe hanging behind the door. Chuck your things out when you've got them off and I'll set them by the fire to dry.'

With her nose in her glass, she trekked off to the bathroom, her soggy shoes making little sucking noises as she moved. Presently, her bare arm came around the half-open door and dropped her wet clothes in a little pile, then the door was closed. He picked them up and set a couple of upright chairs close to the fire so that he could drape the clothing over them, then he stuffed the toes of her shoes with newspaper and put them in the hearth.

He poured himself a drink and sat in an armchair to wait. Her skirt was already steaming when she returned. She looked pink and warm and David's over-large robe made her appear more child-like than ever, if that were possible. Her hair was concealed in a turban made from a towel.

'That's better!' he said. 'Something to eat? I regret that I have no hamburgers, but I have cheese and biscuits and I'll make you some cocoa.'

'Cocoa?'

'*Chocolat.*'

'Mmm! Yes please. I like very well the *chocolat.*' She put her head on one side in a perfectly charming gesture of mischief. 'Almost as much as the hamburgers,' she added with a grin.

It transpired, David soon learned, that she also liked the fruit cake, *and* the shortbread biscuits, *and* the ham sandwiches, *and* the cornflakes. Hers was the healthiest appetite he had ever seen on a woman, yet she wore it with amazing slimness and grace. At last, even she could eat no more and, with a sigh, she pushed away her plate and empty cup.

David surveyed her across the kitchen table with wry amusement. 'And now, perhaps, *Mademoiselle* has the strength to tell me what has been happening to her.' As Nicole recounted some of what had been done to her, David lost his amused look and became quite angry. Although too embarrassed to be able to go into every detail, she was able to make clear to him the manner in which she had been used and abused. At the end of the recital she said, 'And this mad woman also smacks my *derrière*!' She stood up, turned her back to him, and raised the back of the robe to reveal her bottom, severely bruised, with clear handprints already turning blue.

The child-like, naive innocence of this action made him catch his breath. Standing on tip-toe, leaning back and craning over her shoulder in an attempt to see herself, she made a picture which any painter would have given his eye teeth to create. Suddenly becoming aware of what she was doing, Nicole blushed and covered herself. 'Excuse me, David. I did not think. It was not proper, that. To show myself so.'

He hastened to set her at her ease. 'Not at all, Nicole,' he said, keeping a perfectly straight face. 'It was most proper that I should know how badly you have been treated. Rest assured that you may safely leave this matter to me. You shall sleep here tonight, and tomorrow, we will get you home to your father.'

'But, David, again I have no money!'

He shrugged. 'For me, money is not a great problem. Certainly, I have enough to help a friend in this small way. Tomorrow, we will put you on a coach at Victoria Station and that will take you to Paris. Can you be met there?'

'But certainly! Fôret-sur-Marne is only a short drive from Paris. If you will permit me to make telephone to my father, Louis will pick me up.'

'Louis?'

'He drives my father.'

'Oh, I see. Tomorrow, then, you go home. Tonight, you sleep.'

'You have a room for guests?'

'No. You will use my bed. The sheets were changed this morning and I'll lend you some jammies.'

'Jammies? What is it, the "jammies"?'

'Pyjamas. Same word in French.'

'Ah!' She giggled. 'At home, I shall no longer wear the pyjamas. I shall wear the jammies, then everyone will know that I have travelled to England.'

He laughed.

'And you?' she asked. 'Where do you sleep?'

'I shall sleep in an armchair beside the fire. I shall be most comfortable, I assure you.'

He went into the bedroom with her, selected clean pyjamas from the chest of drawers and tossed them on the bed. To his surprise, she came to him and, standing on tip-toe, planted a quick, soft kiss on his cheek. 'Thank you, David. You have been so kind. Good night.'

'*Bonne nuit, Nicole. Dors bien.*'

He went out, closing the door softly behind him. He sat down in the armchair and picked up his drink. He had lied through his teeth. Trying to sleep in that armchair was like trying to be at ease on a rock-pile. He finished his drink and squirmed to find the least uncomfortable position. That kiss on the cheek had made him feel a hundred years old. With all the women he had known, why had he not taken the obvious opportunities for sex which were open to him with this one? He could have offered to kiss her bottom better. He could have put his arms around her to comfort her and she would have responded. Perhaps the answer lay in the fact that he had, automatically and without thought, used the personal pronoun '*toi*' when hoping that she would sleep well, as one does when addressing an infant. In spite of her age and the maturity of her body, she was a child.

This was a nice little French girl. And a nice little French bottom! He chuckled to himself and fell asleep.

The smell of frying bacon woke Nicole in the morning. She put on David's robe and shoved her feet into a pair of his slippers, which were huge on her tiny feet. She shuffled awkwardly into the kitchen, where David was wielding a large frying pan with some dexterity. He turned as she came in. She was a cute picture in the giant slippers and robe, the rolled-up arms and legs of his pyjamas falling down over her wrists and ankles. 'Aha! Just in time. I was about to come and drag you out by the leg. Full English?'

'Pardon?'

'An English breakfast. We don't fool around with coffee and rolls, you know. Every Englishman worthy of the name starts the day with a Full English, fried. That's two eggs, sunny side up, bacon, sausage, fried bread and fried tomatoes, with a big mug of strong English tea. I insist that you force yourself to eat this national delicacy.' He shovelled such a breakfast onto her plate and placed it on the kitchen table before her, together with a rack of thick toast, marmalade and, of course, tomato ketchup.

Fascinated, but pretending not to look for fear of unnerving her, he watched this massive pile of food, topped by a liberal application of ketchup, disappear inside her slender frame. 'It is permitted to wipe the plate with one's toast, should one wish to do so,' he observed gravely. She did wish to do so.

At last, Nicole had finished everything in sight and wiped her lips on her napkin. 'It is good, that,' she said. 'I like very much the Full English.'

She grinned. 'And the cocoa. But I think most of all, I like the jammies.' She pinched up some of the loose material at her wrist. 'Are they not beautiful?'

David thought that, on her, a coal sack would be beautiful,

but he refrained from saying so. 'That may be so, *Mademoiselle*, but it is now time to take off the beautiful jammies and get into your clothes. They're dry and, unless you get a move on, you'll miss your coach. Hurry now, and we'll telephone your father before you leave.'

It was with a twinge of genuine regret that he watched her coach pull out of the station. He watched it for a long time until it was completely lost in traffic, then headed for home. Somehow, he felt, his flat would never be quite the same as it had been last night.

A few days later, he received a letter with a French postmark. Opening it, he discovered a banker's order, reimbursing all of – and more than – the money he had spent on Nicole. Some phrases in the letter caught his attention. 'My daughter is not wise in the ways of men. I shall be forever in the debt of such an honourable English gentleman. Nicole speaks often of her kind Uncle David and his English jammies.' Uncle David! That made him feel two hundred years old. He shook his head ruefully, then stopped and looked more closely at the signature. 'Noel – Comte de Fôret.' He whistled softly. That was interesting. Daddy was somebody important and probably rich into the bargain. David had already decided that Jane was a perfect candidate for a visit to the Castle of Despair. Matrilla would be very likely to extend an invitation to the Comte to witness Jane's re-education and Monsieur le Comte might well decide to make a donation to the worthy cause of righting wrongs!

How to entrap, Jane, though? That was a knotty problem with which he had been wrestling for some time. Someone so heavily into lesbianism would be unlikely to respond to his boyish charm. That train of thought reminded him of someone else who had, so recently, found him completely resistible. He really needed Pandora's help on this one, but could he bring himself to present his dented ego for more damage? Making up his mind, he drew a deep breath and reached for the telephone.

'Pandora? It's David. David Corby.' Deliberately, he made his voice neutral and businesslike.

Her response was neither. 'David! How lovely to hear you. I've been hoping you'd phone. I was scared I'd frightened you away for good!'

He was much encouraged. The very sound of her voice brought memories flooding back and they were not all embarrassing. That face. That hair. That figure! How much sweeter would the conquest be if he really had to work for it! 'What do you mean, frightened me away?' he lied. 'Oh, that! I had a good laugh about it when you'd gone. So did the charwoman who found me in the morning.'

She giggled. 'Oh dear! It was naughty of me, wasn't it? I don't know what came over me. I'll make it up to you, I promise.'

David found his body stirring in response to the images his mind was producing of Pandora 'making it up to him' and he thrust such thoughts aside. This was business! 'Look, I need a favour. Can you help?'

'I certainly owe you a favour, don't I? What's the problem?'

Quickly, David outlined Nicole's story and Jane's part in it. 'Our Southern entry port seems right,' he concluded. 'But I can't think of a way of getting her there. Can you?'

Pandora thought aloud. 'I agree with you that she is an ideal candidate and that the Southern entry port is right. I'll do a spot of sleuthing and find out something about her habits – where she goes; what clubs she uses. She's strictly lesbian and into B and D, isn't she? We'll have to use that as a lever. Let me see . . . Yes . . . I think that would work. Look, David, leave this one entirely to me.'

'Really? That's handsome of you. I'll owe you one.'

'You will! And I'll expect you to give me one next time we meet!' She rang off hastily, before he had a chance to fully absorb that *double entendre*. For a moment, he cursed himself for not having been quicker on the uptake and pursued the fleeting opportunity with an invitation to drinks or dinner. Then he shrugged and grinned. This was not a girl to be taken by storm. Softly, softly, catchee monkey. He could wait. He recaptured his mind's image of her, naked in the anteroom. She was worth waiting for!

Nine

The lights in the nightclub were dim; the music smooth and easy. Lovers danced, moving slowly and fondling each other, occasionally kissing. From where Pandora sat on her high stool, she could see the action reflected in the long mirror behind the bar. The scene was no different from that to be found in any nightclub, except for the fact that there was not a man in the place. All the couples were women. She waited until the barmaid came her way, then held up a finger. 'G and T. Ice and lemon, please.' She turned to the young, blonde girl on her right. 'What will you have, Melissa?'

'I'll have a rum and coke, please.'

'No you won't!' said Pandora testily. 'It makes your breath stink. You'll have a Screwdriver. And mind what I told you. If you get pissed again tonight, it won't just be another spanking. It will be a knickers-down thrashing with the cane!' She turned and smiled apologetically at the well-built woman on her left. 'You have to keep them in order, you know.'

'Oh yes. I know. Mine too!'

'Really!' Pandora leant forward so that she could inspect the pretty redhead sitting on the woman's left. 'It's good to find another strict disciplinarian. God knows what some women let their partners get up to. Caught this one' – she nodded towards Melissa – 'kissing some total stranger once. It was a while after that before she could sit down, I can tell you!'

The woman jerked a thumb in the direction of the redhead. 'Funny, I had the same trouble with this one, just recently. I dealt with it, though.' She turned to her companion. 'Your bum still smarts a bit, doesn't it, Karen?'

Blushing furiously, the redhead murmured, 'Yes, Jane.'

'Jane and Karen, eh!' Pandora held out her hand. 'I'm Pandora and this is Melissa. Pleased to meet kindred spirits. Drink?'

'No, we're OK, thanks.'

The barmaid brought the drinks she had already ordered and Pandora paid for them before resuming the conversation. 'Actually, just between the two of us, I'm not sure that I'm not doing her a favour when I spank her. I think she enjoys it. How about yours?'

Jane nodded vigorously. 'Mm! No doubt about it. Makes her feel safe to have a strong arm about the place.'

Pandora leant forward with a beckoning motion and lowered her voice to a confidential whisper. 'What Melissa really enjoys is to be hung up by the feet with her legs apart while I spank her pussy. Have you ever done that?'

Jane was not only impressed, but turned on. 'Sounds good to me, but no, I haven't.'

'It's great! You should try it next time you're at the club.'

'The club? This club?'

'No, silly. *The* club. You know.'

'No, I don't.'

'My God! You mean you don't know about the club. I thought every couple with your preferences knew about it.'

'Well, I don't,' said Jane. 'What's it all about?'

'Well,' said Pandora, lowering her voice again, 'they have all this wonderful apparatus. Whipping benches and pillories, racks and chains. I could hardly hang Melissa upside down in an ordinary flat, could I?'

'No, I suppose not,' said Jane thoughtfully.

'And there is also a system which allows you to watch other women disciplining their partners. It costs a little more, of course, but I enjoy it.'

Jane was breathing heavily now, and Pandora could see her thighs moving uneasily under her black business skirt. 'Where is this place?'

'Wait a minute,' said Pandora. 'I do believe I've got a leaflet with me, somewhere.' She rummaged through her handbag. 'Ah, here it is. The Wicked Lady Fitness and Social Club. That's just a front, of course. The real action goes on in the back rooms.' She passed the leaflet over. 'When you phone, mention my name. And so they'll know that you don't want just an ordinary membership, give them the password.'

'Oh, what's that?'

'Tell them you want to visit the Castle.'

'I want to visit the Castle,' Jane repeated, memorising the phrase. 'OK. Right! Thanks very much, Pandora.'

'You're welcome, I'm sure!' she said.

The red decor and the strange smell of incense were making Karen very nervous so that her grip on Jane's hand was almost painful. 'I don't like it, Jane,' she whispered. 'It's spooky.'

'Oh, shut up, Karen. Don't be such a baby. You'll make me cross and with what I've got planned for your bottom already, that isn't a good idea.'

Just then a young, dark-haired woman, naked except for a gauzy scrap of material about her waist, appeared. 'Good morning, ladies. Come with me, please.' She led the way down the red-carpeted passage and opened a door which led into a tiled room with a glass shower compartment. 'For reasons of hygiene, it is a requirement of the club that all our ladies should shower before going on into the Playrooms.'

She addressed herself to Jane. 'This is your bathroom. Your partner's is next door. All our ladies have private bathrooms. You will find that the shower is automatic. It won't operate until the door is closed. The temperature will be pleasant as soon as you turn it on. You can then adjust it a little to suit your preference. Please take your shower now, and when you are ready, press the bell beside the door and I will come for you.' She smiled and went out, taking Karen with her.

Jane looked about her. Such a bathroom had obviously

cost quite a bit. The shower was unusual and she inspected it more closely. It was made entirely of glass, except for the tray at the bottom. Even the side against the wall had a glass panel. The shower head was different because it was very large and fitted flush to the glass roof, instead of projecting. The controls were also recessed into gold-plated concavities. She stripped, placing her clothes on the bench and hooks provided, then went over to the shower. She pulled open the heavy glass door and operated the controls. Nothing happened. Of course! It wouldn't work with the door open. She stepped inside. There was no handle on the inside of the door but, even as she searched for one, there was a soft hiss of air and it closed, automatically. A very expensive shower indeed! She was pleased. She operated the controls again. Nothing happened! She twiddled them furiously, still without effect. Exasperated she pushed at the door to get out. It wouldn't open!

The bathroom door opened and the girl who had brought her there came in with another, similarly dressed. Jane instinctively covered her pubes and breasts with her arms but they took no notice of her.

She banged on the glass. 'I say! This thing's not working! I seem to be stuck in here!' They came over but, instead of trying to open the door, one went to each side of the shower and pulled on it. It moved as if on castors and they trundled it into the centre of the room.

Now Jane was furious. Careless of her naked state, she used both fists to pound on the glass and screamed, 'Damn you, women! Can't you see I'm stuck in here. Get me out at once!' For all the difference that made, she might as well have been making no sound at all. Suddenly a chill struck her. Something was definitely wrong! She inspected the glass panels more closely and, for the first time, saw that they were double layers, with an air gap in between. The shower was soundproof!

The girl who had brought her to the room stooped and did something at the base of the shower. Jane heard a whirring sound and felt a draught of cool air coming up through the drain beneath her feet. Looking down, she saw a glow of light from a translucent panel in the shower tray. The other girl left the room for a short while. When she came back, she was lugging a large amount of flat cardboard. Working together, they opened it out into an extremely large sheet, vertically creased. Holding it between them, they passed on either side of the shower, wrapping the cardboard around it so that its creases coincided with the corners of the cubicle. Then, the only light Jane had came from the glass roof and the panel under her feet. When the cardboard was folded and fixed over the top, even the light from the roof was lost and she was left in the gloom to wonder what was going to happen to her.

For a long time, it seemed that Jane's cardboard-covered glass prison had lain on its side. Mercifully, the transition from vertical to horizontal had been gentle, as had all the movements which, she presumed, showed that she was being transported in some fashion. At least, with the cubicle on its side, she had been able to lie down at full length and it was good to have light and air. The shower head, she had discovered, doubled as an extractor for the fresh air which came in through the drain, so any worries she had about suffocating were dispelled. Now, at last, the cubicle was being raised to the vertical again, with the same care as before. She moved with the transition, allowing herself to slide down the slope of the glass until her feet found the shower tray and she was able to stand. Now the cardboard was being removed and the glare of light made her blink for a moment.

The shower was now standing in some sort of office with a large desk, which was flanked by two other desks. Three women were staring at her. One was unusually tall and wore a tight-fitting, purple dress. The other two wore only filmy skirts. They were not the same two had had trapped her in the cabinet. One was dark and the other was very fair. Jane covered her vital parts with her hands and arms and shrank back from their curious gazes. In her transparent cage, there was nowhere to hide. She pressed herself against the far side, but the tall woman moved round behind her and Jane knew that she was staring at her back view. She hadn't enough hands to conceal her pubes as well as her bare buttocks and she was uncomfortably aware of the fact that she had not trimmed or waxed lately. Her pubic hair was unusually luxuriant and would be plain to see sprouting profusely in the division between the cheeks of her bottom. Her only means of defence against their invasive eyes was to sit down on the floor of the shower and curl herself into a ball, hugging her knees with her arms.

The women smiled and moved away. There was a large box of tools on the desk. The two bare-breasted girls selected some and went to the back of the cubicle. Jane could not work out what they were doing, but it soon became clear when they removed the two shower controls, leaving, in their place, two metal-lined holes. Suddenly, Jane could hear sounds outside her cell again.

The tall woman was now seated behind her desk. 'Now that you can hear me,' she said, 'I can tell you that you are in the Castle of Despair. I am Matrilla, the Ice Queen, and these are my hand-maidens, Marla and Luna. You have been brought here for punishment and re-education.'

Jane scrambled to her knees and put her mouth to one of the holes. 'Damn you, woman! Who do you think you are? Why have you brought me here?'

'I have just told you,' said Matrilla calmly. 'For punishment and re-education. I will be more specific. You have been brought here because you are a bully who enjoys humiliating and hurting people. More specifically, you have violated an innocent young girl. That is the reason for your punishment. Your re-education is necessary to bring about a change in the way you treat people who love you.'

Jane was furious. 'What right do you have to lecture to me?'

Matrilla's eyes bored into her and Jane quailed in spite of her anger. 'I have the right which comes with power and control. Not the sort you think you exercise. You will find that my power is to be feared; my control total.' She nodded to the girls. 'One hour, please.' They came up to the cubicle and started to push it out of the room.

Jane scrambled to her feet. 'Wait a minute! What's happening? Where are we going?' She received no reply.

The journey along the corridors to the Great Hall was not a happy one for Jane. To be naked in public is the stuff of nightmares for most women and she was no exception. Everyone who passed sniggered and pointed in a humiliating way and, by the time they arrived at their destination, she was again curled into a ball on the bottom of her transparent prison. If she had thought that shaming, the next hour was even worse. Left in the centre of the hall, she was stared at and commented on by crowds of people. Much as she disliked contemplating what else was to happen to her, she could not help being glad when the girls returned to fetch her and wheeled her back to the office. They pushed her close to the desk so that she could hear Matrilla more clearly.

'Humiliation is only part of the punishment process,' the Ice Queen said. 'You will find that it gets a great deal worse. I have in mind –' She was interrupted by the shrill ringing of the telephone on her desk. She picked up the receiver. 'Yes? What? All of them? Very well. I will come at once.' She put down the phone. 'Marla! Luna!' She hurried out of the room and the two girls followed her, closing the door behind them.

Left alone and unobserved, Jane got up and stretched her cramped limbs. She turned round slowly, taking in all the details of the office. What the devil did that bitch intend to do to her next? Suddenly, her eyes fell upon the desk. God! Those tools were still lying there and her prison had been pushed sufficiently close to give her a chance of reaching them. With a hammer or a screwdriver, she might be able to break out of her glass case before they came back. Hastily, cursing herself for having wasted time in looking around, she knelt and thrust her arms through the holes left by the removal of the shower controls. Her fingertips scrabbled in vain. The tools were fractionally out of reach. She pushed madly against the glass wall in an effort to extend her reach, grinding the side of her face and her breasts against the cold, shiny surface. Yes! No! Yes! Just a tiny fraction more and she would . . . Clack! The metal rims around the holes closed like handcuffs, trapping her upper arms. She tugged, feverishly, but was unable to pull them back. She was trapped in a kneeling position, her arms waving outside the cubicle, but the rest of her even more confined inside.

With her face turned as it was, she was able to see the door opening. The three women went behind her, to a position where she could only just see them out of the corner of her eye and she realised that there was now nothing she could do to impede their view of her backside. She squirmed uncomfortably, and tried to tense her muscles to close the gap which they must be staring at. She felt a cool draught on her and a soft hiss of air as the door opened. She kicked out with her legs as best she could, but met with only thin air.

Matrilla drank in the plight of her nude victim with a fierce thrill which sent twinges of lust right through her. She devoured the acres of exposed skin with her eyes, allowing them to drift over the broad buttocks and down the stocky legs. This woman was naked right down to the soles of her feet. She was trapped and helpless. Not only that, she was kneeling, which was a posture of subjugation and submission which Matrilla found particularly satisfying. She thought the woman must be particularly humiliated by having her excessive pubic hair on display. She had noticed how she had tried to conceal it before. She considered, head on one side. Perhaps just one more twist of the knife was needed.

'My, you *are* hairy down there, Jane!' she said. She was gratified to see a scarlet blush spread over her captive's face. Enough? Perhaps not. 'In fact,' she went on, 'I don't think I've ever seen a woman with so much pubic hair as you have. I really must have a memento of the occasion. Luna, fetch some tweezers!'

Jane was incredulous. 'What!' she exclaimed. 'You can't possibly mean to . . .' She broke off as she saw Luna take a pair of tweezers from the desk drawer and come back with them in her hand, realising that Matrilla was indeed deadly serious. 'My God! You can't!'

'One of the many things you will come to realise, Jane,' said the Queen, 'is that I can do anything to you and with you. That is what I meant by power and control. Believe me, this is only a tiny demonstration. Marla! Luna! Hold her legs!'

Jane kicked out again, but with no more effect than before. She felt her ankles being grasped, then her legs were forced apart and trapped firmly between the thighs of the girls as they sat on them. Matrilla knelt between them and stared at the pinioned, squirming nudity so enticingly presented. She felt herself close to spontaneous orgasm. The sight of that hair and the knowledge of what she was about to do made her breath short and uneven. She must contain herself and not rush. She must spin out this divine moment, to be savoured at leisure, later.

'Open her!'

Jane screamed as she felt hands on her bottom cheeks, forcing them apart and holding them there. Her face flamed again. The eyes on her were like a physical touch. Not only her pubic hair, but the whole of her anal area and most of her vagina was on display. The shame of being exhibited in that fashion was enormous.

Matrilla was speaking again. 'Now, Jane, you can help me here. I have never researched this before. Tell me, is it more painful if I pluck a hair from here . . .' She reached forward and selected one from the many which adorned the side of Jane's buttocks. With a sharp tug, she plucked it.

Jane leapt in pain, as much as she was able. 'Ow! Damn you! You bitch!'

'. . . Or is it worse if I choose one really close to that little brown hole, like this!'

'Ouch! Oh God! Oh God!'

'But you have such a lot to choose from that it is quite confusing. Perhaps I should take one from lower down. Maybe one of those which so becomingly adorn the lips of your secret place. Here!'

'Aagh! Ow!'

Matrilla tired of her game. The infliction of pain was

pleasant enough, but it bore no comparison to the thrills of anticipation and power. Her level of arousal was dropping. If she wanted to reawaken it, she would have to move on to the next stage. She got up and went back to her desk.

Through the glass against which her face was pressed, Jane watched Matrilla warily. She saw her collect an assortment of black leather belts, two metal cylinders and a bottle which appeared to contain oil. Uncomprehending, she continued to watch her until she passed out of sight to her rear. Moments later, she felt fingers on her body, probing through the thick, black hair at the entrance to her vagina. She wriggled her bottom, but the groping continued and she felt the lips which hid her sex being held and pulled apart.

'What are you doing? Don't do that! What . . . Oh my God! No! What is it?' Something cold, hard and slippery was intruding upon the warmth of her vagina. Further and further in it went, while she humped her body in ineffectual contortions in an effort to prevent this obscene violation. The movement stopped and she stopped struggling, pulling on the thing experimentally with her vaginal muscles, trying to evaluate the sensation. To her disgust, she found that the object inside her, together with her helplessness, were having an erotic effect on her and thoughts of orgasm were flitting through her mind. She thrust them resolutely aside.

Now she felt the cold trickle of oil at the base of her spine. Hands spread her cheeks again and she shivered as she felt the oil run down over her sphincter. A finger massaged the oil in that place, rubbing in tiny circles. She felt her nipples pricking into involuntary erection and her vagina sucked more greedily at its lodger. She was embarrassed that this movement might be transmitted to whatever part was still protruding and so might be visible to the eyes behind her. She tried to stop it but for as long as the finger moved, she knew she would be unable to control herself.

The finger stopped and she sighed with relief. However, it was not removed, just positioned centrally and held there. She held her breath, waiting for what might happen. The finger began to press. It wasn't possible! They couldn't be going to . . .! They were! The pressure became greater and she tried to use muscular control to prevent it from going further. It pressed again and she quivered with the effort of holding her bottom closed against it. The pressure increased still further until, with a sudden, elastic spasm, she was penetrated. She tried to tell herself that she had not deliberately opened herself to it, but was distressed to find that she could not decide if that was true. The oily finger moved in a most delicious way, rotating and plunging. No! Not delicious! She was furious with herself for thinking that, even for a moment. How could such a degrading thing be anything but horrible! If only her bottom would keep still and not insist on moving and pressing itself back upon the intruder! She knew that her clitoris had erected itself and that moisture was leaking past the obstruction in her vagina. That had to be a reflex reaction. It was nothing to do with being sexually aroused at all.

The finger was removed. Thank God! Her ordeal was over. They had enjoyed their fun and she hadn't disgraced herself by coming. She relaxed, then tensed again as something else pressed in the same place. This time it was cold, hard and slippery. It pressed again, intent on following the path stretched and oiled by the questing finger.

'No! Please no! Not with that, whatever it is. It's too big! It won't go. I can't take it! Don't do it! Don't! Oh God!' With the full length of the thing inside her, she stopped twitching and heaving. She knelt, trembling, as she sought to expel it from her body. She could feel the skin around her sphincter stinging with the stretching it was forced to do to encompass the girth of the thing. She hardly noticed the belts being passed around her body and between her legs. She only knew that the girls were releasing her arms and that she could, at last, remove them from the holes and stand up. She did so slowly and carefully. The hard cylinders in her vagina and anus were uncomfortable when she stood fully erect. She looked down at herself, noticing for the first time the broad belt around her waist and the strap between her legs. She pulled at it, but it was fastened with padlocks and she knew that without the keys, she would never escape from it.

She turned and walked awkwardly out of the glass cage, glad to be free of it after such a long time. Matrilla was sitting behind her desk again, a small remote control device in front of her. Jane went over to the desk and leant her hands on it to obtain some relief from her discomfort.

'Why have you put this thing on me? Is it some sort of chastity belt?'

'No,' said Matrilla, 'it's not, as you will soon discover. And from now on, you will address me as "Madam".'

'What!' said Jane. 'You must be joking! If you think I'm going to . . . Oh! What's happening! Get it off me! Stop! For God's sake, stop!' She fell on her knees, tugging furiously at the belts which fixed the twin instruments of titillation inside her.

Matrilla switched off the Activator and watched Jane, who remained on hands and knees, panting heavily. 'You were saying?' she enquired smoothly.

Jane looked up at her. 'What is it?' she asked.

Matrilla looked at her for a full two seconds then pressed the button again. Jane collapsed and rolled into a ball, screaming and clawing at herself until Matrilla switched the Activator off.

Wearily, Jane dragged herself to her hands and knees again.

'Do you fully understand the importance of the correct form of address now, Jane?' said Matrilla, her hand straying near the button.

Jane's head dropped. 'Yes, Madam,' she murmured hoarsely.

'Excellent! Then we understand one another. The Activator is just one of the many means of control I have at my disposal. It was convenient to have you so fitted because I don't want the inconvenience of having you carried to your next place of punishment. I'm sure you will be happy to walk, rather than have me press this button again, won't you?'

'Yes, Madam.'

'In fact, I suspect you would do anything I told you to do, wouldn't you? Or do you need another demonstration?'

'No, Madam, please!'

The Queen leaned forward, her voice quivering with sexual pleasure and excitement. 'That's what I mean by control! Your experiments have been puny by comparison. While you use canes and physical force, I hold all your actions under the tip of my little finger. How dare you consider yourself to be dominant! You don't even begin to understand the word.'

The Queen got up and came round to the side of the desk. 'You may crawl over here now, and lick my shoes.' Obediently, Jane crawled forward on hands and knees and bent to the task she had been set. Matrilla watched her for a while. This evidence of submission was nice enough, but she found she wanted to move on to better things. For a while she toyed with the idea of having Jane service her with her tongue, or beg to have her head shaved, but neither of these notions were exactly right. Time to move on.

'Very well. You may get up now. Follow me. Do not cover your body with your hands and keep up.' She picked up the remote control and waved it at Jane to emphasise the order. Without looking back she left the office, followed by Marla and Luna.

It was not easy to keep up with them. They walked briskly, while Jane, because of the discomfort of the Activator even when it was not switched on, could manage only a stooping hobble. Being able to take only short paces, she found that she had to trot to keep them in sight, which had a disconcerting effect on her breasts. They were full but sagged a little, lacking the musculature of youth. In consequence, they jounced and joggled, swinging from side to side, yet she dared not support them with her hands, so that they became the cause of some amusement to the people she passed.

The three ahead of her disappeared through double doors and, when Jane followed them, she found herself in a large room with a polished wooden floor. The group had stopped and she hobbled up to them, looking around fearfully at the array of apparatus on display.

'This is the Training Room,' said Matrilla. 'It is here that the next phase of your re-education will take place.' She pointed to a steel-framed chair with padded leather back, seat and arms. 'Sit!'

Jane went over to it and sat down with obvious difficulty as her weight came on the cylinders inside her. Marla and Luna strapped her in at wrists, elbows, knees and ankles. The chair was much wider than usual, which had the effect of spreading her legs apart.

Matrilla inspected their work and nodded, satisfied. 'Lean forward!' she commanded. Jane did so and Marla reached behind her and released the Activator belt.

'Take your weight on your arms!' Jane obeyed and Luna knelt beside the chair. She released a catch and slid the seat sideways from under Jane's body, exposing her bottom. Slowly and carefully, she withdrew the metal cylinders. For Jane, the sensation was almost as bad as having them thrust into her. Nevertheless, her gasps of sexual stimulation were mingled with sighs of relief at being relieved of their internal pressure. Luna replaced the seat and Jane settled herself onto it with a much greater degree of comfort than before. Working quickly, the two girls passed straps across her lower stomach and above her breasts, buckling her in so that she could not slide or bend forward.

Matrilla inspected those straps too. 'Are you perfectly comfortable?' she asked.

Jane thought that a very odd question in the circumstances, but replied civilly enough, 'Yes, thank you, Madam.' In fact she found she *was* comfortable, apart from the minor inconvenience of not being able to move. The padded leather was soft and the headrest sloped backwards slightly.

'None of your straps are too tight? You have no feeling that your circulation is restricted?'

'No, Madam.'

'Good! That sort of discomfort is not part of this training. You will be in that chair for the next three days, waking and sleeping, therefore your comfort is important.'

'Three days!' Jane was so appalled at the prospect that she only just remembered to add, 'Madam'.

'Yes. Three days. During that time you will be fed at regular intervals. Starvation is not part of the punishment, either.'

'But what about . . . I mean . . . There are things I must do, Madam.'

'Of course there are. It would be strange to expect your normal bodily functions to cease. Now that *is* part of your punishment. Whenever you feel the need to answer the call of nature, of whatever sort, you will inform the girl who will be with you. She will remove the chair seat and provide a suitable receptacle below. You will then perform your function before an invited audience of men and women.'

'Oh no! Please, Madam. I can't do that!'

'Not only can you, you will! Your diet will ensure that you are capable of a bowel movement every day. Three days; three movements. If you do not produce that number in three days, your stay in the chair will be extended until you do.' Matrilla watched her captive carefully as the full extent of the humiliating, degrading awfulness of what she would have to do sank in. She saw the signs of it on Jane's face and became orgasmic again. She fought hard to prevent any sign of her inner tumult of sexual excitement from showing.

To heighten her pleasure she added, 'And while I think about it, there is a detail I have forgotten. With that mass of hair, your audience will be deprived of a good view of everything they should see. Luna; please remove the seat so that Marla can trim her a little. Not a complete shave, Marla. Just cut back that bush on either side of her sex so that it is clearly visible.'

As Marla knelt between her parted thighs, snipping at her dense black pubic hair, Jane began to sob. 'Please, Madam. I beg of you. Something else. Please, oh please, punish me some other way. I will serve you any way you like, but don't do this thing to me. I can't bear it.'

The Ice Queen felt her vagina liquifying and leaking.

Abject surrender! Begging! It was marvellous to see. If she didn't have an orgasm soon, she felt she would burst. She watched Marla complete her task and could hardly wait for Luna to replace the seat. Only then, to conceal what she felt, was she able to take refuge in action, moving on to the next stage. Luna fetched her a jar and, dipping into it, she smeared Jane's breasts, nipples and vagina.

Jane looked down at herself while the ointment was applied. 'What is it, Madam? Please tell me. What have you done to me?'

Matrilla stepped back. 'We'll just wait a few moments and that will save me an explanation. It will also enable you to understand why this punishment is called "The Tantalus".' She watched, fascinated, as the unbelievable sweetness stole over Jane's body. First, that look of uncertainty. Then, the next stage of disbelief. The dreamy expression of pure, unalloyed sexual pleasure. The Queen waited patiently through all of those, waiting for the one she wanted. That was it! The realisation that the incredible yearning, craving, longing for orgasm was not going to be satisfied.

Jane groaned, rolling her head from side to side as if in terrible agony, her eyes rolling back in her head. 'Oooh! Touch me! For pity's sake, somebody touch me!'

The fire in the pit of Matrilla's stomach blazed hot and bright. Just one more coal to put on it now. She signalled to Luna, who brought a long flexible dildo. She plugged its wire lead into a socket in the arm of the chair and switched it on. It buzzed, and its vibrations were clearly visible.

She knelt between Jane's widely parted legs and Jane looked at it with joy written all over her face. 'Yes! Oh yes!' she moaned. 'Quickly, please! Please hurry!' Luna clamped the artificial organ to the front edge of the chair so that it stuck up at an enticing angle. Jane struggled to inch her buttocks forward and almost reached it. Satisfied that this was the total extent of Jane's movement, Luna adjusted the instrument so that it remained just half an inch beyond that, then finally locked it in place. Jane shrieked with frustration, tossing her body about within the narrow confines of the straps. Try as she might, she could not reach the buzzing, vibrating object of her most abject desire.

The sight was too much for Matrilla. She had to leave! Now! Immediately! The liquid running down her legs told her that she could delay no longer. 'Luna, you stay here!' she said. 'Marla, come with me. I have a job for you!' She left hurriedly, leaving her victim to squirm and suffer.

Ten

Helen Crombie took off her earrings and set them down on the dressing table in front of her, then rubbed the earlobes which had been compressed all evening and were now protesting at the discomfort of a rapidly returning blood supply. From where she sat, she could see in the illuminated mirror not only her own reflection, but that of her husband, Henry, now balancing unsteadily on one leg as he removed his evening dress trousers. He was a thickset man. At thirty-two, he was a little older than she and his body showed the early signs of obesity which self-indulgence brings. She sighed, wishing that Henry wasn't quite such the life and soul of the party. At the one they had just come from, he had led the raucous conversation with risqué jokes and had had just a little too much to drink, which accounted for the fact that he had just toppled onto the bed in his efforts to undress.

She studied her reflection in the mirror. Still reasonable for her age, she decided, but maybe a bit too serious. She pulled at the loose skin near her eyes in an effort to make the tiny lines disappear. The other women at the party had been much more glamorous. They had no problem with wrinkles; particularly Eleanor Stacey. She was far too sexy for her own good, or anyone else's. Ellie had been all over Henry like fly-paper all evening and her husband, Jack, had shown no sign of caring. Henry, of course, had lapped it up. To be the centre of attention delighted him. To be the centre of an attractive woman's attention was even better.

She spoke over her shoulder. 'How was Ellie, Henry?'

'Oh, you know, darling. She was fine.'

'You spent a lot of time with her.'

'Of course I did. She and Jack are our friends.'

'Your friends, Henry,' she corrected. 'You didn't spend much time with Jack, though.'

'That's because he was sniffing round you all night. Fancies you. Didn't you know that?'

Jack had made that perfectly clear. Jack fancied himself as a ladies' man. He wore heavy gold jewellery and talked about his money and his Mercedes at every opportunity. Helen found everything about him to be thoroughly repellent, but was always too polite to say so, not wishing to spoil the friendship which Henry obviously wished to cultivate.

'What is it that you like so much about them, Henry?'

He came up behind her and placed his hands on her shoulders, bare above the cocktail dress. 'They're a couple that's really with it. Modern. Swinging. We could be like them, if you tried a bit.'

'You want me to be like Ellie?'

'You know what I mean, old thing. You're all right, but a bit behind the times, you know.'

Helen thought, If he calls me 'old thing' just once more, I'm going to put starch in his underpants for the next six months.

She smiled at that thought and Henry misinterpreted it. 'That's better! It's just a matter of getting with it and flowing with the tide. We should talk to them about how it's done. We can do that tomorrow night. I've invited them over for drinks.'

'Oh!'

'Now that's just what I mean. Don't be so po-faced and old fashioned all the time. Live a little!' He slid his hands down over her shoulders and into the front of her dress, fondling her breasts. 'Hurry up and come into bed. Don't bother with your nightie. I'll only take it off again. I want you tonight.' He moved away, took off the rest of his clothes and climbed into bed, naked.

Helen started to take off her make-up. It was a pity there

wasn't a bit more romance about Henry. There it was! The matter-of-fact assertion which allowed no argument. He had decided that he was going to have her and he would, no matter what she thought about it. She was by no means averse to sex. In fact, she hungered for it with a passion. The trouble was that Henry's version of that delicate, delightful pastime was not to her taste. A hasty grope, a sudden lunge, a bit of shoving and grunting and it would all be over, leaving her deeply unsatisfied. She wasn't exactly sure what she wanted, but she knew that there must be more to sex than that. She sighed and completed her work on her face. Maybe tonight things would be different. Or was that a triumph of optimism over experience?

She took off her clothes and folded them neatly on a chair, then went around picking up Henry's discarded trousers, socks and shirt, to put them in the laundry basket. She was aware of his eyes on her nakedness as she moved about the room and that pleased her. At least her body was still worth looking at and as long as that persisted, there was always hope. She turned back the covers and slid into bed. On one elbow, she reached to put out the bedside light. As she did so, Henry turned towards her and she felt his hand clutch at her groin.

Oh Henry! she thought. Why can't you, just for once, creep up on me with soft, gentle kisses on my face and neck, then my breasts and stomach? Even my feet! Why do you always have to go straight for the main course, when there are so many starters we would both enjoy?

She sighed deeply, turned onto her back and opened her legs. The sigh was taken by Henry to be a sign of arousal and he heaved himself on top of her. She reached down between parted thighs to guide his erect member to her vagina. This was the only time she got to touch his penis. Henry didn't fondle her and he didn't care to be fondled himself. Indeed, she hardly ever got to see that part of him. When she did, it was a matter of glimpses, accidentally obtained. She would have liked to spend a little time with it in her hands, exploring it, but she knew that would not be approved. She just pulled it into position and he thrust it in to its full extent. She was not really lubricated, so the manoeuvre did not cause as much of a thrill as it might have done. He withdrew a little, then thrust again and continued to pump his buttocks, driving his penis into her at every stroke.

Her body responded by lubricating and the sensation became quite pleasant. She sorted through the file in her mind to see with whom she would have sex tonight. Charlton Heston? Timothy Dalton? Sean Bean? She allowed herself to dwell, pleasantly, on wiry bodies, thin hips and taut buttocks. Now her own passion was rising and what was being done to her was exciting. For a few brief seconds she enjoyed their coupling, then Henry gasped, shuddered and came. He withdrew immediately without waiting for his organ to deflate. He rolled away from her and turned his back. 'Mmmm! Lovely!' he said sleepily. Very shortly after that, his deep breathing told her that he was fast asleep.

She waited a few minutes until she was quite certain that small movements would not wake him before she began to masturbate. This was the part of sex she most enjoyed. Her time. Without any sort of obligation to her partner, sex could be anything she decided it should be. She rubbed her clitoris slowly in dreamy circles while the fantasy came upon her. She was never quite certain what sort of kingdom it was that she inhabited, but knew that she was the Queen and the most beautiful woman in the land. Thousands of men sought her favours, but only one whose beauty could match her own dared to look into her face. All others were instantly struck blind. This special man was, even now, coming up the golden stairs towards her golden throne. She smiled at him and he stared her steadily in the face. He was golden all over, hair, body and clothing. As he drew nearer, she raised her feet up onto the front edge of her throne and splayed her legs, displaying her golden treasure to him. A shaft of golden light spread from it and illuminated him. He sank to his knees in front of this glory, leant forward and began to lick her with his long, hot, golden tongue. Faster and faster, licking along her golden labia and tickling her golden clitoris.

Sometimes, she could make this dream last a long time by slowing her masturbatory movements. This night, she was hungry for satisfaction and rubbed harder and faster. Before climax, the golden man would mount her and insert his long, golden shaft into her excited vagina. He was doing that now, and she felt herself on the brink of orgasm. Suddenly, the image changed, and she was now the golden person, looking down at her own naked body, knowing just what needed to be done to maximise the stimulation. She reached under her own body and felt for her bottom hole, massaging it in quick circles which sent excited tremors through her whole pelvic area. She thrust faster and faster into her vagina and rubbed harder and harder. Her climax came and she longed to thrash about with the pleasure of it. With Henry asleep alongside her, she had to confine herself to little gasps and shudderings. Keeping her hand between her legs and still manipulating herself very gently, she turned onto her side for sleep.

The following evening found Helen bustling about, preparing for their visitors. There was a bit more to 'having them over for drinks' than Henry imagined. The whole house had to be dusted and vacuumed. Snacks, cheese, peanuts and crisps had to be obtained and she had to check that there was a sufficient quantity of drink in the house to satisfy probable requirements. She was finished at last and stood back to admire her work.

Henry said, 'Have you put out the cards?'

'Cards? I didn't know they were coming to play cards.'

'Well, they are.'

'Really Henry, you might have warned me. I could have looked up the rules to refresh my memory. You know how bad I am at card games.'

'Don't worry about it. I'll see we play something simple.'

'If I'd known, I could have got a table ready.'

'Well, you know now. Do it now!'

She scurried about and found the green baize cloth they used for card playing. They did not possess a card table but made use of a more sturdy one, simply covering it for the occasion. This was most inconvenient for Helen because she had already used that table for snacks and now she had to clear it and put them elsewhere. She stood again for a while, checking that all was now as it should be after the upheaval. At that moment, the doorbell's chimes announced the arrival of the Staceys. The routine of greeting called for little brushes of cheek to cheek and kissing noises in the air. Was Helen mistaken, or was Ellie Stacey just a little too enthusiastic when kissing Henry, and were Jack's hands just a shade too squeezy when he embraced her?

They all sat down and drinks were passed around. The usual sort of opening conversation was gone through; the men on the subject of football and politics; the women on each other's clothes. Then it was time to move to the card table.

'Poker?' asked Jack.

'Ooh, lovely!' said Ellie.

'Right!' Henry said. 'Poker it is!'

Helen's heart sank and she resisted the impulse to kick Henry under the table. Poker was the game at which she was quite useless. Not only did she have to keep asking what beat what; her personality was such that she found herself unable to dissemble. Whether she had a good hand or a bad one, her facial expression was guaranteed to reveal the fact.

To her total astonishment, she won the first hand with three sevens. She won the second with a pair of twos and the third with King high. She was elated. She had never had such a run of luck before. She lost a couple of hands after that, then won three more in succession. It really seemed as though she had got the hang of poker at last and she began to bluff bad hands into winners in a way she never thought she could. The level of her drink sank and Henry topped it up for her. The pile of peanuts in front of her grew, and so did her confidence. Jack and Henry were swapping rude stories, Ellie was laughing uproariously and even Helen found herself smiling at them. For once, she was having a good time. Maybe the Staceys weren't so bad after all.

Presently, Henry said, 'Playing for peanuts is a bit dull. How about we play for clothes? Strip poker.'

Jack replied, 'All right with me. What about you Ellie?'

'Fine with me,' said Ellie, giggling. 'I've got nothing I'd be ashamed to show.' She met Helen's eyes across the table with a brazen stare.

All eyes turned on Helen. 'Come on, darling,' said Henry. 'Don't be a spoilsport. What do you say?'

Helen hesitated, irresolute. Every instinct told her to refuse, but she didn't want to be a wet blanket and besides, she *was* on a lucky streak. What finally decided her was that look of Ellie's and the stress she had placed on the fact that *she* had nothing to be ashamed of. As if Helen had! The cheek of the woman!

'All right,' she heard herself saying. 'How does it work?'

'Just one item of clothing is the only bet allowed. No buying or raising. We lay the hands straight down, as dealt. Winner stays at the table. The three losers take something off and put it on that armchair over there, OK?'

Helen gulped nervously, wondering what she'd done. 'All right.'

She lost the first hand, but was gratified to see that Ellie lost too.

They went to the armchair with Henry and each took off a shoe. Ellie won the next hand and put her shoe back on again. It seemed to Helen that her luck had run out. She did not win a single hand. When any of the others lost, they seemed to win the next hand and regain their item of clothing. She didn't, and the consequence was that her supply of clothing was dwindling much faster than theirs. With the removal of her pantihose, she found herself reduced to just knickers and brassière and the cold hand of panic clutched at her heart.

'Would anyone like coffee?' she enquired in a trembly voice.

'Not right now, darling,' Henry replied and dealt.

Helen breathed a sigh of relief. Three tens! A potential winning hand at last. With a gleeful snigger, Ellie laid down three jacks.

Helen folded her arms over her breasts. 'Henry! I can't! I just can't!'

Henry was sympathetic. 'What do you think, Jack, Ellie? She's been having a bad run. What say we give her a chance?'

'All right with me,' said Jack. 'What about you Ellie?'

'Oh yes! We ought to give her one more chance to change her luck. We'll lend her the bra for now. If she wins the next hand, that's OK, but if she loses, then she owes us the panties as well as the bra. And, as interest on the loan, she ought to stand on the table to take them off.'

Helen said in a small voice, 'Can't I just stop playing now, dear?'

'Stop playing? Of course you can't. We've all been taking the same risk. You can't be a spoilsport, just because you're losing.'

There was that word again. Spoilsport. Helen nodded in dumb misery and the cards were dealt again. With a sick certainty, she picked up her hand. Nine high! It was resoundingly bad. When the cards were laid down, hers was the lowest hand of the four. She looked all around the table, hoping to see some glimmer of compassion, but found none.

In particular, Ellie's expression was one of smirking, hard-eyed triumph. 'Come on, then,' she crowed. 'Up on the table and strip off!'

'No! Please, no!' Helen clung to the seat of her chair, but that did not save her. Henry and Jack came and stood on either side of her.

'Play the game, old thing.' She really hated Henry at that moment.

'Yes, you can't welsh on a bet,' added Jack.

The two men nodded to one another, then each grasped an arm and lifted her onto her feet. She felt herself propelled upwards. Her foot touched the seat of her chair and then she was standing in the centre of the table, not quite certain how she had got there. She gazed down, as if through a mist, at the litter of cards and the leering faces about her.

'Off! Get 'em off!' they began to chant.

Helen gazed imploringly at Henry, but saw only gloating anticipation in his face. Slowly and reluctantly, she reached behind her and unclipped her bra. She lowered it down her arms and let it fall, protecting her bare breasts with her arms.

Henry said, 'Now the knickers. You have to take those off as well.'

'Yeah! We want a full strip!' Ellie's voice betrayed the fact that she had consumed a little too much alcohol.

Frozen, Helen could only stand and shake her head. There was no way she could bare her body to them.

Ellie put the poison in. 'If it was me who wouldn't pay up on a bet, Jack would spank my bottom.' She looked at Henry. 'But then, Jack's a real man. He doesn't stand any nonsense.'

Henry rose to the bait, as Ellie had known he would. 'Right, then. She gets a spanking. Give me a hand!' He made a lunge for Helen, who screamed and backed away, only to have her ankles trapped by Jack. For a moment, she teetered, arms waving, then toppled off the table. Jack and Ellie caught her and held her until Henry came and took her by the waist. He dragged her over to the sofa and fell backwards onto it, holding Helen across his knees.

He had some trouble hanging onto his screaming, squirming wife. 'Come and help me, then!' he said. Jack and Ellie came over and joined in the struggle. Jack took Helen's wrists in his fists and pulled her arms out straight, while Ellie sat on her legs.

Henry raised his hand, but Ellie stopped him. 'Wait a minute. It's not a real spanking unless it's on the bare bum, is it?' She hooked her fingers into the waistband of Helen's knickers and pulled them down, exposing her white buttock cheeks. 'That's better. It's all ready for you now.'

Henry began to spank the naked bottom so invitingly posed for him. Helen's screams and wriggles increased until it looked as though she might break free of her tormentors.

'Stop again, Henry!' Ellie said. 'She's making too much

noise.' She pulled again at the knickers which were now around Helen's thighs. Helen pressed her legs together, but could not prevent her panties from being taken off, leaving her completely naked. Ellie picked up one of her own stockings and went to Helen's head. Reaching down, she shoved the knickers into the screaming mouth, silencing the yells, then, before Helen could spit them out, she bound them in place with the stocking. She took Helen's wrists from Jack and bent her arms behind her back. Using Helen's tights, she bound each wrist to the other elbow, so trapping Helen's arms behind her, yet clear of the target area of her bottom. Going to her feet again, she passed the last stocking around the thrashing ankles and bound them together.

'OK, Henry. Carry on! See if you can make it as red as Jack makes mine!'

Henry resumed his spanking and the naked flesh of Helen's upturned bottom danced and wobbled as each blow fell, rapidly turning from white to red. To Helen's relief, he stopped after a few more. She lay across his knees, his left arm about her waist making escape impossible. She was very aware of her humiliating exposure to the eyes of Jack and Ellie and her face was as red as her bottom with embarrassment.

Her shame increased enormously when she heard Ellie say, 'Looks as if you've warmed it up all right, Henry. Mind if I have a feel.' Helen felt Ellie's hand stroking her bare bottom, then felt fingers dipping into the crevice between her thighs. She heaved in furious indignation and made muffled protests into the knickers which filled her mouth.

'If your arm's tired, Henry, I can give her a few more for you.'

Helen froze. Surely Henry couldn't allow her to be spanked by this woman. He could. Helen received four stinging slaps from Ellie. Maybe Ellie was spanking harder than Henry, or maybe her bottom area was already sore. Whatever the reason, Ellie's slaps hurt much more than Henry's. At least though, the spanking seemed to be over and Jack hadn't joined in.

There was the hated Ellie's voice again. 'When I've been naughty, Jack draws on me with lipstick. Do you think we ought to do that, Henry?' Craning her head round, Helen saw Ellie go to her purse and take out a lipstick. Her skin crawled as she felt Ellie write something across her back at shoulder level. Later, in the bathroom, she found that it was the word 'Spoilsport'.

Ellie was a little drunk, with power as much as with alcohol. 'I know!' she cried. 'Noughts and crosses!' Helen felt her draw a grid pattern on her bare back and shuddered. There was nothing she could do to prevent them playing their game out to the end and soon her back, bottom, thighs and legs were covered in lipstick scrawl. They heaved her over and it was, somehow, worse that they could now see her pubes and breasts. She endured as best she could as they covered the front of her body with lipstick, even her face. She thought that she would always remember Ellie's face as she took pains to ensure that her own turn took place on breasts and nipples.

At last they tired of their maltreatment and Henry carried her over and placed her in an armchair, then went back to Ellie on the sofa. They began to kiss and cuddle, while Helen could do nothing but watch. After the poker game, neither had been wearing a full complement of clothing and they soon abandoned the remainder on the floor. Naked now, they grappled on the sofa. Jack came over to Helen and crouched at her feet. He ran a caressing hand up her leg and then began to stroke her stomach and breasts. She shook her head violently.

'What's the matter, Helen?' Jack asked. 'Henry said you were up for a bit of wife-swapping. Changed your mind?' He reached up and removed her gag.

For a while, she said nothing, while she worked her mouth and jaw to get rid of the stiffness. 'Just let me loose, Jack. I need a bath.'

She could see that he was genuinely puzzled. 'You mean you didn't know about this? Henry and Ellie said you did.'

'Then, among other things I could name, Ellie is a liar and so is Henry.'

'Crafty sods!' he said, admiringly. 'I know she and Henry fancy each other and I thought you fancied me. Never mind. I'd give her a spanking tonight, if it wasn't for the fact that she'd enjoy it.'

Over his shoulder, Helen could see Henry and Ellie licking and sucking at each other and she felt that she didn't want to be present for the inevitable coupling. 'Come on, Jack. Be nice to me now. Let me go so that I can get cleaned up.'

'If I do, will you be nice to *me?* Let me scrub your back?'

Helen thought about this. She just had to get out of that room and into the bath. Jack was her only chance of doing that and besides, she would never be able to reach the marks on her back without help. After all, he had already seen all that she had to show him. She made up her mind. 'All right, Jack. A back scrub. But that's all. No hanky-panky. Agreed?'

'Agreed!' he said. 'Nothing you don't want me to do, Helen.' He untied her and helped her to her feet. As they went, together, towards the bathroom, Helen could not resist looking back. Henry and Ellie were on the floor, now. Henry's bare bottom was pumping up and down between Ellie's parted thighs and her legs were locked across his back. She turned her eyes away and followed Jack into the bathroom.

Helen filled the bath and stepped in, sinking gratefully below the surface of the hot water. She sat up, soaped a flannel and scrubbed at her face and neck and Jack knelt beside the bath to watch. She rinsed off and soaped the flannel again. She handed the flannel to Jack and leaned forward. 'All right, Jack. Do my back for me.'

He took the cloth from her and covered her back with suds, then rubbed gently. She craned over her shoulder. 'Is it coming off?'

'Most of it, but I might need to scrub a bit. Would you mind?'

'No. Just get the stuff off me.' She felt that she could not be free of Ellie's malevolent spirit until every scrap of lipstick was gone.

'I think that's got it all,' he said at last. 'Look, what about your bottom and the backs of your legs? Suppose you turn over and I'll do those as well.'

She gave him a long, suspicious look, but there was sense in what he proposed, so she rolled over and got up on her knees. He washed her all over while she posed acquiescently. There was no doubt that it felt good to be lathered and soaked with hot water. In spite of the fact that it was Jack, she found herself responding to his movements with reciprocal swaying of her hips. Her breasts hung down, still lipstick-marked, soapy water dripping from her nipples.

'You know, Helen, you have a gorgeous body,' Jack murmured.

'You mean it's better than Ellie's?'

'Ellie's a pretty woman. You're a beautiful lady.'

Helen was not deceived by this outrageous flattery, but it pleased her, nevertheless. She pretended not to notice when Jack's hand, without an intervening flannel, dipped into the crevice between her reddened bottom cheeks. His finger rubbed to and fro across her anus and her mind fled back to her masturbation fantasies. He was no golden man, for sure, but what he was doing was definitely exciting. His hand slid down and forward and he massaged her pubic region from underneath. She drew a deep breath of pleasure, then caught his wrist. 'I think you'd better stop, Jack. I can reach that bit myself.'

'All right, but why wash yourself when someone else will do it for you? Why don't you lie back and let me do the front?'

The image returned to her mind of Henry and Ellie enjoying themselves. Why shouldn't she have some pleasure, too? She made up her mind and rolled over, lying back to make herself available to him. She watched as the washcloth moved over the whole of the front of her body. It was pleasant enough on stomach and thighs, but when it passed across her breasts, as it did many times, the roughness of the material stimulated her nipples into erectness so that each subsequent pass increased the sensation tenfold. A voice inside her said, 'The hell with you, Henry. I'm going to lie back and enjoy it.'

Aloud, to Jack, she said, 'You know I'm not going to let you have me in spite of all this, don't you?'

'That's OK,' he answered. 'You don't know me well enough yet. I'm happy to wait. We've given you a raw deal tonight, though and I'd like to make it up to you. I like touching you, if you like to be touched, and that's enough for now.'

Those terms were acceptable, she thought. A fair trade for all the humiliation of the evening. She relaxed and let him do what he would to please her. Part of her mind was curious to see whether he would be able to guess, without being told, what she liked best. She found that his ability in that direction was uncanny. He rubbed slippery, soapy hands over her belly and thighs and massaged her vulva under the water. She sighed and moved her hips in lazy circles, vastly stimulated.

Presently, he made her kneel again and inserted two very soapy fingers into her vagina from the rear while he massaged her clitoris from the front. Waves of pleasure coursed through her and she felt orgasm approaching. When he removed the fingers from her sex and played with her anus again, she wriggled her bottom in delight. At precisely the right moment, he increased the pace of his clitoris masturbation and penetrated her rectum with the extreme tip of a soapy finger. She came to climax with a glad shout, jerking her buttocks back toward his hand, her head craned upwards; the neck cords standing out for what seemed ages with the strain of tensing her stomach muscles to cope with her powerful contractions. It was the best orgasm she had experienced for years.

She stayed where she was for quite a while, getting her breath back. Jack continued to rub her back and bottom gently and passed his hands to and fro across her breasts. This was not a bit like sex with Henry, who rolled off her and went straight to sleep, and she found herself thinking kindly of Jack, who was rapidly turning out not to be the man she had thought him to be when she had so heartily disliked him. She reached out a hand to him and he helped her out of the bath. He wrapped her in a towel and patted her dry, but he did not attempt to kiss her. She appreciated that.

She covered herself with the towel and secured it by twisting it into a roll above her breasts. The germ of an idea was creeping about in her brain and she considered it pensively. Henry and that bitch Ellie were engrossed in each other, outside. It would give Henry something to think about if she spent an excessively long time in the bathroom with Jack, wouldn't it? And, after all, Jack wasn't really so bad. He had been decent to her and given her a nice orgasm. Perhaps he deserved a break!

She made up her mind. 'Why don't you take a bath, Jack?'

'What? Are you serious?'

'Sure, why not? You remember the children's game. Well, I've shown you mine. Now you show me yours.' To make her point clear, she put the plug back in the bath and turned on the water.

She watched him undress with considerable interest. When he got to his last garment, his undershorts, he turned his back.

'No, don't do that, Jack. I'd like to see your body, if you don't mind.'

Obediently, he turned back again, dropping his shorts and stepping out of them. She stared at him. His penis was circumcised and of average length, but quite thick. It protruded from a bush of black hair which was the same colour as that which covered most of his body. She had known he would be hairy and that made him satisfyingly different from Henry.

'Seen enough?' he said, and she realised that she had been disconcerting him with her stare.

'Yes, thank you. The bath's full. Why don't you get in?'

He climbed over the side and sat down. She knelt beside the bath. 'Want me to do your back?'

'Yes please.'

She took the soap and worked up a lather. Even as she applied it to his back, she knew that her object was not to wash him clean. It was simply to have the feel of his body under her hand. She slid her hand gently to and fro, caressing; not scrubbing, and enjoyed the slippery contact between them. Presently she said, 'You'll have to lie back in the water to wash off the soap. He slid his bottom forward and lay at full length in the bath. The water was not deep enough to cover him completely and his penis was exposed. It was, she noticed, only half erect and she felt a sudden longing to see it in its full state of tumescence.

'You washed my front. Do you think I ought to wash yours?'

He nodded and she soaped her hands again. She started with his chest, passing her hands lightly in small circles. After only a short time she noticed that he gave a little jump every time her palms passed over his nipples and that these had grown from tiny bumps into quite large projections. It had been so long since she had touched a man's body in that way that she could not recall if that was a normal reaction or not. His penis had grown a little more and she could no longer resist the temptation. Renewing the lather on her hands, she slid them down over his stomach and took this fascinating object in her right hand. He gave a great leap and drew in his breath, sharply.

She looked up from what she was doing. 'All right, Jack?'

'Yes, thank you. Very nice.'

She smiled and returned her attention to her fascinating new toy. There could be no doubt about its state of erection now and she was pleased about that. It wouldn't have been much of a compliment to her otherwise. She studied it intently. She had been wrong to think of it as average. It scored higher than that. She massaged it slowly and carefully, her thumb on top, instinctively applying gentle pressure to the area facing her, just below the glans. He stirred under her ministrations and she knew that he was appreciating what she was doing. His half-floating testicles caught her attention and she took them in her soapy left hand, lifting and stroking, causing him to utter a groan of pleasure.

Suddenly annoyed by the opacity of the lather, she took

a double handful of water and splashed it over him, washing the soap away. She put both hands on the edge of the bath and rested her chin on them, drinking in the view. His neglected organ was twitching and jerking all by itself. She admired the redness of the abrupt ledge which separated the head from the rest of his penis. Inside me, she thought, that would cause the most delightful sensations as it pushed past sensitive places. There was a sudden prickle in her nipples and she felt her lower stomach contract. On a sudden impulse, she loosened her towel and leaned forward so that her breasts hung down inside the bath, its enamel cold on their warm undersides. As she soaped her hands again she felt his hand on her, caressing her breasts, and that pleased her.

She took his penis in her right hand again and put her soapy left hand between her own legs, feeling for her clitoris. She fingered herself while she resumed her gentle massage.

'This looks awfully dirty to me, Jack. I think I'm going to have to rub a lot harder to get it clean, don't you?' He nodded, unable to speak.

She gripped harder and rubbed faster with her right hand, while her left set up just the sort of circular motion she liked around her love button. Now he was grunting and convulsing, his hips making involuntary pelvic thrusts into her hand. A tremendous sense of power swept through her. She had a sudden yearning to see him completely out of control in the throes of ejaculation; to know, at last, exactly what it was like when a man did that. She had never seen Henry's sperm. Well, tonight, she was going to see Jack's.

She felt the first faint pulsings of movement in his soapy penis and increased her own masturbation movements. She knew she was as close to orgasm as he was. She cast around in her mind for that extra stimulation which would trigger his explosion to coincide exactly with her own.

'That's right, Jack,' she crooned. 'Isn't it lovely? Look at me. I'm doing it to you and I'm going to make you come, aren't I? I'm going to take you all the way; no stopping.

Look at my nice breasts. They're for you to play with, Jack. Touch me! Touch my nipples, Jack. Make me come, too. Pull my nipples, Jack. Pinch them! Harder! Hurt me! Make me feel it, Jack! That's right! Now Jack! Now! I want to see that cream! Give it to me! Yes! Yes! Yes!'

In the midst of her own climax she had the enormous satisfaction of seeing his whole body contort, his face distorted in a grimace which might have been pain and his penis pumping and pumping again, shooting a mighty fountain of white semen far up his body, almost into his face. He slumped and she slowed her movements in both hands, coming down very slowly from the mountain she had climbed. After a little while she stirred again, scooped up water and washed his stomach and chest for him. Beat that, Ellie, she thought.

That night as she sat before her mirror, applying her night cream, Helen noticed Henry staring at her, curiously.

'Want to tell me what happened in that bathroom?' he said.

She looked back at his reflection with wide-eyed innocence. 'Why, I took a bath, dear. What else would you do in a bathroom?'

'But Jack was in there with you.'

'He was just being kind. You and Ellie had already stripped me naked. There was nothing extra for him to see, was there?'

'Then why did he say just before he left that he couldn't understand why I was willing to pass you around?'

'Did he say that? Wasn't that nice of him? He's an outrageous flatterer, you know.'

'So nothing happened.'

'I told you, dear. I took a bath.'

'Hmm!' Apparently satisfied, he went on, 'You see, that's just what I was talking about.'

'What is, dear?'

He came up behind her and put his hands on her shoulders. 'That is. I give you the opportunity to swing and you don't. You don't even get steamed up about me and Ellie. Do you know how ordinary and suburban that makes you?'

'Oh dear! Do you really think so?'

'Yes, I do. You ought to do something about it. You know. Make yourself less dull. Live a bit. Why not talk to your sister about it? She's a swinger, if ever I saw one. She'll put you straight.'

'Do you think that would be a good idea? I *am* having lunch with her tomorrow.'

He patted her on the head. 'Of course it's a good idea, old thing. In fact I insist on it. You tell Pandora all about it. I'm sure she'll set things straight.'

'Mmm! Perhaps you're right, dear. I'll do that.'

David Corby was in mid-shave when the phone rang. It was a sunny morning anyway, but the weather seemed to improve enormously when he heard Pandora's voice.

'Hallo you!' he said. 'Calling about that one I owe you?'

She laughed, causing his heart to beat a little faster. 'Yes, actually,' she said. 'But down, boy! Not in the way you mean. I really need you to help me out in the same way I helped you. I've got a pair who need shipping but I don't see how I can get at them myself.'

'Anyone we know?'

'Well, strangely enough, one of them is my brother-in-law. That's part of the problem. I don't want him to suspect that I had anything to do with it.'

'Understood,' he said. 'If one is a man, I shouldn't have any difficulty in getting close enough to do the business. Just tell me about him and his habits and leave it to me. Southern entry port again?'

'Mmm, yes! It seems to work well.' She quickly sketched in details while David took notes.

'OK, then. Consider it done,' he said. 'I say! Things really get going when we put our heads together, don't they?'

'Heads together is quite nice,' she said. 'Personally I've always preferred tails to heads.'

She put the phone down quickly, leaving him to work out whether that was a double meaning or a double-double meaning.

'Oh dear. Do you really think so?'

'Yes, I do. You ought to do something about it. [illegible]'

[illegible]

He patted her on the head. [illegible]

'Mmm. Perhaps you're right, dear,' Pippa said.

David Cobb was in an expansive mood [illegible]

[illegible]

'Anyone we know?'

[illegible]

'Understood,' he said. [illegible]

[illegible]

'OK, then. Consider it done,' he said. [illegible]

'Heads together,' [illegible]

[illegible]

Eleven

In the dim red light which was the only illumination in their small crate, Henry Crombie and Ellie Stacey were engaged in a bitter argument. For quite a while after their capture, Ellie had been too shocked by the suddenness of it to be able to do a lot of talking. One moment they had been happily squatting on cushions, anticipating a sexy peep-show. The next, the top part of the side walls of their tiny cubicle had folded inwards to meet in the middle and a panel had slid across the only exit, turning that cubicle into the four foot square box in which they now found themselves.

Now, though, Ellie had recovered sufficiently to find her voice and Henry was wishing that her trauma had continued for a while longer.

Henry, you're a pervert!'

'I don't know what you're talking about. I don't know why you keep saying that I had something to do with this.'

'You're weird. That's why I say it. This is the sort of thing that gives you the hots.'

'*I'm* weird? Who was it who was bursting to see some strange woman get her bottom spanked?'

'Only because you suggested it in the first place.'

'But I only suggested it because this chap at the club told me about it.'

'Who?'

'I don't know. David somebody or another. I don't even know if he was a member.'

'Well, you must have been bloody stupid to have believed him. Who in their right mind would expect to find a sex show at a fitness club? I don't know how you could have been so daft.'

Henry was beginning to get angry himself. 'If it's so daft, why were you all for it with your tongue hanging out? I didn't have to twist your arm, did I?' His tone softened and he reached out to squeeze her arm. 'Look, old thing. I'm just as mystified as you are, but at least we're together, eh?'

Somewhat mollified, she replied, 'Well . . . I suppose I've got to believe you. Mind you, though. If I ever find that you did have anything to do with this, you can say goodbye to your balls, Henry.' She snatched her arm away. 'And don't call me "old thing" if you know what's good for you.'

'Come on, Ellie. Try and get some rest. We've got these cushions to lie on and we don't know how long we'll be in here.' He made her lie down and arranged himself alongside her.

When he went to put his arm around her, she pushed it away. 'Oh no! You must be bloody joking! Get off me!'

In that manner, alternately dozing and bickering, they whiled away their journey. The first indication they had that the journey was at an end was when their crate had remained stationary for some time. They were waiting for it to start moving again, as it had done on previous occasions, when the panel which had covered their cubicle exit slid back an inch. For the first time in hours, the lights and sounds of the outside world intruded into their prison.

A girl's voice said, 'When the door is opened, the man is to come out first.'

Ellie put her face close to the crack. 'We both want to come out.'

The voice said, 'When the door is opened, the man is to come out first.'

'Suppose we say we don't like the idea?'

'Then I shall close the door, go away, then come back and say the same thing in an hour's time; then again an hour after that; then again an hour after that; then again . . .'

Henry shoved Ellie to one side. 'Don't be an argumentative bitch all your life, Ellie!' He put his mouth to the crack. 'All right!' I'll come out first.' The door opened just wide enough for him to scramble through. As soon as he was out, it slammed shut again, returning Ellie to soundproofing and the red light.

Henry climbed slowly to his feet, stiff after such a long time in such a small space. He had been prepared to do battle against a mighty foe. It was disconcerting to find himself confronted with a diminutive but very cute brunette who wore nothing except an almost transparent waist-cloth. She smiled at him. He looked around him. He was in a bare room whose only furniture was a hard wooden bench against one wall. Various doors led off this room. Above one of them a light was flashing, 'Enter'.

'Please follow me, Master.' It was obvious that she would have been completely shocked by a refusal and her mode of address was reassuring to the point of being a turn-on. He followed her into what proved to be a large office containing three desks. There were three people already in the room and he allowed his eyes to rove appreciatively over two of them, because they were in the same near-naked state as his guide. The woman in the purple dress behind the centre desk looked up from her file and smiled at him.

'Won't you sit down, please, Henry.'

He hesitated, but could see no harm in listening to what the woman had to say, so he took a seat in the large upright wooden chair she was indicating. 'Look, what's this all about?' he said.

'It's very simple, Henry. I am Matrilla, the Ice Queen. This is the Castle of Despair. You have been brought here for re-education.'

'There's nothing wrong with my education.'

'Ah! He that knows not, but knows not that he knows not,' said the Queen sadly.

'What?'

'It's a quotation, Henry, but never mind. I am not talking about your academic education, which is no doubt excellent. I am talking about your sexual prowess. That certainly needs some adjustment.'

'Is this a joke?'

'Far from it, Henry. My information is that you are sadly lacking in that department. We can remedy that. You may find it quite a pleasant process. For instance, if I told you that during your stay here you will be having sex with girls like these' – she waved at her companions – 'that would not displease you?'

He looked around him at the lush acres of delicious flesh on display before he answered slowly, 'No . . . I suppose not.'

'Good! Then you will stay with us for a few days? It is a free service. You will have your own room and your own personal body servant. A young woman, of course.'

Henry brightened perceptibly. 'I think I can spare a few days.'

'Excellent! You have made a wise choice.'

'But what about Mrs Stacey?'

'Ellie? Yes, it was unfortunate that she was with you and had to be brought here as well. She will, of course, be returned immediately. Gala will show you to your room now. No, not through the anteroom, Gala. Use the other door.'

Gala led Henry away. When he had gone, Matrilla beckoned to Luna and Marla and they went out into the anteroom. The door of the crate was facing the office. Matrilla went behind it while Luna opened the crate's door about two inches. As she did so, Matrilla said loudly. 'I'm just glad the plan worked, Henry. As you said, she is a sexy little thing and we shall have a lot of fun with her. You will have your usual room of course.' She opened and closed the outer door, noisily.

Inside the crate, Ellie put her mouth to the crack and screamed, 'Bastard! Pervert! I knew it was you all the time! I'll get you for this, Henry Crombie, you see if I don't!' Matrilla smiled and signed to her girls. They closed the crate and wheeled it away on its castors.

Henry followed the dark-haired girl along the castle's corridors, his eyes fixed on the twin moons of her bottom as it swayed about under its flimsy covering. 'Are you my personal servant, Miss . . .?'

'I am Gala, Master. No, I am not yours. That privilege has been given to another.'

'Oh!' Henry was disappointed. 'What's she like?'

'She is young, Master; in her twenties. She has a lot of very fair hair. She is Scandinavian; Swedish, I think. Do you wish to know any more, Master?'

Henry mentally congratulated himself. 'No, that will do to be going on with.'

Gala stopped outside a door and opened it. Henry went inside, then stopped. 'It's a bit spartan, isn't it?' he asked. The room was large, but had no furniture except a metal-framed cot against one wall. The walls were bare and so was the floor. In one corner, there was a wash basin with a cupboard below, some towels on rails and flush toilet, completely unconcealed. In the other stood a very large, tiled shower tray with spray head above, likewise uncurtained. It looked more like a cell than a room.

'I'm sorry, Master. There is much demand for our rooms. If you will be patient, I'm sure a better one will be found. Please wait here. Jotunda, your personal servant, will be here in a moment.' She went out, closing the door behind her.

Henry sat down on the bed and looked around him. Not much of a room, but he had stayed in worse in his time. He bounced experimentally on the bed. Not much of a bed, either, but it would certainly be adequate to lay a young Swedish girl on. Jotunda, eh? He had fallen on his feet, he thought. He looked up as the door opened. It was several seconds before his brain could act upon the information it was receiving from his eyes and allow his jaw to drop. The girl who was entering was completely naked except for a leather band across her forehead to control her long blonde hair. However, it was not her nudity or her blondness which caused his amazement. It was the fact that, although the doorway was a standard six feet six inches in height, she had to stoop a little to pass under the lintel. It also seemed that she had to turn slightly sideways to get her shoulders through the width. She had none of a woman's usual pear shape. Hers was an inverted triangle.

The breadth of her upper body made her head seem disproportionately small. On any other body, the face in that head would have been considered attractive, with intelligent, bright blue eyes and a snub nose. Below mighty shoulders, bulging biceps increased her width. Where breasts ought to have been, huge pectoral muscles rippled in their place. Her only concession to femininity in that area were her nipples; too large for a man. His gaze passed downwards over the washboard musculature of her flat stomach and rested on her thighs. Not soft and inviting, but great thews of solid muscle. Except for a small area around her forehead, cheeks and nose, she was covered all over with a down of light gold hair which thickened to profusion at armpits and crotch.

She pointed a blunt, powerful finger at him. 'Henry?'

He scrambled off the bed. 'Yes?'

She rapped with her knuckles in the centre of her chest, producing a dull, booming sound. 'Jotunda!'

Henry felt a little faint. 'Oh my God!'

She pointed at him and then at herself. 'You! Me! Sex! Yes?' To make the point, she formed a ring with her left thumb and forefinger and stabbed through it with her right.

'Er, no. I don't think so, thank you,' he said, backing nervously towards the far wall.

She threw back her head and laughed. 'Henry not dress, now,' she said and to render her meaning clear, made gestures as though she was shedding non-existent clothing.

'No, really! I don't think so,' he said, then as she advanced towards him, still laughing, he continued. 'Keep away. I'm warning you!' He clenched his fist and, as she came within range, swung at her face. It was probably a mistake to aim at a target so far above his head. She waited, coolly, until the blow was a couple of inches from her, then slipped it with a dexterous body swerve and countered with a professional choppy punch to his solar plexus. Winded, he dropped to his hands and knees, gasping for air. She grasped his belt and the back of his jacket and picked him up as easily as if he had been made of polystyrene foam. Carrying him to the cot, she dropped him on it face down and, with a nimble leap sprang onto the bed herself and straddled him, facing his feet, her hindquarters grinding against the back of his head, forcing his face into the pillow. He twisted his head to get air and felt the damp curls of her pubic hair against his ear. Her hands went under his mid-section and he felt his belt being unfastened. His arms were trapped under his shins and there was nothing he could do except kick his legs as he felt his trousers and undershorts being pushed down his body to mid-thigh level.

She pulled his shirt up to bare his backside. 'Henry bad! Clap arse!' she said and proceeded to beat his buttocks with the flat of her hard and horny palm. She gave him six stinging smacks, then stopped. 'Henry good; no clap arse, yes?'

He said nothing, so she gave him three more smacks. 'Henry good; no clap arse, yes?'

'Yes! *Yes!* All right! Henry good!' he said. 'Just get off me.'

She jumped lightly off the cot, beaming. 'Not dress, now,' she said, and went through her unpeeling routine. Henry climbed reluctantly off the bed and removed the rest of his clothes. She stooped, hands on knees, to inspect his flaccid penis, which brought her head about level with his own. Looking into his face with a nose-wrinkle of disapproval, she held up a thumb and forefinger with a gap to indicate size.

'Little, no?'

'No!' he said, glancing down, offended.

She placed the flat of her hand against his chest and gave him a push which set him flying backwards. The backs of his knees caught the edge of the cot and he sat down with a force which made the springs creak. She scooped up his dangling legs and flung them onto the bed. Leaning over him, she placed her left hand in the centre of his chest, pinning him while with her right she grasped and masturbated his penis, rubbing it roughly into erection. In spite of his revulsion, he could not control his body's response to her actions and had to watch himself rising to full growth. She climbed onto the cot with him and straddled him again, this time facing his head. Reaching under herself for his organ, she guided it to the cavern of her sex, then settled down hard onto it, engulfing it completely and grinding her pubic hair against his. She reached forward and picked up his hands, placing them over her nipples and making circular motions with them. He deduced that she wanted her nipples rubbed so, to humour her, he continued the movement, even after she released her grip, noting the strange feel of the myriad fine hairs under his palms. She nodded and smiled, putting her hand between her legs to manipulate her clitoris.

He could tell by her frown that she was not completely pleased with the sensation she was getting. She suddenly stopped and leant forward, extending her tongue as far as it would go and making licking movements. She pointed at him and then at her genital area. 'You do!' she said.

'What?' said Henry. 'I don't understand.'

She nodded enthusiastically. 'Yes!' she said. She waggled her tongue again and pointed at his mouth. 'You!' She pointed to her crotch again. 'Me! You do!'

Comprehension came. Henry was aghast. 'Oh my God, no!' he said.

She threw back her head and laughed again. Removing herself from his penis, she reversed her position and faced his feet, her shins trapping his arms again and her sex posed above his face. He stared up at the protruding, rubbery lips in the forest of golden curls and her woman smell consumed him. She lowered herself slowly onto him and he turned his head aside.

She reached forward and took his testicles in one mighty fist. Squeezing gently, she said, 'You do!' When his head did not move, she increased the pressure on his testicles and said again, 'You do!'

He groaned. 'All right! All right!' He turned his face upwards again and the pain in his groin diminished. She lowered herself again and he took a few, tentative licks at the division of her sex.

She tightened her grip again. 'In!'

'Oh! Ah! All right!' He extended his tongue as far as it would go and probed upwards, getting hairs in his mouth, until he could separate her labial lips and stick his tongue inside.

She slid backwards until his tongue rested on her clitoris, then said, 'You do!'

Obediently, he licked and sucked at this protuberance which, in her, was almost as big as a small penis. She sighed and let go of his testicles. She grasped his organ again, masturbating it hard and fast. His face was suddenly drenched with slippery fluid, but he stuck manfully to his task. Now her backside was heaving, grinding her pink slit to and fro across his nose. Her movements were frantic and her approaching orgasm communicated itself to him. He felt his erection swell and pulse in her hand. Just as she wriggled in climax, he came, too, jets of semen flying up and splashing onto the front of her body.

Jotunda got off him and, leaving him to get his breath back, went to the shower. She revolved under the spray, soaping her hairy body and washing his spend from her chest. Glistening with water, she came back to the bed and stood looking at him. 'You wash now!'

'No, that's all right. I'll do it later.'

'Now!'

'Thank you,' he said with dignity. 'I'm not dirty.'

She grabbed his legs and hauled him off the bed. He managed to break his fall by grabbing at the bedclothes, but lost them as she marched backwards to the shower towing him behind her as easily as other women pull shopping trolleys. Unceremoniously, she dumped him on his back on the tiles, then straddled him, looming over him, terrifying in her gargantuan stature. Her stomach muscles tensed and a stream of golden urine emerged from her equally golden crotch, raining hot on his skin. She shuffled forward, still straddling him, so that it approached his face and he wriggled desperately to avoid it. Her capacious bladder enabled her to subject him to this humiliation for quite a while. When the stream finally stopped, she stood staring down at him. 'Henry dirty now!' she remarked drily and turned on the shower.

She soaped him all over and washed it off, then washed herself again. She threw him a towel and he dabbed at himself, watching her warily as she dried too, rubbing her hair briskly. That done, she ran her fingers through it, drawing it back off her face, then replaced her leather headband. That seemed to be the limit of her coiffure and wardrobe.

Jotunda went to the little cupboard under the washbasin and stooped to open it. When she stood up she had two pairs of leather cuffs in her hands. Each pair comprised a large cuff and a smaller one, linked by a short length of chain.

'What are those for?' Henry asked, deeply suspicious.

'Put on!' she said.

'Oh no!' he said, backing away. 'You're not going to put –'

He got no further. Dropping the cuffs at her feet, she dived forward so suddenly that Henry was caught off guard. She grabbed his left wrist in her huge left fist and tugged him towards her, straightening his arm and turning him to his right. She slammed the flat of her right hand behind his left shoulder, starting him off on the beginning of a giant circle with herself at the centre and his straight left arm as the radius. Round and round he went in a stooping stumble, forced lower and lower by her right hand on his shoulder, until he lost his balance and sprawled face down on the floor with his left arm still fully extended. She put her right knee on the nerve centre behind his left upper arm, freezing him into immobility while she groped for the cuffs and buckled one onto his left wrist. Holding onto the chain attached to the cuff, she released his arm and backed over his body to kneel in the small of his back, pinning him down while she reached down for his left ankle. She pulled it up and secured the other cuff to it. With his left wrist cuffed to his left ankle, she was able to get up and deal with the other side of his body in a similar manner at her leisure until Henry lay on his face, his arms drawn back behind him and his knees bent by his restraint.

Jotunda stepped across him and stooped. Locking her fingers under his waist, she lifted him into the air as if he was as light as a feather. 'Stand!' Thus suspended, he found he could swing his arms and legs down and get his feet underneath him. When she was satisfied that he had his balance, she released him and went back to the cupboard while he, perforce, remained where he was in a humiliatingly stooped position, unable to straighten up because of the chains which joined his ankles to his wrists.

When she came back, she had an oversize dog collar and lead. She fastened the collar round his neck and tugged on the lead. 'Walk!' she commanded. With hesitant, experimental steps, he tried to obey and found that he could just about manage to hobble along in this position. 'Walking' was not a correct description. A very undignified waddle was closer.

When he saw her opening the door, he stopped dead. 'Please no, Jotunda!' he said. 'Not outside! I couldn't. Really!'

She frowned and wagged a finger at him. 'Henry bad, clap arse,' she said. She dropped the lead and came beside him. Reaching under his body, she grasped his penis firmly to hold him steady, then administered six more burning spanks on his helplessly presented bottom. It had not recovered from its previous treatment, so those slaps stung like mad. When she picked up the lead again and said, 'Walk!' he did not demur, but waddled along as best he could behind her. That slow journey through the long corridors burned itself into Henry's memory. Quite apart from the discomfort of moving in such a doubled-up position, there were the giggles and comments of everyone they passed to contend with. In spite of what might be in store for him there, he was happy to be back in Matrilla's office again, away from eyes other than those of the four women who occupied the room with him.

When the Queen nodded to her, Jotunda removed his cuffs and Henry stood up, rubbing his wrists and stretching his aching back. Matrilla pointed to the high-backed chair. 'Please sit down again, Henry.'

Mindful of what Jotunda could force him to do, he seated himself without question.

Matrilla said, 'The first stage of your re-education is now complete, Henry. We can move on to the next, which might be more pleasant.'

He was indignant. 'Education? How can you describe what I've been through as education?'

'It wasn't education, Henry. It was incentive. In all educational processes there has to be one of those. The child hopes to get a school prize; the student hopes for a degree; the candidate hopes for a better job. In your case, the hope will be that you don't have to spend any more time with Jotunda! She has dealt with you leniently, by my order. If you go back to her, there are other less amusing pastimes in which she likes to indulge.'

Henry's skin crawled at the thought that his ordeal had been considered lenient and amusing. However, he cheered up considerably when Matrilla went on. 'You will transfer now to a proper room and Gala will attend you. I advise you not to waste your stamina on her, for tonight you will be visited by the first of many ladies, for whom you will provide sexual services. I see that idea appeals to you, but do not jump to any conclusions. It will be your function to please and completely satisfy these ladies. They will score your performance out of ten and report to me. At first, a five will keep you away from Jotunda. Later, a score of eight or more, three times in a row will be needed.

'In order to achieve scores like that, you will have to become familiar with those things which most appeal to your partner at the time. They will all have slightly different tastes, so yours will be a constant learning process. You will find that asking them to tell you what they like will not be very helpful, although you can do a certain amount of that. Too much, though, is a real turn-off for any woman. If she likes something which is a little bizarre, you will embarrass her by making her express her taste in words. Most of what you learn must be done intuitively, by watching how she responds to certain things; experimenting and observing reactions. From what my files tell me, it will take several visits to Jotunda before you get the message. Any questions?'

Henry shook his head. 'I think I understand.'

'If you prove to be better than I expect, I might give you a treat. I might have Jotunda bound and delivered to you for your pleasure.' Correctly interpreting his nervous glance, she said. 'It's all right. She can't understand. She speaks only a few words of English. I'll bet you'd like to cane her bottom, Henry, after all the things she's said to you.'

'You bet I would!' he replied with feeling.

'How many strokes do you think she should have, Henry?'

'As many as she deserves,' he said, 'and that means going on until my arms get tired.'

'Well, we'll see how you get on. Now you may put on this robe and slippers and go with Gala.'

As Henry followed his guide out of the office, his expression was extremely thoughtful. When he was gone, Matrilla reached into her desk drawer and switched off her tape recorder.

As she was being wheeled away in her crate, Ellie was furious. With herself, for having got mixed up in this bizarre business but, most of all, with Henry who, she was sure, had betrayed her. The crate stopped, the door opened and Ellie found herself looking out into a bare cell with just a wooden sleeping bench and basic toilet arrangements. It did not look very inviting but it was, at least, larger than her present prison, so she crawled out. Immediately the door of the cell hissed and slid shut behind her. She turned and beat on it with her hands, yelling to be let out but if anyone heard, they took no notice. It was some hours before she was visited again, during which time she grew very hungry. That feeling was uppermost in her mind when a small panel in the door opened and a girl's face looked through.

'Hey! What about some bloody food?' said Ellie.

'I have some for you here, Mistress,' the girl replied.

'Well, give it to me, then.'

'I'm afraid it is on a tray, Mistress, which means that I have to open the door. I am not permitted to do that unless you are secured.' She dangled handcuffs and ankle cuffs through the trap. 'If you will put these on, I will serve you at once.'

'What!' said Ellie. 'Not bloody likely!'

'It seems a shame to waste such good food, Mistress. I have a cocktail for you and a salmon mousse; tender sirloin steak, with Bearnaise sauce, mushrooms and new potatoes, then a very nice . . .'

The borborygmi in Ellie's stomach grew deafening. She capitulated. 'Oh, all right. Give them here.' She sat on the bench and fixed the ankle cuffs and handcuffs on herself, clicking them shut. The girl inspected her through the panel, then the door slid aside and she came in with a large tray. She set it on Ellie's lap and removed the white cloth, then the silver dish-covers, to reveal everything she had promised, and more. She left, closing the door behind her. Ellie picked up the cutlery provided and dug in with a will. It was not easy to eat with her hands cuffed, but her appetite easily set aside that small problem. There was even, she found, a flask of excellent coffee to wash it all down with. It was only when she was wiping her mouth on a napkin that a thought struck her.

She set the tray aside and hobbled to the door. 'Hey!' she shouted. 'Hey! What about a key to take these things off with?' There was no reply.

A short while later, the door opened again. This time, the girl who had brought her dinner was accompanied by another who was wheeling an invalid chair. 'Please sit in the chair, Mistress.'

'Like hell I will,' Ellie replied.

'As you wish, Mistress, but where we have to go is quite a long distance and it will be uncomfortable for you to walk or be dragged.'

Ellie eyed the girls. They looked strong enough to be able to accomplish their threat, particularly since she was fettered, hand and foot. What they said had an irrefutable logic to it. She sat in the chair. They wheeled her out of the cell and along corridors. Only then did Ellie begin to appreciate the vastness of the place she was in. They came to a door, opened it and went in. It was a large room, some thirty feet square and completely bare of furniture. In the centre of it was a raised dais, about eighteen inches high and carpeted in grey to match the rest of the room. It was six feet wide and ran almost the whole length of the room, only a narrow walk-way being left at either end.

With one at either side, the girls lifted her out of the chair, then one stood in front of her and took hold of her handcuff chain, raising her arms away from her body. The other girl reached around Ellie's waist and passed a leather belt around her, buckling it at the back.

Alarmed, she struggled. 'What are you doing?' Neither replied. They held her easily and pulled her across the room until she was facing the dais. The girl behind her pushed her forward. Tripped by her ankle cuffs, she fell to her knees. The girl holding her handcuffs walked backwards, climbing onto the platform as she did so, forcing Ellie to shuffle forward on her knees until the dais stopped her. Further pulling resulted in the upper part of her body being stretched, face down on the raised portion, then the girl behind her padlocked D rings at each side of her belt to staples in the platform. When they stepped away, Ellie found that she could move her arms and legs as far as the cuffs allowed. What she could not do was to raise her hips from their draped position over the edge of the raised section.

She stretched herself around to look at her captors. 'What is this? What's the idea?'

They did not answer but one went to the wall and pressed a button. There was an electric hum above her and Ellie looked up to see what appeared to be a thin plywood curtain descending from the ceiling above her. There was a padded, arched, cut-out section in its bottom edge which coincided exactly with her waist so that, when it came to rest on the platform, it was as though there were now two rooms. Ellie's upper body was in one section and her bottom half was in the other.

The two girls were now out of her sight in the room behind her. 'Hey!' she shouted. 'Hey! What's going on?' There was silence, broken only by the sound of the door closing.

Pandora and her sister Helen sat side by side in comfortable chairs in front of Matrilla's desk, watching her complete her reading. Finally, she looked up. 'I think I have it all straight,' she said smiling. 'Just a couple of points to make sure about. You say you don't want to see Henry's re-training?'

Helen shook her head. 'No. I can't see the point.'

'Very well. As you wish. I hope you will feel the benefit of it in years to come. Now; about Ellie.'

'That's different,' Helen replied. 'I'd like to see her get what she deserves.'

'Would you like to beat her bottom yourself, or watch it done?'

'Do you know,' said Helen slowly, 'I'd rather like to do it myself. After all, she spanked me.'

'And suppose I tell you that we can not only arrange that but at the same time ensure that Ellie doesn't consort with Henry again.'

'That would be wonderful, but I don't see how –'

'Here, all things are possible,' said the Queen. 'There are a couple of things which are important, though. All the time you are in the room with Ellie, you are to make no sound. And I have to assure you that the person you see will be Ellie, although it will be difficult to tell. Now come with me.' She went to a corner of the room and collected a small trolley on which there rested what appeared to be a small hi-fi set.

'What's that?' asked Pandora, mystified.

'You'll see. Let's just call it edited highlights.'

She took them to the room in which Ellie was secured, opening the door quite noisily. Helen looked around her. To her eyes, it appeared to be a very long, narrow room. The left-hand wall was carpeted up to a height of about eighteen inches. Above that, the wall seemed to be made of wood. From a hole in the centre of that wall, where carpet met wood, the lower half of a body, dressed in a flowered skirt, was protruding.

Suddenly, from the other side of the wall, she heard Ellie's voice. 'Who's that? Is somebody there? Answer me!' The protruding bottom wriggled impatiently.

Matrilla laid a finger to her lips and switched on the hi-fi, poising her finger over the 'Play' button. Loudly, she said, 'Come in Henry. This is the room where we have Ellie, all fixed up for you as you asked.'

'Henry? Is that you back there, you bloody pervert?' Ellie called.

Matrilla pressed the button. Her own voice, perfectly reproduced, filled the room. 'I'll bet you'd like to cane her bottom, Henry, after all the things she's said to you.'

'You bet I would!' Henry's voice was charged with emotion.

'How many strokes do you think she should have, Henry?'

'As many as she deserves,' came the reply, 'and that means going on until my arm gets tired.'

Matrilla switched off the machine and said, 'Very well, Henry. So you shall. Here's the cane. I'll just leave you to get on with it.' She opened and closed the door, remaining inside, then handed Helen a cane and nodded towards the flowered skirt.

Ellie, speechless with outrage during the recent exchange, suddenly found her voice again. 'Henry Crombie! Don't you dare touch me! I'm warning you, you'll be sorry?'

Helen approached her victim. She found herself trembling with excitement at the thought of what she was about to do and was surprised to find that the excitement she felt was definitely sexual. Her vagina was twinging in a most peculiar manner. She stooped to grasp the hem of the flowered skirt, then laid it back, rolling and tucking it so that it was only a thin width of material above Ellie's haunches. The mighty shriek which this occasioned on the other side of the wall was music to her ears. Ellie's legs thrashed about, but she was severely hampered by the ankle cuffs. Ellie was wearing tights with panties underneath and Helen rejoiced as she hooked her fingers into the waistband and tugged them down to mid-thigh, leaving the panties in place. She found that this location did not satisfy her. She wanted Ellie to be as naked and exposed as possible, so she tugged again.

The accompanying screech was well worth the effort, she thought. Ellie actually helped her with her task. Had she kept her legs together and her knees on the floor, it might have been more difficult. As it was, by flailing about, bending and straightening her legs, she brought her knees off the floor and made it easy to drag the tights right down to her ankles.

Now for the moment Helen had dreamed of. She was going to pull Ellie's knickers down and leave her bottom bare. She savoured the moment, running her fingers around inside the waistband for quite a while, listening to the squeaks of rage and fright. With cruel slowness, she tugged them down, a little at a time, jerking to expose a fresh area of pink skin, then waiting until the wriggles subsided a little before she jerked again. At mid-thigh, she tired of this game and yanked them all the way down to the ankles in one movement. The round, womanly contours with the intriguing nest of pubic hair below set her vagina watering again.

As she picked up the cane, she remembered what Jack had said about Ellie; that she enjoyed a spanking. Well, enjoy this one, Ellie, she thought. With all her strength, she brought the cane down across that hated bottom.

'Oh God! Oh Jesus, Henry!' Ellie burst into song immediately.

With a fierce joy, Helen struck again, then again and again.

Four red weals had appeared on that wobbling, pink mass. Even if there had been silence, it would have been obvious that the pain was excruciating. Ellie's yells merely confirmed what Helen's eyes told her. Now Helen was clear in her mind about what she wanted. She wanted to rid herself of all the resentment she had felt about the Henry and Ellie affair. She wanted to pour out her hatred on that naked posterior; to see it completely reddened and on fire; to know that Ellie would not sit down in comfort for some weeks to come. Mad with rage and passion, she slashed wildly wanting to cover the whole area, even the small of her back and the backs of her thighs.

She hardly heard Ellie, now sobbing and groaning, 'Aaagh! Ouch! Ow! Mercy! No more! I'll be good, Henry! Forgive me! Please, no more!'

Suddenly, Helen felt her wrist grasped and held firmly. She paused, arm raised, slowly coming back through the red mist to understand where she was and what she was doing. For the first time she really saw and understood the reality of that twitching, convulsing mass of red stripes. Pandora was holding her wrist and, with finger to lips, was shaking her head. Helen dropped the cane and Pandora led her out of the room. Outside, the storm broke. Helen burst into tears, leaning her head on her sister's shoulder. Pandora held her, stroking her hair. 'There, there. It's out now. It's gone.'

Twelve

Jane stirred uneasily in her chair, moving as far as her straps would allow in an effort to ease her cramped limbs. She had lost all track of time and wondered vaguely if she was soon to be washed again. That, at least, broke the monotony. She had found that the shame of her bottom being bared by having the seat removed so that she could be cleaned underneath was somewhat offset by the fact that it gave her numbest places some respite. Also, she had contrived to have two orgasms as a result of her vagina being touched with a soapy washcloth. Perhaps, if she was lucky this time, the girl would linger a fraction too long in that area and she would be able to get off that way again. The most difficult thing to bear had been those occasions when she had been obliged to call for the commode. By drinking as little as she could, she had been able to reduce her output to a minimum, thus reducing the number of grinning faces she would have to see. She was astute enough to know that there was nothing to be gained by refusing solids. She shuddered and turned her mind away from remembrance of the audiences who watched her evacuate them.

She looked down at her own body, seeing the remains of food which had been dribbled down her breasts and stomach – deliberately, she thought. She knew that her face was similarly smeared, although she could not see it. Between her legs, the dildo was still buzzing and vibrating as it had done since she was put there. Seeing it reminded her again of how badly she needed a climax and she tried hard to control the desire to scream with frustration. She succeeded, perhaps more easily than she expected. That meant that about two hours had elapsed since the last application of cream to her breasts and vagina. With no watch, she judged time by the extent of her desire. It was always there but faded from unbearable to nagging as the effects of the salve wore off.

Griselda, her current watchdog, got up from her chair and left the Training Room. That meant that it was either to be food or a wash, she could not remember which. When the girl came back with a basin and towels, she knew that it was the latter. She submitted, eagerly, to the touch of the warm water on her, washing away the foul fragments of food. It was refreshing to have her face and neck washed. By habit, she took her weight on her arms to allow Griselda to pull the seat away from under her and sighed with relief as the pressure on her bottom was eased and she felt cool air on it. She tried to jerk her body up and down on the cloth as it cleansed her bottom and sex. No luck this time! If only they would do that just after the salve had been put on, she felt that she could have come at a single touch.

Griselda patted her dry, powdered her and replaced the seat. 'There, Mistress! Nice and clean, ready for the Queen.'

'The Queen?'

'Yes, Mistress. She is coming to see you today.'

At that very moment, the double doors opened and Matrilla swept in, closely followed by her faithful lieutenants. She surveyed Jane, hands on hips. 'Your three days are over. Have you enjoyed the Tantalus?'

'No, Madam.'

'Good. I hope that will encourage you to behave in such a way in future as to make it unnecessary for you to revisit us.' She turned to Griselda. 'She has performed the necessary number of functions?'

'Yes, Madam.'

'She has had no orgasm?'

'Two, I'm afraid, Madam. She was hardly touched at all, but she has been very worked up and they were impossible to prevent.'

'When was the ointment last applied?'

'Two hours ago, Madam.'

'Very well. Let it be put on again, now, then unstrap her.' She smiled at Jane. 'Your yearning for completion is about to be satisfied.'

Jane could not really believe that she was to be allowed to touch herself, but half a hope was better than none at all so she put up with the cream with better grace than usual. Griselda released her straps and Jane made as if to get up.

'Better not!' said Matrilla. 'Luna and Marla will help you, lest you fall.'

The two hand-maidens on either side of Jane helped her out of the chair and she found that Matrilla's advice had been good. The pain in all her joints was great, her legs were like rubber and she felt a little faint after such a long period sitting down. They supported her and walked her gently up and down for a while, until she began to feel more normal. With that normality came the familiar effect of the cream. An overwhelming lust for sexual satisfaction.

Matrilla had been watching her carefully, judging the moment. 'Would you like a dildo now, Jane?'

Jane hoped this was not a cruel joke at her expense. 'Yes please, Madam.'

'Then you shall have one,' said Matrilla. 'It's over here!' She led the way to a piece of apparatus which looked rather like a vaulting horse, except that it had a saddle. It was unlike an ordinary saddle in that it had a very high front and rear, so that whoever sat in it would be unable to move backwards or forwards. Set in the centre of the saddle was a long, flexible dildo. There were no stirrups. Griselda brought over a set of steps and put them alongside the horse.

'There it is,' said the Queen. 'Just climb up and it's all yours.'

Deeply suspicious, but spurred on by her intense craving, Jane approached the steps. All three girls helped her to mount them. The moment when she put her leg over the saddle and allowed the artificial organ to sink deep inside her was sheer bliss. Three days of frustration were swept away in a moment by the huge orgasm which hit her the instant the thing entered her. She squirmed herself down onto it and slid her hand between her stomach and the front of the saddle to fondle her clitoris so as to be able immediately to repeat the sensation. The joy and relief she felt was indescribable as she quickly obtained a third climax. She was so intent on her pleasure that she did not notice that the steps had been removed and that Luna and Marla, working between them, had tied her ankles together underneath the leather belly of her man-made mount.

Matrilla spoke. 'Is that nice, Jane?'

Almost speechless, Jane stammered, 'It's truly wonderful, Madam. Thank you! Thank you!'

'Then we must increase your pleasure, mustn't we? This horse is one which is used to train riders. It moves. With these controls, I can make it duplicate the movements of a walk, trot, canter or gallop. Let's try the walk first.'

She operated the controls and the horse began to move with an easy lope which swayed Jane's body and set up sympathetic rhythms as she moved on the dildo upon which she was impaled. She moaned and stroked her breasts to increase the sexiness of it.

Matrilla altered the movement to a trot. Without benefit of stirrups, the jerkiness of the motion jounced Jane up and down on the rubber penis. She cried out with excitement and came again, rolling her head in ecstasy. She lost count of the number of orgasms she had experienced. Now, they were more difficult to achieve and the time between them lengthened.

At last, she felt she could stand no more. 'Enough!' she cried. 'Enough!'

The Queen switched off the mechanism and the horse came to a standstill. 'You've had enough?'

'Yes, thank you, Madam.'

'You don't want me to make the horse trot any more?'

'No, thank you, Madam. I'd like to get off.'

The Queen stared at her. 'This is an important point in your re-education programme, Jane. It is now that you learn that when someone does something you don't want them to do, they are being cruel and unfeeling.'

She set the mechanism to 'trot' again. Jane tried to support herself by pressing down on the saddle, but that did not prevent the up and down motion inside her. In fact, it seemed to make it worse and she came to her peak again very quickly.

Soon she was screaming, 'Mercy! No more! Mercy, please, Madam! I can't do any more.'

Matrilla switched off the horse and Jane slumped, panting. Matrilla drove home the lesson remorselessly. 'When you do things to your partner which she does not like, you are treating her as I have just treated you. Do you understand that better now?'

Jane sobbed. 'Yes, Madam.'

'I know that Karen enjoys a certain subservience and it is none of my business how a couple choose to enjoy themselves. However, it is a matter for both to decide what is enjoyable and what is not. I have placed a loaded gun in Karen's hand and it is pointed at you. It is a phrase: "I don't like this game." If she says that, and you persist in what you are doing to her, you pull the trigger and shoot yourself in the foot. The matter will be reported to me and you will be back here for further training. Do you understand?'

Jane nodded dumbly.

'Then it is time for you to go home. Release her!'

She did not wait to see Jane taken, half-fainting, from the horse. She left the room. She opened the next door along the corridor and went in. A handsome, white-haired gentleman rose to meet her.

'Monsieur le Comte. You have enjoyed what you have seen?' She gestured towards the large one-way window which commanded a view of the Training Room.

He bowed. 'Thank you, *Madame*, it has been a privilege.'

'You are satisfied that the matter of your daughter's mistreatment has been dealt with?'

'In an exemplary fashion, *Madame*. I am quite satisfied.'

'Have you enjoyed your stay with us. Nadia has served you well?'

His eyes sparkled. 'Ah! What a little treasure, that one. I have been made to feel young again.'

Matrilla smiled. 'It was our pleasure, *Monsieur*.'

In the Queen's office, Grace was polishing the floor. This had been her work for part of each day, among other, more demanding and humiliating tasks. Her instructions were to shine it until she could see her face reflected it in and it had, she estimated, almost reached that stage. She was wearing a skimpy, sexy, maid's outfit. Made of wet-look black material, it was so short that it hardly covered her bottom at all, even when she was standing. Kneeling, as she was obliged to do, and forbidden to wear knickers, she was well aware that everything she possessed was on view and jiggling enticingly for the entertainment of the two girls whose job it was to watch her work. She did not particularly care. Her mind was filled with thoughts of the coming evening, when the mysterious stranger would come to her in her room, as he had come every night. She could still feel him in her and his hands on her skin and she tingled at the recollection of the things they had done. She longed to hear his voice and to see him. That was the single part of the relationship which was unsatisfactory to her. The sex was fantastic every time! She was unreasonably happy and only just stopped herself from humming a tune while she polished.

Matrilla came into the office and stood behind her, watching her for a while, before going across to her desk and sitting at it. Presently she called over to her. 'Grace. Stop that now and come here.'

Grace got up, stretching her back wearily, and came to stand in front of the desk. 'Yes, Madam.'

'Sit down, Grace.'

By habit, Grace moved towards the wooden chair, but the Queen indicated the more comfortable one closer to her desk, so she sat there.

The Queen stared at her for a long time, making her feel

rather uncomfortable. Finally, apparently content with what she saw, she said, 'I think it's time you went home.'

'Thank you, Madam.'

'Yes,' said Matrilla. 'I think your training is almost complete. Do you think you have learned anything?'

'You know, Madam,' she said, slowly, 'I really think I have. I have had some horrid experiences, and they have made me more aware of the way I affect others. That was what you intended, wasn't it?'

'If you understand that, you have learned well. Tell me though, have all your experiences here, without exception, been horrid for you?'

Grace blushed a little. 'Well . . . no.' Greatly daring, she went on, 'Oh Madam, could I know the name of the man who comes to me in my room every night?'

'Why do you want to know that. Is it not sufficient that he pleases you? What more do you want?' said Matrilla.

'It's hard to explain,' Grace replied. 'I want to know what he looks like, of course, and I'd like to be able to find him again. But, more than that, I want to know what he thinks about. Does he like me? Does he play golf? What are his politics? Does that sound silly?'

'Not in the least. It shows that you have come to understand more than you know. The meeting of two bodies for sex without a meeting of minds at the same time, is gratifying, but only in the same way as masturbation is gratifying. In fact, it *is* masturbation, except that you are using someone else's hand.'

'I see. But can't you tell me who he is?'

'I'm afraid not.'

Grace was downcast. 'But how will I ever find him once I go home?'

'Who knows? If you have affected him in the same way as he has affected you, perhaps *he* will find *you*!'

'Do you think so?'

'It could happen,' Matrilla said, 'but now let us turn to thoughts of your final examination. There is a test for you to pass. This one, though, is a little different. In everything that your training has called for so far, you have been physically restrained by cords or chains, or driven by threats of pain. In this test, you will be subjected to the most severe restraint of all.'

'Oh, what's that?'

'You will be asked to undergo yet another humiliating ordeal which will be hard for you to bear. If you do not bear it, there will be no punishment. Indeed, you may refuse to undergo it and nothing will happen to you. You will still go home. That is why I said "asked" instead of "ordered".'

'I don't think I understand.'

'Think about it. The greatest restraint of all is self-control. Are you now the old Grace, or are you this new person. The only way you can find out is to volunteer for this test and see it through to the end. If you fail, your only punishment will be that you know you failed. If you refuse, your punishment will be that you recognise that you have not changed at all and are still the same selfish person you were when you came here.'

'I think I see.' Grace mulled it over in her mind, then her chin came up. 'I accept.'

Matrilla smiled. She had noticed the omission of the formal address, 'Madam', but did not comment on it. Grace was leaving and Lady Crendall was coming back. So be it! 'Well done!' she said. 'Go with Luna and Marla now. They will prepare you for your test.'

Alone in the office, Matrilla went to a side door and opened it to admit a handsome, well-dressed man. She ushered him to the chair by her desk. 'You heard that, Sir Malcolm. Your wife has much appreciated your visits to her room each night.'

He nodded. 'She has said as much at the time, but one is never sure of things said in the heat of passion. I owe it all to you and the instruction I have been given here. She owes you a lot, too. I never thought she could behave as she did just now. I was quite proud of her.'

'With every reason, Sir Malcolm. I'm sure she will pass with flying colours. I'm only sad that I am so convinced I shan't see either of you here again. Will you tell her tonight?'

'Yes, I think I will. We can go home together then.'

Matrilla rose. 'Good luck to you both. Now I must go and supervise the final exam.'

When she got to the Great Hall, Grace was already there with Luna and Marla. Grace was wearing a robe and they were standing in the centre of a large square of plastic which had been laid on the floor. A circle of curious onlookers stood around.

Matrilla addressed the crowd. 'You have seen many displays of cruelty in this hall. Today, the ordeal is to be one of humiliation. The woman will start by displaying herself to you. Take off your robe, Grace!'

With slightly trembling hands, Grace obeyed, opening the robe then slipping out of it and handing it to Luna, who took it to the side of the square and put it down.

'Display yourself! Put your hands behind your back and spread your legs! You will observe that the woman has been shaved, indicating that she has been shamed before. You are invited to feast your eyes on this particular part of her body and imagine what that must have been like for her.'

Grace's face was red with embarrassment as many pairs of eyes concentrated on her bald mound.

'She will now demonstrate that the shave was thorough, extending everywhere. Turn round, Grace. Part your legs and touch your toes.'

As she adopted this position, Grace's face burned even brighter. She could see her audience through her legs and knew that they were staring at what she was so conspicuously revealing. She fought to control her overwhelming wish to run and hide.

'Stand up again and turn to the front, Grace. Ladies and gentlemen, the woman will now submit to having her body painted, from head to toe, with treacle, while you watch.'

Grace's head jerked round and she stared at Matrilla for a moment, then set her shoulders and resumed her previous position. Luna and Marla fetched two large buckets and a pair of brushes from the side of the circle and set them down beside Grace. They dipped the brushes into the brown, sticky substance and waited.

Matrilla nodded. 'Very well. Begin!'

Luna said, 'Hold out your hands, please, Mistress.' Grace did so and watched as Luna and Marla laid a large brushful of the treacle in each palm and worked it in between her fingers. The feel of it there was dreadful and gooey. She shivered at the thought of what it would feel like elsewhere. When they had finished her hands, front and back, Luna said, 'Put your hands on your head, please, Mistress.'

That was, perhaps, the crisis for Grace. It had not occurred to her that the stuff would get in her hair. It was the point at which she almost quit, but then steeled herself and placed both her sticky hands firmly on her head, feeling the stuff squish into her scalp. She felt the treacle running down her body as they daubed it lavishly under her arms. After that, it was easier, even when the sticky brushes intruded upon her most intimate places. They had her bend over while they applied it between the cheeks of her bottom and smeared it liberally between her legs. They made her put her hands down while they painted her face and neck and she felt her arms sticking to her body in a most uncomfortable way.

Finally, they seemed to be satisfied and stepped away, leaving her to stand completely covered in brown treacle which crawled oozily down her skin. Then, to her horror, she saw that the final indignity was to come. They lifted their buckets and poured the remains of the stuff over her head. It glued her hair flat to her scalp and ran in shiny rivulets over her face and breasts. Mercifully, her eyes were closed by then, so she was unable to see them come towards her with bags of feathers, which they threw over her. The feathers stuck to the treacle, making her look like a ridiculous and oversized chicken.

Her first inkling that the test was really over was when the girls came to her with a basin of water and washed the treacle and feathers away from her face and eyes, so that she could see. As they wrapped her robe about her and led her away, she became dimly aware of applause.

As she was passing Matrilla, she paused, head high. 'Well?'

Matrilla inclined her head gravely. 'Well done, My Lady,' she said. 'You may call me Matrilla.'

'Why are they clapping, Matrilla?'

'Because they all knew the nature of the test. That you were fighting your most dangerous enemy; yourself. They saw you win and they are pleased for you. You may go home proudly now.'

'Yes,' said Grace, 'but not before tonight, please!'

Matrilla smiled. 'No, my dear. Not before tonight.'

'Oh, Pandora. Do you really think I dare?' Helen gazed apprehensively at her sister.

Pandora had no doubt about it. 'Of course you do. Why shouldn't you have a bit of fun with a nice man while you've got the chance. Just what do you think Henry's doing right now?'

'Yes, but I won't know him.'

'All the better. You don't want to be involved in a romance. You just want a bit of the other to cheer you up. Anyway, look at it this way. Think how much better you'll be for Henry with a bit of outside experience. "What should she know of Henry, who only Henry knows?" and all that.'

'Is that a quote?'

'Well,' said Pandora. 'Kipling didn't put it quite like that, but it's what he meant, I'm sure. Oh, come on, Helen. It's what this place is all about. Lots of women would give anything for the opportunity.'

Helen was wavering. 'I have wondered what it would be like with someone else.'

'Good!' Pandora took that as an affirmative. 'Now, let's make you look like a million dollars and smell like two million. I've got a very slinky housecoat you can borrow and I have the most sinful perfume imaginable. It's called *Bitch on Heat*, to go with his *Rampaging Bull* after-shave.'

'Really?'

'Oh God, Helen. You are so gullible. You wouldn't like to buy Tower Bridge, would you? Come on. Let's get you ready.'

Some time later, Pandora inspected her work. Helen's hair and make-up were impeccable. The peach silk house-coat suited her complexion beautifully. 'Nothing underneath?' she asked.

Helen blushed. 'No, Pandora.'

'Come on. Open up! Let me see.'

Shyly, Helen unfastened the belt and held the garment open. Pandora regarded her nudity. 'Just had to check to see that you hadn't chickened out and put passion-strangler bloomers on. Nothing worse for a chap than losing the circulation in his fingers because of knicker elastic round his wrist. I guess you'll do. No, wait a minute. Don't put it away yet.'

She went to the dressing table and fetched something. 'Open up! Stand still!' She dipped her finger into a little pot. 'Just the merest touch of rouge on the nipples. Drives 'em potty, that.' She rubbed in slow circles. 'Don't wriggle! You'll smudge!'

'It feels funny.'

'If it's funny when I do it, it's going to be hilarious when *he* does! All right. Put 'em away. Right. He'll be here presently and I don't want to be in the way. I've got other fish to fry, so you've got the room to yourself all night. Take your time and enjoy it. Don't panic!' With a quick kiss, she was gone.

The soft knock at the door made Helen almost jump out of her skin. As she went to open it, she found that her heart was pounding and she felt a little sick. She opened the door and the visitor stepped inside. She was not exactly sure what she had been expecting, but this young man did not fit any of her preconceptions. He was in his mid-twenties, she judged, of average height and with very blond hair. He was dressed in a smart but casual jacket, white silk shirt and grey trousers.

'Mrs Crombie? I am Andrew. You were expecting me, I believe.'

At the third attempt, Helen managed to croak, 'Come in.'

He followed her into the centre of the room, where she

turned and faced him. They stared at one another in silence for long seconds, then he smiled and said, 'These moments are so difficult, aren't they? Look, I know that all the rooms are equipped with a drinks cabinet. Why don't you sit down and let me get you something.'

She subsided gratefully into an armchair and he went to the cabinet. 'I'm having a vodka and orange juice. How about you?'

'Isn't that funny. That's what I drink too.'

He brought her drink over and seated himself opposite her, on the other side of the low table. She sipped her Screwdriver and the spirit braced her to say what she felt she had to.

'Andrew. I'm sorry, but I really don't think I can do this.'

'Oh?'

'No. Look, I'm really sorry, but it's the notion that you have been sent here. I mean it's all so sort of . . . tacky, if you know what I mean.'

He leaned forward. 'Helen. May I call you Helen?' She nodded, and he went on, 'I have a confession to make to you. I am not the man who should have come to you this evening.'

'You're not?'

'No. His name is Jason. He is much bigger and stronger than I am, which is why he has the job of looking after lonely ladies. I am not employed in that way. I work in the accounts department. For the past few days I have seen you moving about the castle with your sister. I thought that you were so different from the ladies who usually come here; so cool, so self-possessed. So beautiful. I felt that I wanted to get to know you, but then I found out that you were married and, of course, I had to respect that. When I heard that Jason was being sent to you, I couldn't believe my luck. I seized the opportunity and bribed him to let me come in his place. I'm so sorry that I tried to deceive you and I can see that my presence here is upsetting you. Please believe that I would not dream of causing any further distress to a lady I so much admire. I'll leave at once.'

He set his drink down and made to rise, but she stretched out her hand and put it on his. 'No! Wait a minute, Andrew.' She thought for a moment. 'You thought I was beautiful?'

'If you think differently then you haven't looked in the mirror lately. Even now, with the table between us, my mind is reeling with the thought that I might have had the chance to kiss you.'

Helen's nipples were prickling and she felt a distinct warmth where she sat. She played for more time to consider her emotions. 'Really?'

'Yes, really. I'm sorry if that offends you.'

'No,' she said faintly. 'No, it doesn't.' The seat of her chair was quite uncomfortable now.

'And I'm ashamed to tell you that the thought that you are probably naked underneath that housecoat is driving me mad. Feeling as I do and knowing that I will never see you without it is hard to bear.'

Helen looked down at herself. Her nipples were creating huge bumps in the peach silk. The source of the chair's heat must be steam, because it felt damp, now, as well as hot. Her voice trembled as she said, 'I don't know, Andrew. Never's a long time.'

'You mean you wouldn't mind if I kissed you?'

'No,' she said gently. 'I don't think I'd mind that at all.'

He stood up and came around the table. She stood up to meet him and then she was in his arms and he was kissing her face, her lips, her neck, whispering sweet endearments.

He let her go and stepped back. 'Helen, dearest. Take off the housecoat.' As though in a dream, she loosened the sash and slipped it off her shoulders, letting it fall to the carpet behind her and revealing her body to him.

He stared at her. 'My God, you are so beautiful. I had not dreamt . . .' Then she was in his arms again and this time, his kisses rained down on her breasts, her nipples, then back to her lips again. For long moments they clung together before he stooped and, gathering her knees over his arm, he swept her off her feet and carried her to the bed. He laid her down, tenderly, then stepped back to remove his own clothes, never taking his eyes off her. She lay on her back and watched him. His body was beautifully slim, almost hairless and tanned to a golden-brown all over. His penis was already erect and was just as beautiful as the rest of his body. She raised her knees and spread them wide. He came to the foot of the bed and knelt on it; her golden man. She knew what he would do before he did it. She watched his face grow closer to her vagina and almost screamed in anticipation. The touch of his golden tongue on her sex brought her to immediate orgasm, yet that did not disappoint her. She felt herself capable of many more.

She felt his golden body slide smoothly on her bare belly, then his mouth was on her nipple, his tongue and teeth driving her to a second orgasm. His golden penis penetrated the entrance to her vagina and she welcomed it in, sucking and pulling at it with all her strength. She came to orgasm twice more before he came inside her. He lay on top of her for a long while, gently easing his now semi-rigid organ in and out, creating for her the most delicious aftershocks. When he finally withdrew, she rolled onto her side. He put a protective, loving arm about her and soon she slept.

Andrew allowed his arm to go numb under the weight of her head so that she would be well asleep and not disturbed by its removal when he left. To while away the time, he worked on his report to the Queen. The standard line about being an ordinary employee obsessed with her beauty had worked well, as it usually did with shy clients. That deserved a mention. He turned his mind to thoughts of tomorrow. He was booked for the ageing spinster in 32B. The strategy would have to be different with her. Perhaps a wickedly incestuous hint of a mother's love for the son she never had? He would ask Matrilla and they would work on it together.

bed. He laid [illegible]. She seemed [illegible]
move his wet clothes, [illegible] taking [illegible] of him. She lay on her back and watched him. [illegible] was [illegible] and [illegible] over. [illegible] all [illegible] just as [illegible] his body [illegible] and [illegible] wide. He came [illegible]. He [illegible] her golden [illegible] he had [illegible] before in the [illegible] in [illegible]. The [illegible] on his [illegible] to [illegible] orgasm, [illegible]

[illegible] a sudden [illegible] something [illegible] his mouth [illegible] her nipple [illegible] tongue and teeth [illegible] him to a second orgasm. [illegible] the entrance to her vagina and she [illegible] it [illegible]. She [illegible] to orgasm [illegible] for a long while, gently [illegible] and out, [illegible] delicious [illegible]. When he finally [illegible] him about her [illegible]

[illegible] to go while under the weight, [illegible] that she would be [illegible] sleep and [illegible] when he left. [illegible] report to the Queen. The [illegible] work, but [illegible] did with [illegible] turned his mind to the [illegible] of tomorrow. He [illegible] looked [illegible] would have to be [illegible] love for the [illegible] thought [illegible]

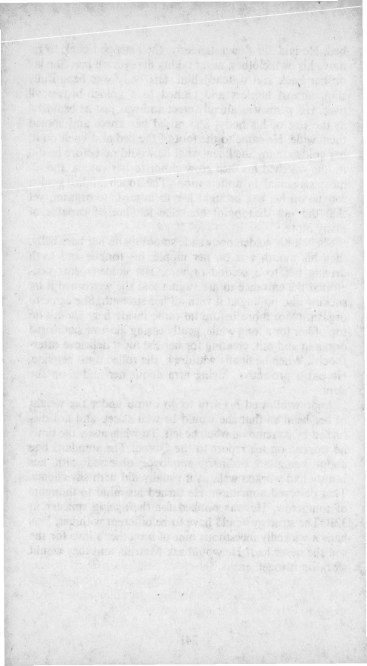

Postscript

David Corby made his way back along the corridors from the restaurant to his room. He had dined alone, yet lingered over the meal because there was little to hurry for. At first he had resented being asked to give up sweet little Nadia, until he learned that she was to be with the Comte de Foret. If he had to give her up for anyone, he would rather it should be Nicole's father than anyone else. Good luck to the old boy!

He opened the door of his room and went in, then stopped in amazement, the door handle still in his hand. Pandora was lying face-down on his bed, reading a magazine. She was stark naked and one foot was wiggling, pensively, in the air.

She looked up and smiled. 'Hello, David.'

He closed the door and set his back against it. 'Hello. What are you doing here?'

She pushed her magazine away and rolled over, away from him, onto her back. She stretched, pushing her arms far above her head, knowing that doing so set off the muscles which supported her breasts and made them project provocatively. She raised one knee and swayed it from side to side so that he got tantalising glimpses of the joys between her thighs. 'I've been waiting for you, David. You swore that one of these days, you were going to fuck my brains out and I swore to you that one of these days I was going to let you. Well, it's one of these days and I'm here to fulfil my part of the swear. I've brought my brains with me. Is it one of these days for you, too, David? Are you going to keep your half of the swear?'

He walked towards the bed, unknotting his tie while he drank in the perfection of her naked, peachy skin, so perfectly contrasted with the patch of brown hair at her crotch; the darkly swollen nipples set on perfect curves of woman-flesh. 'Hang on to your brains, Pandora,' he said. 'It's one of these days.'

Please send me ____ copies of the 1996 Nexus calendar @ £5.50 (US$9.00) each including postage and packing.

Name: ____

Address: ______________________________________

____

____

____

☐ I enclose a cheque or postal order made out to Nexus Books

☐ Please debit my Visa/Access/Mastercard account (delete as applicable)

My credit card number is:

_ _ _ _   _ _ _ _   _ _ _ _   _ _ _ _

Expiry date: __________________________

FILL OUT YOUR ORDER AND SEND IT TODAY!

NEW BOOKS

Coming up from Nexus and Black Lace

Nexus

The Spanish Sensualist by Josephine Arno
October 1995 Price: £4.99 ISBN: 0 352 33035 X
Julia's seemingly impossible task is to persuade the stubborn Don Lorenzo Alvarez de Quitana to lend some of his fabulous pieces to a London art exhibition. Don Lorenzo accepts, but on one condition: that she joins his exclusive group of Hedonists. And in order to do that, she must pass five arduous tests of her sensuality.

The Ice Queen by Stephen Ferris
October 1995 Price: £4.99 ISBN: 0 352 33039 2
She strides through the corridors of the Institute of Corrective Education with a whip in her hand and a sneer on her face. Her gaze strikes terror into any man or woman unlucky enough to be placed in her care. She takes no excuses and gives no quarter. She is Matrilla, the Ice Queen; and she has just received a new batch of sinners to correct.

Demonia by Kendal Grahame
November 1995 Price: £4.99 ISBN: 0 352 33038 4
Hundreds of years ago, Demonia and her vampire acolyte Sinitia struck terror into the hearts of young men and women all over the country, stalking the beautiful in order to drain them of their sexual energies. Now they have woken in the heart of modern London.

Melinda and Sophia by Susanna Hughes
November 1995 Price: £4.99 ISBN: 0 352 33045 7
In this, the fifth and final volume dedicated to the beautiful blonde submissive, Melinda enters a new domain where she is subjected to the whims of the Master's cruel wife Sophia. Even more merciless is the courtesan Bianca, who takes in instant fancy to Melinda's youthful charms.

BLACK
lace

Led on by Compulsion by Leila James
October 1995 Price: £4.99 ISBN: 0 352 33032 5
A chance visit to a country pub on the east coast turns into an orgy of revelry when Karen becomes ensnared in Andreas's world of luxury and fast living. With the help of the devine Marieka and a multitude of willing and beautiful slaves, he throws the best and most depraved parties in town.

Opal Darkness by Cleo Cordell
October 1995 Price: £4.99 ISBN: 0 352 33033 3
Twins Sidonie and Francis share everything: clothes, friends, a love of the arts – and a rapacious appetite for sex. They set out together on a grand tour of Europe with the intention of discovering new pleasures. But in the hypnotic Count Constantin and his gorgeous friend Razvania, they may have taken on more than they bargained for.

Rude Awakening by Pamela Kyle
November 1995 Price: £4.99 ISBN: 0 352 33036 8
When you are used to getting everything you want handed to you on a plate, abduction must come as something of a blow. So Alison and Belinda discover as they are stripped, bound, and forced to comply with the wishes of their cruel but intriguing captors.

Jewel of Xanadu by Roxanne Carr
November 1995 Price: £4.99 ISBN: 0 352 33037 6
Raised as a nomad in the Gobi desert, Cirina is used to meeting strangers. Antonio, on a quest for a Byzantine jewel, is special – but their blossomimg relationship is cut short when Tartar warriors remove Cirina to the pleasure palace of the Kublai Khan.

NEXUS BACKLIST

All books are priced £4.99 unless another price is given. If a date is supplied, the book in question will not be available until that month in 1995.

CONTEMPORARY EROTICA

THE ACADEMY	Arabella Knight	
CONDUCT UNBECOMING	Arabella Knight	Jul
CONTOURS OF DARKNESS	Marco Vassi	
THE DEVIL'S ADVOCATE	Anonymous	
DIFFERENT STROKES	Sarah Veitch	Aug
THE DOMINO TATTOO	Cyrian Amberlake	
THE DOMINO ENIGMA	Cyrian Amberlake	
THE DOMINO QUEEN	Cyrian Amberlake	
ELAINE	Stephen Ferris	
EMMA'S SECRET WORLD	Hilary James	
EMMA ENSLAVED	Hilary James	
EMMA'S SECRET DIARIES	Hilary James	
FALLEN ANGELS	Kendal Grahame	
THE FANTASIES OF JOSEPHINE SCOTT	Josephine Scott	
THE GENTLE DEGENERATES	Marco Vassi	
HEART OF DESIRE	Maria del Rey	
HELEN – A MODERN ODALISQUE	Larry Stern	
HIS MISTRESS'S VOICE	G. C. Scott	
HOUSE OF ANGELS	Yvonne Strickland	May
THE HOUSE OF MALDONA	Yolanda Celbridge	
THE IMAGE	Jean de Berg	Jul
THE INSTITUTE	Maria del Rey	
SISTERHOOD OF THE INSTITUTE	Maria del Rey	

JENNIFER'S INSTRUCTION	Cyrian Amberlake	
LETTERS TO CHLOE	Stefan Gerrard	Aug
LINGERING LESSONS	Sarah Veitch	Apr
A MATTER OF POSSESSION	G. C. Scott	Sep
MELINDA AND THE MASTER	Susanna Hughes	
MELINDA AND ESMERALDA	Susanna Hughes	
MELINDA AND THE COUNTESS	Susanna Hughes	
MELINDA AND THE ROMAN	Susanna Hughes	
MIND BLOWER	Marco Vassi	
MS DEEDES ON PARADISE ISLAND	Carole Andrews	
THE NEW STORY OF O	Anonymous	
OBSESSION	Maria del Rey	
ONE WEEK IN THE PRIVATE HOUSE	Esme Ombreux	Jun
THE PALACE OF SWEETHEARTS	Delver Maddingley	
THE PALACE OF FANTASIES	Delver Maddingley	
THE PALACE OF HONEYMOONS	Delver Maddingley	
THE PALACE OF EROS	Delver Maddingley	
PARADISE BAY	Maria del Rey	
THE PASSIVE VOICE	G. C. Scott	
THE SALINE SOLUTION	Marco Vassi	
SHERRIE	Evelyn Culber	May
STEPHANIE	Susanna Hughes	
STEPHANIE'S CASTLE	Susanna Hughes	
STEPHANIE'S REVENGE	Susanna Hughes	
STEPHANIE'S DOMAIN	Susanna Hughes	
STEPHANIE'S TRIAL	Susanna Hughes	
STEPHANIE'S PLEASURE	Susanna Hughes	
THE TEACHING OF FAITH	Elizabeth Bruce	
THE TRAINING GROUNDS	Sarah Veitch	
UNDERWORLD	Maria del Rey	

EROTIC SCIENCE FICTION

ADVENTURES IN THE PLEASUREZONE	Delaney Silver	
RETURN TO THE PLEASUREZONE	Delaney Silver	

FANTASYWORLD	Larry Stern	
WANTON	Andrea Arven	

ANCIENT & FANTASY SETTINGS

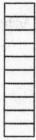

CHAMPIONS OF LOVE	Anonymous	
CHAMPIONS OF PLEASURE	Anonymous	
CHAMPIONS OF DESIRE	Anonymous	
THE CLOAK OF APHRODITE	Kendal Grahame	
THE HANDMAIDENS	Aran Ashe	
THE SLAVE OF LIDIR	Aran Ashe	
THE DUNGEONS OF LIDIR	Aran Ashe	
THE FOREST OF BONDAGE	Aran Ashe	
PLEASURE ISLAND	Aran Ashe	
WITCH QUEEN OF VIXANIA	Morgana Baron	

EDWARDIAN, VICTORIAN & OLDER EROTICA

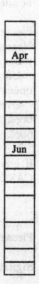

ANNIE	Evelyn Culber	
ANNIE AND THE SOCIETY	Evelyn Culber	
THE AWAKENING OF LYDIA	Philippa Masters	Apr
BEATRICE	Anonymous	
CHOOSING LOVERS FOR JUSTINE	Aran Ashe	
GARDENS OF DESIRE	Roger Rougiere	
THE LASCIVIOUS MONK	Anonymous	
LURE OF THE MANOR	Barbra Baron	
RETURN TO THE MANOR	Barbra Baron	Jun
MAN WITH A MAID 1	Anonymous	
MAN WITH A MAID 2	Anonymous	
MAN WITH A MAID 3	Anonymous	
MEMOIRS OF A CORNISH GOVERNESS	Yolanda Celbridge	
THE GOVERNESS AT ST AGATHA'S	Yolanda Celbridge	
TIME OF HER LIFE	Josephine Scott	
VIOLETTE	Anonymous	

THE JAZZ AGE

BLUE ANGEL NIGHTS	Margarete von Falkensee	
BLUE ANGEL DAYS	Margarete von Falkensee	

- -

Please send me the books I have ticked above.

Name ....

Address ....

....

....

.... Post code ....

Send to: **Cash Sales, Nexus Books, 332 Ladbroke Grove, London W10 5AH.**

Please enclose a cheque or postal order, made payable to **Nexus Books,** to the value of the books you have ordered plus postage and packing costs as follows:

UK and BFPO – £1.00 for the first book, 50p for each subsequent book.

Overseas (including Republic of Ireland) – £2.00 for the first book, £1.00 for the second book, and 50p for each subsequent book.

If you would prefer to pay by VISA or ACCESS/MASTERCARD, please write your card number and expiry date here:

....

Please allow up to 28 days for delivery.

Signature ....

- -